POE

An Alexandra Poe Thriller

ALSO BY

BRETT BATTLES

ROBERT GREGORY BROWNE

JONATHAN QUINN THRILLERS
THE CLEANER
THE DECEIVED
SHADOW OF BETRAYAL (U.S.)/
 THE UNWANTED (U.K.)
THE SILENCED
BECOMING QUINN
THE DESTROYED
THE COLLECTED

TRIAL JUNKIES THRILLERS
TRIAL JUNKIES
NEGLIGENCE

STANDALONES
KISS HER GOODBYE
WHISPER IN THE DARK
KILL HER AGAIN
DOWN AMONG THE DEAD MEN
THE PARADISE PROPHECY

LOGAN HARPER THRILLERS
LITTLE GIRL GONE
EVERY PRECIOUS THING

PROJECT EDEN THRILLERS
SICK
EXIT NINE
PALE HORSE
ASHES

STANDALONES
THE PULL OF GRAVITY
NO RETURN

For Younger Readers

TROUBLE FAMILY CHRONICLES
HERE COMES MR. TROUBLE

POE

Brett Battles
and
Robert Gregory Browne

An Alexandra Poe Thriller

ONE

May 4th
Paris, France

HE THOUGHT THERE might be a problem when they didn't hear from Six.

It was a routine status check, each of the spotters responding as requested:

"Zeta One, clear."

"Zeta Two, clear."

"Zeta Three, clear."

"Zeta Four, clear."

"Zeta Five, clear."

Then radio silence.

A full seven seconds of it.

McElroy's gut clenched as he keyed his mic. "Zeta Six, report."

More silence.

"Zeta Six?"

Three more seconds of nothing, then a sharp *pop,* followed by, "This is Six. Sorry. Was repositioning. I think I have him."

McElroy exhaled, telling himself that these things happened, that Six was a good man and should be given a bit of slack. But that feeling of possible difficulties had not abated, and he wondered for a moment if they should abort the entire operation.

No.

He was simply letting paranoia get to him and he couldn't give in to it. Not when they were this close.

He tapped Duncan's shoulder. "Put Six on center

screen."

With just a few keystrokes, Duncan switched the image in the main surveillance monitor to the feed coming from Zeta Six's camera—a shot from the top of a building on the west side of Rue Danton, showing the small plaza in front of the Saint-Michel metro station near the entrance of the Latin Quarter. It was six p.m. on a Friday evening, and the area was packed with the usual swarm—tourists out enjoying the city and locals trying to find their way home.

Not the optimum situation, but then McElroy hadn't set the schedule.

"Zeta Six, identify subject," he said.

"Comin' atcha."

A translucent gray grid appeared over the feed, then a red dot zipped across the screen and planted itself on the back of a man walking across Boulevard Saint-Michel, away from the camera.

"You sure that's him?" McElroy asked.

"I think so. Got a quick shot of him coming out of the metro station. Sending you that now."

A moment passed, then Duncan's computer terminal dinged softly.

"Play it," McElroy told him.

A smaller, unused monitor flickered to life with Six's shot of the metro entrance. The man he had tagged was in the middle of a pack of exiting commuters.

Duncan paused the image and pushed in. Stonewell's surveillance gear was cutting edge, compact, and ultra high-def, so little quality was lost as the image was enlarged.

The man on the screen was solidly built and had a rugged, timeworn face that McElroy had committed to memory years ago.

His pulse kicked up a notch.

"That's him," he said, then keyed his mic. "Raven spotted. All teams, Raven spotted. Entering on Rue de la Huchette. Six has him tagged. Zeta Five, stay alert."

Using the digital tag, the spotters synced their systems to

pick the target out of the crowd.

"Got him," Five said. "On Huchette now."

Duncan switched Zeta Five's feed onto the main screen.

"Grab team, stand by," McElroy said.

His orders from Stonewell were to snatch Raven *and* the man he was meeting. Both were wanted by the US government, and their captures would reflect well on the organization, not to mention earn it a generous bonus on top of its usual service fee.

There was only one small problem. The Latin Quarter was a warren of narrow pedestrian streets that weaved around centuries-old, multistory buildings like crooked trails through a dense forest. All were already filling up with hungry tourists. Because of the twists and turns, sight lines were a bitch, with dozens of nooks and recesses where their targets could hide from view if they even remotely suspected they were being followed.

Raven had chosen his meeting place wisely.

There was also the not insignificant fact that Stonewell's entire operation was off the grid. The French government was kept in the dark, a decision made by Stonewell's executive committee and passed on to McElroy.

It was one that he fully supported, however. No way the French would've allowed them to move forward, especially given the short time frame involved.

The radio crackled. "Zeta One to base. Hawk sighted. Exiting taxi on Rue Saint-Jacques."

McElroy shifted his focus to Zeta One's monitor in time to see a blond, powerfully built man walking away from a taxi at the curb. He had bleached his hair, but it was Hawk all right. Stonewell had obtained only one halfway decent picture of him, but McElroy recognized the intense eyes and that jagged pink scar on the right side of his neck.

In some circles within the US intelligence community, Hawk was considered the bigger catch. He would undoubtedly possess information about terrorist organizations throughout Europe and the Middle East that would be paying off for years.

But the real prize was Raven. It wasn't so much because of what the man might know, but because of what he represented. His capture would be satisfying to Stonewell's clients.

Deeply satisfying.

And to McElroy himself.

"Both targets on site," he told everyone. "Grab team in position."

One of the small monitor feeds was focused on the front of the restaurant where the two men were reportedly scheduled to meet. It was down a side street, deeper into the Quarter, and flanked by two other restaurants.

Within moments, the members of the grab team joined the steady stream of tourists on the cobbled walkway. Two of them, a man and a woman, approached the restaurant and paused outside the door as if they were trying to decide whether this was where they wanted to eat. They were the backup, just in case either Raven or Hawk got that far.

McElroy glanced at the monitor tracking Raven. The man's progress had slowed because of the crowd, and he was still at least a couple minutes away from the restaurant.

Hawk's path, on the other hand, was clearer, and it looked as if he would reach the meeting location first—if he were allowed.

"Hawk approaching from the south," McElroy reported. "Turning your way...now."

Hawk disappeared from Zeta Two's monitor and reappeared on Zeta Three's. The road went straight for about twenty-five feet, bent to the left, then sharply back to the right before passing by the restaurant.

Hawk entered the bend, and slowed as he reached the tight turn.

"Now!" McElroy commanded.

Just as Hawk made the turn, four members of the grab team closed in around him, and before he even realized what was going on, one of them stuck a needle in his arm, pumping enough Beta-Somnol into him to knock him out for hours.

The others caught him before he could fall, propped him up between two of them, and dragged him back out of the Quarter, five happy friends who had started drinking a little early.

McElroy allowed himself a smile at how seamlessly it had all gone.

But the celebration didn't last long.

"I don't see Raven," one of the spotters said. McElroy wasn't sure which.

He whipped his gaze back to the main monitor, and noted that the red dot that had been marking Raven's position was gone.

Fuck.

"Who had him last?" he asked Zeta team. They were the spotters, while Omega team was on the ground for the grab.

"I did. Zeta Five."

"What happened?"

"Don't know. I had him on Huchette. He turned off and Zeta Four should have picked him up."

"Never saw him," Zeta Four reported.

That didn't make sense. Once Raven had been tagged, Zeta Four's camera should have automatically been able to pick him up.

"Everyone, eyes open! Find Raven." McElroy grabbed Duncan's shoulder, gripping it harder than he realized. "Replay the feeds for Zetas Five and Four. He's got to be there somewhere."

Duncan started with Five's view first, picking it up fifteen seconds before Raven would make his turn. The target was walking at the same pace as before, moving around those who had stopped in the road, and getting out of the way of those moving faster than him. Then, just before he reached the intersection—

"Play that back," McElroy said.

Duncan did as ordered and McElroy studied the screen.

"Look there," Duncan said. "He hesitated."

Indeed, Raven had. It had been only for a second, but it was a definite hesitation. *Why would he…*

McElroy's breath caught in his throat as a possibility occurred to him.

It can't be, he thought. To Duncan, he said, "What time did he pause?"

Duncan checked his computer screen. "6:06:17."

"And when did Hawk get taken down?"

Another check. "6:06:15."

Shit.

"What happens when he gets to the corner?"

Duncan started the video again. Right before Raven arrived at the corner, he reached up, grabbed the top of his jacket, and started to pull.

"What's he doing?" McElroy asked, more to himself than anyone.

Duncan replied by switching over to the recorded footage from Zeta Four. The area that Four had been tasked to cover ranged from the corner to where the road angled slightly right about fifty feet before the restaurant. This, unfortunately, meant there was a section of dead space, about three or four feet in length, right at the corner—if one kept tucked to the wall.

Apparently Raven had.

He should have appeared immediately on screen, but there was no one there.

"Where the hell is he?" McElroy said.

Duncan seemed flustered. "I don't know…he should be—"

Before Duncan could complete his sentence, someone appeared down near the end of the street for a fraction of a second before heading back onto the other road. Duncan stopped the video, rewound several frames, and zoomed in.

Raven.

"He must've taken his jacket off when we grabbed Hawk," Duncan said, surprised. "But how could he know?"

The digital tag had keyed in on Raven's jacket—its

material, color, size—and that's what each of the other surveillance rigs would pick up on. Without it, the spotters would have to make their own visual identification until a new tag was created.

Feeling his gut clench again, McElroy keyed his mic. "Raven is on the loose, heading east on Rue de la Huchette. All teams move in to intercept!"

The feeds from the spotters' cameras began bouncing up and down, as the men hustled to reposition themselves so they could try to get eyes once more on Raven and assist the grab team.

McElroy barely maintained composure as he waited for someone to spot the target.

Finally, Zeta Three called in. "I'm on Huchette, east to Rue Saint-Jacques. I don't see him anywhere."

"He must have made it out already," McElroy said. "Everyone fan out. Check taxis, buses, pedestrians. He's got to be out there. We can't let him slip through."

But after five minutes of no further sightings, McElroy feared his instincts had been correct.

After ten, he knew it.

Raven was gone.

TWO

EVEN IN THE tensest situations, the sound of Deuce's voice was reassuring. At that very moment, he was shouting breathlessly in Alexandra Poe's wireless earpiece.

"Look alive," he said. "He's coming your way!"

"Good," Alex whispered.

Barely a second later, she heard Charlie Wright's footsteps pounding toward her down the alleyway. He was repeating something under his breath like a mantra, his tone panicked, but she couldn't make out the words.

Then a second set of footsteps entered the far end of the alley—Deuce, his ragged breaths still in her ear as he followed Wright, cutting off any potential retreat. Wright must have heard him, too, because the mutterings became louder and more frantic. "Oh, God. Oh, God. Oh, God. Oh, God. Oh, God."

It wasn't the most original plea Alex had ever heard, but people like Wright weren't exactly known for their creativity.

She waited until he'd closed the distance between them to a couple dozen feet, then she stepped out from behind the Dumpster and pointed her Taser at him.

"Hold it right there, Charlie."

"Holy shit!" Wright cried.

He was big man who wouldn't have looked out of place on the front line of a football team, so stopping wasn't exactly a simple thing. He tried to skid to a halt, but stumbled over his own feet and fell onto the cracked asphalt.

Alex shoved her Taser into its holster as she rushed over,

and then jumped onto his back, straddling him before he even had the chance to roll over. Grabbing his arms, she pulled them toward her so she could cuff his wrists with a plastic zip tie, but he suddenly shoved upward and tried to stand.

Out of sheer instinct, Alex threw an arm around his neck so she wouldn't fall off. He clawed at it, gasping for air, and twisted around in a circle until he was able to knock her to the ground.

With a thick splash, she landed half in, half out of a muddy, water-filled pothole, groaning in pain as her left butt cheek hit the jagged edge of the pavement.

"Jesus!"

As Wright started to run again, she pushed herself back to her feet, and grabbed for her Taser, only to find that her holster was empty. The weapon must have fallen out during the rodeo ride on Wright's back.

She scanned the ground, looking for the familiar shape.

"Dude," Deuce yelled, "for chrissakes, stop! You are *not* doing yourself any favors!" He slowed as he came abreast of Alex. "You all right?"

"Fine," she said, waving him on. "Just go get him!"

Deuce nodded and took off after Wright.

As Alex whipped around, still looking for her Taser, her gaze settled on the pothole she'd fallen into.

"No," she said, hoping her instinct was wrong.

Crouching next to it, she plopped her already muddied hand into the water. A moment later, she closed her eyes and scrunched her face. "Son of a…"

She pulled the waterlogged Taser out of the puddle, and angrily shoved the now useless weapon into its holster, this time snapping the restraining strap into place. Then she lit out after Deuce and Wright.

Both men were out of sight, but she could hear Deuce still breathing heavily in her earpiece.

"Where are you?" she asked.

"Turn left…at the end of the alley."

"You still on him?"

"Ten-four."

Maps. Directions. Layout. These were things Alex had a particular talent for. Study a map for a few moments and it would be committed to memory. So she knew it would only be a couple more minutes before Wright reached Norris Boulevard, the main drag in this little Maryland burg.

Not exactly the most discreet place for a takedown, but what choice did they have?

When she reached the end of the alley and turned left, she could see both Wright and Deuce ahead. A part of her had hoped Wright would be kneeling on the ground, out of breath, but the big man was still running, albeit at a much slower pace. Deuce, leaner and in better shape, had closed to within fifty feet of him and had his Taser out.

"Stop!" Deuce called out. "Right now!"

Ignoring the pain in her gluteus maximus, Alex sprinted down the road in a burst of speed faster than even her partner could achieve, but she was still a half block back when Wright suddenly turned and lunged toward Deuce.

Caught off guard, Deuce fired his Taser, but Alex could see that only one of the needles hit its mark. A spasm shot through the left side of Wright's massive rib cage, but it didn't stop him. He yanked out the needle, and made a grab for Deuce's hand. Deuce jerked away just in time, and landed a blow to Wright's gut with his other fist.

Wright staggered back a few feet, and then leaned forward breathing deeply, his hands on his thighs.

"On the ground!" Deuce shouted.

Wright didn't move.

Deuce took a step closer. "I said, on the ground!"

Wright reached out and swatted at the air, in what was probably meant as a warning. Unfortunately for Deuce, Wright's arm was as long as he was large, and the back of the big man's palm glanced off Deuce's chin.

Deuce stumbled back a few steps, the blow momentarily stunning him.

Wright took a tentative step forward, as if he were going

to take advantage of the situation and run again.

But Alex shouted, "Not another move!"

Wright jerked in surprise and looked back. She was ten feet behind him, her inoperable Taser once more in her hand.

"On the ground," she said.

He hesitated for a moment, then, with a sigh, lowered himself onto his knees.

As Alex moved behind him and secured his wrists, she glanced at Deuce. "You all right?"

He turned his chin toward her. "You think it's gonna bruise?"

She shrugged. "Maybe."

"Cool."

Deuce wasn't like other people.

But then neither was Alex.

Baltimore, Maryland

THE RIDE HOME was uneventful. By the time they got to the station, it was nearly nine p.m.

Artie Cashman, aka Max Cash of Max Cash Bail Bond, was waiting in the lobby when Alex and Deuce escorted Wright inside.

"Well, well, well," he said. "The giant takes a fall. What did I tell you about trying something stupid?"

Wright, not meeting his eyes, shrugged.

"Come on, Charlie, what did I *tell* you?"

Alex nudged her prisoner. "You'd better speak up."

The big man frowned, and mumbled, "That you'd always find me."

"That's right." Max beamed. "And guess what? I did."

Alex could have argued the point, since the only thing Max had provided was an address that turned out to be bogus, but in the grand scheme he was close enough. Charlie had gone rabbit and gotten his tail clipped. And Max was just lucky that Alex and Deuce had been available to do the clipping.

"Let's get you checked in," Alex said.

Max seemed to notice her for the first time. "I see he put up a fight, huh?"

Alex glanced down at her muddied shirt and pants. "No, I always dress this way. Helps me blend in with the losers."

"I think it's working," Max said.

He had already briefed the police before Alex and Deuce arrived, so the transfer of the prisoner went smooth as silk.

Once Wright was off their hands, Max told them, "Come by the office tomorrow and I'll write you a check."

Deuce chuckled, but Alex narrowed her eyes.

"Don't even try," she said.

Max spread his hands. "What? You can come first thing in the morning." He looked at his watch. "That's less than twelve hours from now."

"Max."

"Come on, Alex. You think I carry my checkbook everywhere I go?"

"You *know* the rule."

It was simple: payment on delivery. No exceptions.

He huffed as he pushed a hand into his pocket. "Fine, here." He pulled out a check, and handed it to her. "Buy yourself a garden hose, spray off some of that crud."

She wasn't surprised to see it was already filled out. Max was a notorious skinflint, and more times than not Alex had to play this little game with him.

She nodded at Deuce, and they turned to leave.

"Hey," Max said, "I still want you to come by tomorrow. There's a hearing in the morning and I have a feeling my guy isn't gonna show. If that happens, I want to jump on it right—"

"We're busy tomorrow." A lie, but Alex wasn't in the mood to pick up Max's trash twice in a row. "Come on, Deuce."

Deuce clapped Max on the back. "See ya, dude."

"I'm serious," Max said as they walked away.

"Tomorrow, okay?"

Without looking back, she said, "Not gonna happen."

"Come on, Alex, is that any way to treat one of your best—"

"Alexandra Poe?"

She had reached the door and started to push it open, but that stopped her. She turned toward the voice.

Smiling at her from a dozen feet away was a well-groomed man in a dark gray Armani suit. Mid to late thirties, possibly forty, but not much more, and in decent shape. She wouldn't have called him attractive, but he was passable.

A lawyer, she thought, or something along those lines.

She smirked, then went outside, Deuce trailing behind. She was tired and just wanted to take a hot shower and crawl into bed.

She heard the door open behind them as they walked toward the parking lot.

"You *are* Alexandra Poe, correct?"

Growing annoyed, she quickened her pace.

"I just need a moment of your time."

"Set it up with my secretary," she said as she pulled out her key fob, and aimed it at her Jeep. With a push of a button, the locks popped open.

Deuce circled around to the passenger side, while Alex pulled open the driver's door and climbed in. When she tried to pull it closed, the man in the Armani suit grabbed hold of it, stopping her.

"You're about to lose that hand," she said.

He didn't budge. "I know it's probably not a good time."

"You figured that out on your own? Let go of the fucking door."

With his free hand, he removed a business card from his pocket, and held it out. "When you get a moment, I'd appreciate it if you'd give me a call."

Alex wrenched the door free from his grasp, but just before she could close it, he tossed the card inside. The locks clunked down as she hit the dash button, then she started the engine, punched the gas, and left him standing in the parking lot.

Deuce said, "Looks like the wolves are circling again."

Alex looked over and saw that he'd somehow gotten hold of the business card. He turned it so she could see it.

Taking up the entire left side of the card was an all-too-familiar logo: STONEWELL ASSOCIATES.

The man's name, however, was new to her.

Jason McElroy.

She grabbed the card out of Deuce's hand, crumpled it, and tossed it into the back.

Deuce snickered. "I take it you won't be calling him?"

"Not without a gun pointed at my head."

THREE

SHE DIDN'T GET the alarm to stop shrieking until the second try. Clipping a hand against the clock radio, she hit the snooze button, groaned, and rolled onto her back.

She should have turned the thing off last night, when it was clear she couldn't sleep, but she'd been too preoccupied with the thought of that asshole from Stonewell to do anything sensible.

This wasn't the first time Alex had been approached by the organization. Stonewell was a top-tier defense contractor, and for whatever reason, they seemed to think she should be working for them. She suspected it had less to do with her skills than with the way she looked, being half Iranian and all. Her dark hair and mixed-race features would make it easy for her to pass for a number of different nationalities, which could be quite useful to an international operation like Stonewell.

Alex pushed the covers to the side, sat up, and made sure the alarm was off for good.

To hell with them. She was fine with the way things were, thank you. She was her own boss, could pass on assignments she wasn't interested in, could even take off and do nothing for a month or more if she wanted to. Not that she ever did, but knowing she could was all that mattered.

She stood up, still angry, thinking that if Mr. Jason McElroy hadn't grabbed her door like an overaggressive lunatic, she could have brushed it off. That's what had really set her teeth on edge. Her personal space was very important to her.

More than one person had learned that the hard way.

She thought about taking a shower, but what she really needed was to work this crap out of her system, so she pulled some clothes on, grabbed her gym bag, and headed for the door.

ACKERMAN'S GYM WAS located in a middle-class Baltimore neighborhood that was once good, had gone bad, and was now transitioning back the other way.

Through it all the gym had remained a constant.

The original owner had been an old fighter named Marty "Ace" Ackerman. Marty had never gotten close to a title fight, but had seen plenty of champions either on their way up or their spiral back down—much like the neighborhood, Alex had often thought—and had died at the ripe old age of eighty-six, right there in the gym.

He'd left the place to its longtime manager, Hans Emerick. Emerick himself was getting up there in age, but he still showed up every day, and was more than willing to train Alex whenever she asked.

"Speed bag," he said the moment she walked in. "Fifteen minutes. Then crunches. Five hundred."

His German accent was still thick after all these years in the States. He was a refugee of the Cold War, a promising East German weightlifter who'd escaped through one of the tunnels under the Berlin Wall, something he almost never talked about.

"Ancient history," he'd say, if anyone brought it up.

Alex was the only exception. In her he seemed to see some sort of kindred spirit, and had given her a glimpse of what his life had once been and how terrified he was the night he snuck into the West.

"You have not known fear," he told her, "until you've been alone in the dark and either freedom or death is only a few footsteps away."

Alex had never argued the point.

Just hearing about it was frightening enough.

Changing into her workout clothes, she wrapped her

hands in tape, and headed out to the bag. Within the first few seconds, she could feel her tension begin to drain away. This was exactly what she needed, something to get her blood moving again. Push out the toxins and soak in the fresh oxygen.

Right. Left. Right. Left. Right. Left. The rhythm slow at first, then speeding up to her normal pace. Sweat beaded along her hairline and down her jaw as the knot in her stomach started to loosen.

This was good. Really good.

Emerick let her know when the fifteen minutes were up by clapping his hands twice and saying, "Crunches."

She hit the bag one last time, then moved over to the floor and began torturing her abdomen. She had counted to two hundred twenty-one, grunting with each crunch, when the buzzer at the far end of the room went off.

Someone had entered the lobby.

Emerick, who had been sweeping the area around the boxing ring as Alex worked, leaned his broom against the ropes and went to see who it was.

Alex passed crunch number three sixteen when Emerick came back inside, accompanied by two other men. She assumed they were clients, and didn't pay them any attention.

Three thirty-five. Three thirty-six. Three thirty-seven. Three thirty-eight.

"Alex?"

Three thirty-nine.

She slowed slightly on three forty, and looked over.

"Someone here to see you," Emerick said.

She shifted her gaze to the man standing next to him.

Jason McElroy.

Son of a bitch.

The suit was dark blue today and he was carrying a briefcase, but he wasn't wearing a tie, maybe in deference to his surroundings. He took a few steps toward her, his buddy remaining back by the door to the lobby.

"Good morning, Ms. Poe."

Ignoring him, Alex picked up her pace again. *Three forty-one. Three forty-two. Three forty-three.*

She kept going, right through four hundred and all the way up to five, before she finally stopped. Lying back on the mat, she allowed herself to catch her breath, then hopped to her feet.

"Okay, what next?" she asked Emerick.

He thought for a moment. "Medicine ball."

With a nod, she moved over to where they kept the heavy, oversized ball, picked it up, and acknowledged McElroy's presence for the first time. "You catch."

He blinked at her. "What?"

"I throw. You catch."

"Uh, okay."

As McElroy turned to set his briefcase down, Alex tossed the ball. Sensing the movement, he swung his arms around and up just in time to catch it before it slammed into his hip.

Alex motioned with her fingers. "Come on. Throw it back."

McElroy tested the heft of the ball, and heaved it in her direction. In a single, continuous motion, Alex caught it and sent it back.

"I was hoping we might have that chat now," he said.

She nodded at the ball. "Keep it going."

As he threw it back, he said, "I realize you've been contacted by others from my organization in the past."

Alex made another smooth catch and return. Catching it again, McElroy grunted under his breath. "I know that whatever it was they were asking of you, you turned it down."

"The ball."

"Can't we just talk first?"

She stared at him for a second, then looked at Emerick. "Next?"

Before Emerick could reply, the man who'd been standing by the door said, "I'll toss with you."

Alex had ignored him earlier, assuming he was simply

there to make McElroy look more important. But as he walked toward them, she realized he was more than that.

She knew him.

At one time, she had known him well.

Shane Cooper.

"How you doing, Alex?"

She shot a look at McElroy. "Are you kidding me? Is bringing him along supposed to give you an edge? Is that what you think?"

"I tried to tell him it wouldn't work," Cooper said as he picked up the ball. "But you know suits. They never listen."

He threw it at Alex with more force than McElroy had even come close to achieving. She caught it and returned it equally hard. They continued the back and forth, neither holding the ball for more than a few seconds before sending it off again.

"You didn't answer my question," Cooper said.

"What question was that?"

"How you're doing?"

"I'm fine."

"Me, too."

"I didn't ask."

He smiled. "I know." He tossed the ball back to her. "You're looking pretty good. Maybe a little angrier than before."

"My mood depends on the company."

"Ouch."

They silently tossed for a couple of minutes.

Cooper finally said, "It *is* good to see you."

This time when she caught the ball, she dropped it to the ground and looked at Emerick. "Next."

"I have an idea," Cooper said.

As she started to scowl, he glanced at the boxing ring then back at her. "How about it?"

She stared at him, then shrugged as a short, disdainful laugh escaped her lips. "Your funeral."

While Alex was more than willing to get into the ring

with only gloves on, Emerick insisted they both wear headgear and mouth guards. He also loaned Cooper some shorts, shoes, and a T-shirt.

"This is a waste of time," McElroy said as Alex and Cooper climbed into the ring.

"No one said you needed to stay," Cooper told him.

Alex stifled a smile. She couldn't help liking the fact that Cooper had talked back to McElroy. His willingness to speak his mind even in front of superiors was one of the traits she'd always appreciated. It was good to see he hadn't lost that.

"Four rounds. One minute each," Emerick said.

"Two minutes," Alex told him.

Emerick frowned. "Ninety seconds. Remember, liebchen, this is my gym."

Alex pounded her gloved fists together and nodded. Ninety seconds it was.

They went through the ritual of a quick glove tap in the center of the ring, then separated. Once they were ready, Emerick rang the bell.

Typically, the first several seconds would be spent circling and jabbing, testing each other's defenses. But Alex wasn't in the mood for that. She moved to the middle, making it look like she was going to do the expected, then as soon as Cooper was in range, she let loose a surprise left hook.

He saw it at the last second, and pivoted his right arm to block it, but he was too late. Her blow landed solidly against the head pad that lay across his cheek.

As he staggered sideways, she knew she should move in for the kill, but she held back, not wanting to end it so quickly.

He laughed. "So that's how you want it, huh?" He raised his gloves again. "All right. Let's go."

Through the rest of the first round and all of the second, neither was able to land anything more than glancing blows.

In the third, however, Cooper snuck in a shot to her ribs that nearly knocked the air out of her. But Alex refused to show any weakness, and came at him with a flurry of punches that forced him back against the ropes. If the bell hadn't rung, she was sure she would have had him.

Both fighters were breathing deeply as the final round started. Clothes drenched in sweat, they met in the middle again, their fists held at the ready.

Jabs one way, and the other, all harmlessly knocked away.

As Alex searched for an opening that would allow her to make solid contact, she could sense the seconds ticking off the clock. She didn't want the fight to end this way, not dancing around like this.

She feinted a punch to his stomach, then pulled back, ready to swing at his head, but he'd anticipated the move and left no clear shot. She tried it again, and had the same results.

On her third attempt, she didn't fake a stomach punch, but instead jabbed straight at Cooper's face with her right, and swung another left hook at the side of his head.

Right before her blow landed, he shot a fist up at her now unprotected torso. She hit him a split second before he hit her. Cooper's blow sent Alex backpedaling several feet, while hers knocked him to the mat.

She winced in pain, her ribs undoubtedly bruised, and looked over at Cooper.

"Get up."

He slowly pushed himself up. "That felt good, didn't it?"

"Oh, yeah," she said, ignoring the pain radiating from her ribs.

"You still pack a pretty good punch. I was worried maybe you'd dropped off a bit."

"Nope."

"This is the part where you compliment my skills."

A smirk. "I know."

"Still Alex, I see." He took a breath. "Again? Or are we done?"

"If you're worn out, we can be done."

"Oh, I'm not worn out at all."

But as they raised their gloves, the bell rang.

"You're done," Emerick said. "Both of you."

Cooper held the ropes open so Alex could climb out first. She contemplated letting herself out on another side, but decided to accept the offer. Cooper wasn't a bad guy. There were just some things that were hard to forget.

With Emerick's help, she removed her gloves and pulled off her headgear as McElroy stepped toward her. "So, can we talk now?"

"Don't need to," she said. "Whatever you're asking, my answer's no."

"Ms. Poe, I have some information I'm pretty sure you'll want to hear."

"And I'm pretty sure I don't. But thanks for bringing Cooper by. Haven't had a workout like that in a while."

She started for the women's locker room.

"It's about your father."

She stopped, and slowly turned back. "Don't you dare screw with me, asshole, or I will put you in the ground."

"We have news about him."

"*What* news?"

McElroy smiled. "We know where he is."

FOUR

BAY CITY COFFEE and Treats was one of the recent additions to the neighborhood. It was half a block down the street from the gym in a building that, until recently, had been abandoned for years. Now, the upper floors had been turned into lofts, while a flower shop and a candle store rounded out the businesses on the ground level.

Once they took a table outside, Cooper went in to order their coffee, leaving McElroy and Alex alone.

She said, "All right, you've got me here. Where is he?"

McElroy glanced at the front door. "Maybe we should wait until—"

"*Where* is he?"

A slight hesitation, then, "Yalta."

"Yalta? *Ukraine* Yalta?"

"Yes," McElroy said with a nod. "At least he was a week ago."

"A week ago."

"Right."

"So he's not there now."

McElroy hesitated again. "We can't confirm that."

"So you lied to me when you told me you knew where he was." She got to her feet. "I should have figured as much."

McElroy jumped up.

"Not lied," he said quickly. He was trying for a smile but it came off more like a desperate grimace. "Stretched the truth a bit. But we know where he *has* been. And recently, at that."

Alex was tempted to walk away right then, but the truth was, even if it had been a week since her father was last seen, that was more information than she'd had in over a decade.

She remained standing. "What was he doing there?"

"Meeting with someone."

"Stonewell?"

McElroy scoffed. "No, of course not. We don't meet with…" The words died on his lips as he seemed to realize what he was about to say.

"With who?"

"It's not important."

"I think it is. You were going to say traitors, weren't you?"

He remained silent, confirming what she thought.

She studied him a moment then sat back down. "Why are you telling me this?"

"Because I assume it's something you'd like to know," he said, sinking into his chair.

"Don't even pretend this is a gesture of goodwill. What do you want from me?"

A bell tinkled as the shop door opened and Cooper exited holding three cups of coffee. He placed two on the table and kept one for himself as he sat in the empty seat.

When the others didn't pick up their drinks, he glanced between them. "I take it you've been talking about Raven?"

Alex's brow furrowed. "Raven?"

"Stonewell's code name for your father."

She rolled her eyes. "Oh, that's cute."

Cooper shrugged. "I tried to get them to call you Corvus Mellori, but nobody would bite."

"Corvus what?"

"Little Raven."

She eyed him dully. "I think I may puke."

He gestured to her coffee. "So drink up. It'll do you good."

During this exchange, McElroy leaned down, opened his briefcase, and pulled out a white, nine-by-twelve envelope. From inside he slid out a photo and set it on the table in front of Alex.

The still was taken from an elevated position, but not so

high that the faces were unrecognizable. It was an outside shot of a stone walkway that was either along a lake, or, given that it was apparently taken in Yalta, the Black Sea. Dozens of people were walking by in either direction, but the focus of the shot was a couple standing near the edge. The woman was wearing a conservative dress that went almost all the way to the ground. A scarf was wrapped her head and covered most of her face. Not quite a hijab but the effect was similar, leaving Alex with no way to tell who she was.

She had no such problem recognizing the man. He looked older than the last time she'd seen him, but it was definitely her father. The thing that struck her as oddest was his hair. It was so long. For her entire life, he'd kept it cropped tight to his scalp, but now it looked a little wild and unkempt, and some of the gray was turning white.

The hazards of being on the run.

Alex had to check herself to keep from reaching out and touching the photograph. It really *was* him. "This was taken a week ago?"

"Yes," McElroy said.

"So this woman was who he was meeting?"

"Correct."

"Who is she?"

McElroy reached into his briefcase again and pulled out a file. "That's a good question. She goes by a number of names." He set the file down, opened it, and one by one, pulled out more photographs of her. The outfits changed from shot to shot, but there was always a head scarf that covered all but her eyes. Most of the time they were hidden behind sunglasses. "She's currently using the name Fadilah El-Hashim."

"And what were they meeting about?"

"We're not sure. El-Hashim is associated with a group that launders money for, among others, several terrorist organizations. Not only do they hide the money, but from what we've been able to gather, they're also shrewd investors. Quite shrewd, in fact."

Alex was trying to connect the dots. "So you think she's helping my father hide money?"

"Like I said, we don't know why they were meeting. This image came from a surveillance camera. We only found it and a few others after we learned El-Hashim had met with someone there. What we didn't expect to find was Colonel Poe."

As Alex studied her father's features, all the grief she had held in check came flooding back. He looked tired, and thinner.

Why did you go, Dad?

That was the question she could never answer, one she'd promised herself would be the first out of her mouth if she ever saw him again. Over the years, however, she sensed the possibility of that happening becoming smaller and smaller, and had sometimes wondered if he was alive at all.

Why, Dad?

She raised her head, locking gazes with McElroy. "Okay," she said. "What does any of this have to do with me?"

McElroy started to smile, then stopped. "I'm with special operations at Stonewell. The fugitive retrieval division."

It took her only a split second to see where he was going.

"Whoa," she said, "wait a minute. Is that what this is about?" She pushed away from the table. "You want me to help you find my father and bring him in?" She rose to her feet again. "Thanks for the show-and-tell, asshole, but I think I'll say goodbye."

McElroy hopped back up and grabbed her arm as she tried to walk away. "You completely misunderstand me."

Alex stiffened, her teeth clenching. "Let go."

"I'm not asking you to help me get your father. He's not even on our list."

"Bullshit." She wrenched her arm free.

"It's the woman," he said quickly. "We want to bring her in. She has intel that will help the US government shut down the whole operation she's involved in."

Alex stared at him. "If I wouldn't help you with my father, why would I even consider helping you with this woman?"

"*Because* of your father, of course," McElroy said.

"Meaning what?"

Cooper, the only one still sitting, said in a calmer voice, "El-Hashim is the last person he was seen with. Maybe she knows how to contact him."

"Exactly," McElroy said. "You see now? If you help us retrieve her, you'll have a chance to find out what she knows."

Alex balked. "And pass the info on to you, so you can go after him? I don't think so."

"I told you, he's not even on our list. Stonewell is not a charity. It's a commercial entity. If it's something we haven't been hired to do, we don't do it."

Alex looked at Cooper.

He shrugged. "Hey, it's up to you. But it *is* a chance to maybe find out a little more about him. I'm sure you're curious. I mean, I would be if I were you."

He had nailed it of course, and knew it. She *was* curious. Hell, she was more than curious. She was borderline desperate. Her father had gone AWOL less than a year after her mother's death. Her desire to know why he had left her and her brother behind had dulled as the years passed, but it hadn't gone away. And now, faced with this potential connection to him, her feelings of wonder and anger and loneliness came rushing back like a hundred-foot tsunami.

She stepped back to the table, and picked up the photo without sitting down.

"Do you at least know where this woman is?"

"Still in Ukraine."

"It's a big country."

"We can pinpoint her position to within a dozen feet or so."

Alex raised an eyebrow. "You seem pretty sure about that."

"I am."

"Okay, but what about tomorrow? Or the next day? Or whenever it is we go after her?"

"She's not going anywhere."

"Where exactly is she?"

"I'm afraid I can't tell you that unless you sign on to help."

Alex looked at the image again. This time, it wasn't an older, weary man she saw, but the father she last remembered, grimly holding her hand as they visited her mother's grave. He would be gone the following day, but she hadn't known that then. All she'd known was that he was sadder than she'd ever seen him.

When they had knelt on the grass next to the grave, her father had leaned down and kissed the headstone. Alex had stared at him in surprise. He'd never been one to display much emotion, yet there he was, tears running down his cheeks, and the imprint of his lips gracing the stone next to her mother's name.

"I'm sorry," McElroy said. "Apparently we made a mistake."

He scooped up the file on El-Hashim and returned it to his briefcase. He then held out his hand to Alex for the photo. "I'll make sure no one at Stonewell bothers you again."

She closed her eyes, still grasping the picture. "Hold on."

There was silence, no one moving. When she opened her eyes again, McElroy and Cooper were staring back at her.

"If I say yes," she said, wondering if she was making a mistake, "my rate's a thousand dollars a day, plus expenses, full insurance rider, medical and life. And you hire Deuce, too, at the same rate."

"Deuce?"

Cooper, on his feet now, whispered something into McElroy's ear.

"Oh, right," McElroy said. "Your partner."

"Package deal."

A hesitation, then, "Fine."

He placed his briefcase on the table and opened it back up. From inside, he pulled out a file and removed the sheet of paper it was holding.

"I take it the bump in pay won't be an issue," he said.

Alex took the document from him. It was a one-page, freelance-hire agreement, listing her daily rate at fifteen hundred, plus the requested insurance.

"You're pretty confident," she said.

"Confident, no. Prepared, yes."

"And Deuce?"

"I'll have papers prepped and ready for him when he comes in."

She read everything to make sure there weren't any hidden issues. The agreement seemed pretty straightforward.

McElroy held out a pen. "You can sign at the bottom."

She didn't take it.

"Is there a problem?"

"I haven't said yes yet."

He stared at her for a moment, then reached for the contract, but she kept her hand on it.

"I don't have time for games, Ms. Poe. If you'll please move your hand so we can be on our way."

"I didn't say no, either. I need a little time to think."

"Time is something we don't have."

"You said she wasn't going anywhere."

McElroy frowned. "For now, but that won't last forever."

"How much time do you need?" Cooper asked, his tone considerably more understanding than his boss's. "Would the end of the day be enough?"

McElroy didn't look very happy, but he kept his mouth shut.

Alex thought about it for a moment, then nodded. "End of the day."

FIVE

"PROBLEMS?" EMERICK ASKED.

Alex had no idea what she must look like, but the moment she walked back into Ackerman's, the old man seemed to sense that something had changed.

She answered him as honestly as she could. "I'm not sure."

With a shrug, he tilted his head toward the gym door. "Shall we finish your workout?"

"Not today, Hans. I've got some things I need to do."

She showered, dressed, and was on the road fifteen minutes later. She headed south out of the city, along the same highway she'd driven at least once a week for years now. Passing Riverdale, she caught glimpses of water to the left, where an offshoot of the Chesapeake Bay wrapped its way along the shore. Just before she reached Annapolis, she hopped onto Route 50 and took the Bay Bridge across to Kent Island.

The house was on a quiet road in Stevensville, north of the highway. Like many of the other homes in the area, it was set back from the road on a large parcel of land. Where it differed from its neighbors was the fence that surrounded the property. Most of the homes had none.

Alex pulled up to the gate, and pressed the button on the intercom box.

"May I help you?" a female voice asked.

"It's Alexandra Poe."

The woman said nothing for a second, then, "I don't have you on the schedule, Miss Poe."

"Last minute thing."

"One moment."

With a sudden whine, the gate swung open. Alex drove through and parked next to some other cars, then got out and headed toward the house. Before she reached the front door, it opened, and Mrs. Thornton stepped onto the porch.

"Alexandra. Good to see you." She held out a hand as she always did, and the two women shook. "This is unexpected. Is there something wrong?"

"No," Alex said. "It's...well, I might be going out of town and I'm not sure how long I'll be away, so I wanted to come by first. Just in case."

An understanding smile creased Mrs. Thornton's face. "Of course. But I wish you would have called first."

"Is there a problem?"

"No. But Danny isn't always good with surprises."

"I know how Danny is," Alex said. "I'm sure he'll be fine."

Mrs. Thornton slipped a motherly arm around Alex's shoulders. "I'm sure he will be."

Alex tensed under the woman's touch, but she knew Mrs. Thornton only had the kindest of intentions. The woman couldn't help herself; it was in her nature. She was old enough to have a dozen grandchildren but had none. Ryan, her only child, had been born with cerebral palsy and died as a teenager from complications due to his condition. He had been the inspiration behind Ryan's House, the name Mrs. Thornton had given her home when she'd turned it into a group facility for disabled adults.

She led Alex through the front doorway into the family room that had been converted into a lounge/activity area. Several of the residents were there, working at the table or watching TV.

Alex's brother was sitting on the couch, his attention glued to the SpongeBob SquarePants cartoon on the screen. His lips moved as he mimicked every line, mostly silently, but with the occasional mumbled word slipping out.

She saw the ever-present watch on his wrist, the watch

that had belonged to their father, and suddenly knew she had no choice. If she had been alone in the world, she might've convinced herself she didn't need to see her father again, and turned down McElroy's offer.

But she wasn't alone.

"Danny," Mrs. Thornton said. "Look who's here."

Danny's gaze stayed fixed on the television screen, his mouth still moving.

"Danny, you have a visitor."

Alex's brother had always been able to tune out the world when he wanted to, especially when SpongeBob was on. If there had been a channel that showed nothing else, he would have been just fine with that.

Mrs. Thornton glanced at Alex. "Would you like me to turn it off?"

"No," Alex said. "I'm not in a hurry."

She stepped over to the couch and sat down. "Hey, buddy. I remember this one. SpongeBob and his bubble friend."

It took Danny a moment to process her voice, but when he finally recognized it, he looked at her. "Aleck."

His smile was broad. She opened her arms, and he hugged her.

"Hi, Danny."

"Aleck. You here. Make me happy."

"Make me happy, too."

Danny had been born with Down syndrome. While he was physically two years older than Alex, mentally he was still a small child. Even at a young age, Alex had seemed to sense that it was her job to take care of him, and she'd watched after him ever since. This sense of protectiveness had only increased when their mother was killed and their father, who used to call Danny his "little lieutenant," disappeared.

It had taken their relatives nearly a year to convince Alex to find a place for Danny to live without her once she reached eighteen. Seven years later, she still felt guilty for making that decision. Almost as guilty as she felt for joining the army and leaving him for two long years. But that was something she had to do. She needed to show the military that enlistees from her family, which had a long history with the army, were good soldiers, and by doing so, prove that they had to be wrong about her dad.

Thankfully, Danny never seemed to blame her for anything. His excitement was the same every time he saw her, whether the absence was a day, a week, or several months.

He turned now, suddenly remembering the TV, and started mumbling along again. Alex was happy just to be next to him, happy to have his hand in hers, happy to see him happy.

When the cartoon finally ended, she said, "You want to go outside?"

"French fry?"

"You want French fries?"

He nodded, and half laughed. "Yeah."

After letting Mrs. Thornton know they were going out, Alex led her brother to her car. Danny lived at a pace different than most people's. By the time Alex circled around to the driver's side, climbed in, and belted up, Danny was only pulling his seatbelt on.

She resisted the urge to help him, and watched as he slowly fastened himself in.

"All set?" she asked.

He smiled. "All set."

Dairy Queen was their usual stop. They arrived right before lunchtime, so there were only a couple people in line in front of them.

"You want ketchup with your fries?" Alex knew the answer, but she always asked.

"Three ketchup," Danny said.

"You got it. And to drink?"

"Root beer," he said, almost singing the words. "Root beer. Root beer. Root beer."

That caused a few of the customers to look, but most just smiled when they realized it was Danny.

Alex and Danny's turn came moments later, and soon they were sitting at a table by the window, a hot serving of fries and sodas in front of them.

Alex watched her brother eat, enjoying the pleasure he took out of every bite. There were times when she wished they could talk about whatever came to mind, discuss science and politics, and, hell, even family. But they would never have that kind of relationship. Simple conversations were it with Danny. Anything more and he'd be lost.

As he chewed his fries, he rocked happily side to side. Alex knew he always had a song playing in his head. She wondered which one it was this time. Something from SpongeBob? A Christmas song? "The Hamster Dance"? They were all favorites.

It was at times like this she wished, if only for a little while, she could enter the world he lived in—the simple life he led, the easy joys, and, of course, the easy sorrows. Life where she had to live it was far more complicated. It made her tired just thinking about the difference.

When there were only a few fries left, she knew she couldn't wait any longer. "Danny."

He looked up, grinning.

She smiled. "Good, huh?"

"Goooood," he said, laughing.

"Not so loud, okay, buddy?"

"Not so loud. Sorry, Aleck."

"It's okay. I know you like them."

Danny picked up another fry and dunked it in his glob of ketchup.

"Danny, look at me for a moment, okay?"

He stuck the fry in his mouth, then, in typical delayed fashion, he finally looked at her.

She tried to give him a reassuring smile, but knew it left a lot to be desired. "Look, I...I'm going on a trip. And I'm not sure how long I might be gone."

Danny stared at her, his expression unchanged.

She paused. "Baseball this weekend, remember?"

His face lit up. "Baseball. We go." He was a huge Baltimore Orioles fan. He didn't always understand what was going on, but the pace of the game, coupled with the excitement of being in the stadium, was more than enough to make his day.

"I can't, Danny. Not this weekend. I'll take you when I come back."

His smile faltered. "No baseball?" His eyes began to water, the easy sorrow settling in.

"Yes, baseball," she said quickly, hoping to forestall the tears. "But not this weekend. When I come back." She could see he was trying to understand, so she reached out and put a hand on his. "We'll go. Don't worry. We'll go a lot this year, I promise. Just not this weekend."

"Not this weekend."

"Right." She still wasn't sure if he completely got it, but he didn't cry, so she took that as a small victory.

"Where you go?" he asked.

"On a trip."

He looked at her as if waiting for more. It was one of his traits that made her wonder at times if his comprehension was better than he let on.

Unable to resist his gaze, she said, "A business trip. Overseas."

"Doing?" he asked.

"What I always do. Catching a bad guy."

That usually made him laugh, but not this time. He picked up the last fry, dipped it several times in the ketchup, and set it back down without eating it.

Before she even realized it, the words were out of her mouth. "This person might know where Dad is."

That did the trick. "Dad?"

She bit the inside of her mouth. "I don't kn—"

"Dad here?"

"No. Dad's not here. I don't know where he is."

"Trip to Dad?"

"No, I'm not going to see Dad. I'm sorry, Danny. I

shouldn't have said anything."

"Mom with Dad?"

Alex's heart clenched. It never failed. Every time she mentioned their father, Danny would eventually bring up their mom, too. "No, Danny. Mom's gone. Remember?"

"With Dad?"

"No. Mom's in heaven. Mom…Mom died a long time ago. You remember that. We buried her."

Buried wasn't exactly accurate. What they'd buried was an empty casket. Months later, they had been given a small box of ashes containing the remains of what had been found of their mother's body after a bomb had taken her life. She had been a professor of anthropology at Georgetown University, and was in Lebanon on one of her many academic trips. The bomb had gone off outside a café, killing two others in addition to her. It was officially blamed on Hezbollah, just another moment of violence in a part of the world where it was commonplace. Since an American had died, it had received some attention in the States, but it was soon pushed to the side when a pair of planes smashed into the Twin Towers a couple days later.

Danny was smiling. "Mom in heaven, with angels."

"Yes, with the angels."

"Angels on the box," he said.

"Angels on the box," she repeated. It was something Danny always said when he talked about their mom. Alex had no idea where it had come from or what it might mean, but it seemed to give him comfort, and it always signaled that he was ready to talk about something else.

He picked up the remaining fry and finished it.

"You go see Dad," he told her.

She sighed. "No, Danny. I'm not going to see Dad."

"You go see Dad. Come back we go baseball." He pointed at her, said, "Aleck," then at himself, "Danny," and finally past her toward the door, "and Dad."

She couldn't help but look over her shoulder, as if it were possible for her brother to conjure their father out of thin air, so the three of them could go to a ballgame like they used to do when she and Danny were kids.

But the doorway was empty.

"Baseball when I come back," she said. "Now let's get you home."

ALEX WATCHED ANOTHER episode of SpongeBob with her brother before hugging him goodbye and heading out to her car. She started the engine, but instead of heading out, she retrieved her phone and called McElroy.

"Okay," she said once he was on the line.

"Okay what?"

"I'm in."

He was quiet for a moment. "You're sure?"

"Yes. I'm sure."

"You might want to write this down."

She grabbed a notepad and pen out of the glove compartment. "Go."

McElroy rattled off a set of directions. "Be there with your partner at eight a.m. tomorrow morning."

"Are you going to tell me where this El-Hashim is now?"

"Not until I have your signed contracts in my hand. I'll see you at eight."

The line went dead.

SIX

"DEUCE, LET'S GO!" Alex yelled as she knocked on Deuce's apartment door for a third time.

She heard something bang against it on the other side, then it jerked open.

"Chill, man. I'm ready," he said. He was wearing cargo pants and a blue, unbuttoned short-sleeve shirt over a gray, Jack Daniel's tank top.

"That's what you're wearing?"

He looked down at his clothes. "What? I didn't get any notice about a dress code."

Alex made no further comment. In truth, she was dressed only marginally better than he was—jeans and a black, long-sleeve T-shirt. No logo or picture, though.

They rode in silence through town and onto I-295. Joining the traffic moving southwest toward DC, Alex found herself thinking about her father. It was pretty much something she'd been doing nonstop since she'd said goodbye to Danny, and had made for a very rough, uneven night of sleep.

"Hello?" Deuce said. "Alex, you in there?"

She blinked and glanced over. "What?"

"I asked you a question."

She looked back at the road. "Sorry, I didn't hear you."

"Obviously." He was silent for second, then said, "My question was, are you going to tell me why you changed your mind about Stonewell or what?"

Alex hesitated.

"Please tell me you heard me this time," Deuce said.

"I heard you."

"And?"

"And they need us to help with an extraction."

"That doesn't really answer my question."

"The target, a week ago, she was seen with…my father."

Silence.

"Are you serious?"

Alex nodded. "I've seen the pictures. It was him."

"Holy shit."

Deuce had never met her dad, but as one of Alex's closest friends, he was well aware of the colonel's disappearance.

Neither of them spoke for a moment, then Deuce said, "So we're helping because she might know where he is, right?"

"Right."

He nodded. "I'm cool with that."

"I knew you would be."

Washington, DC

MCELROY CHECKED HIS watch. It was almost eight a.m.

As he paced his office, he fought the urge to look out the window.

Where the hell was Poe?

God help him if she'd decided to back out. He did *not* want to miss this opportunity.

The tip had come in through one of his Eastern European contacts. Fadilah El-Hashim, terrorist money launderer extraordinaire, had been spotted. And being high on Stonewell's acquire list, she immediately became McElroy's priority.

Within an hour, McElroy had dispatched a small team to follow up on the information. The intelligence proved to be good. Excellent, in fact. El-Hashim was still there.

McElroy immediately informed his superiors, and presented them with two options of how to proceed. The first, grab El-Hashim immediately and deliver her to the CIA for interrogation. The second, keep her under observation, see who she met with, and see who else they could net before they brought her in.

When McElroy was pressed for his preferred plan, he said, "It's a risk, but I think it would be a mistake to apprehend her right away."

The directors had concurred and approved option two, making it clear that if El-Hashim were to somehow avoid capture, it would be McElroy's ass in the fire.

The strategy had paid off. Within the first two weeks, they added several new names to their terror watch list, and uncovered a whole new Somalian splinter organization that had yet to show up on anyone else's radar.

But a trip El-Hashim made to Crimea changed everything.

The moment McElroy saw the photos his surveillance team extracted from a security camera along the waterfront in Yalta, he no longer thought of El-Hashim as his number one target. The photos showed the woman in her everpresent hijab, talking to a man.

But not just any man.

To Raven. The son of a bitch who'd given McElroy's team the slip back in May.

If McElroy could bring Frank Poe in, especially after the earlier snafu, the reservations that he knew some of Stonewell's management had about him would disappear, removing the final obstacles to future advancement.

At the same time, it could also backfire on him. If, that was, his bosses knew about the Raven sighting.

While he'd been routinely giving progress reports on the El-Hashim mission, his briefing that day made no mention of the wayward colonel. The only people who knew Raven had been sighted were a limited number of his trusted team members.

Get Poe first, then break the news. That would be best.

To do that, he would have to go through El-Hashim. He knew she must have some way of contacting the traitor, which meant the time had come to bring her in.

He put the nab team in place near her home base in the Czech Republic so they could grab her as soon as she returned from Crimea. Unfortunately, that had yet to happen. Somehow the foolish woman had gotten herself and several of her associates arrested. About the only good thing that had come of this was that the officials in Crimea didn't seem to know who they had. El-Hashim was listed under a false name—A'isha Najem.

It took McElroy less than ten minutes to get over his annoyance, and realize the new situation might actually provide an opportunity. What if he could get someone into the prison to bring El-Hashim out?

The logistics were solved fairly quickly with the old standby combo of blackmail and money. And with the *how* figured out, it became a question of *who*?

The operative would have to be a woman, someone who could think on her feet and blend in with the other female prisoners. While Stonewell did have female security employees, they were few in number and all were assigned elsewhere.

McElroy was looking through the digital archive on Raven when he came upon a mention of the colonel's daughter and everything clicked. Not only had she spent two years in the army before going to college, she now worked as a domestic fugitive retrieval specialist, or, as most called it, a bounty hunter.

She was perfect.

And she had a Stonewell file, too. But instead of containing a gigabyte of information like her father's, her dossier was under one meg, consisting merely of reports on previous attempts by the company to recruit her. All had failed.

That didn't bother McElroy. None of the previous attempts had included the leverage he had.

A link to her father.

As he read through her file again, he saw a cross

reference to another Stonewell employee named Shane Cooper. According to the document, Cooper had served with her in the army.

McElroy worked out a deal to have the man temporarily transferred to his group, thinking that Cooper would have knowledge of Alex that might prove useful.

In the end, it wasn't Cooper's insights that had helped secure her services, but the man's ability to take a punch.

Unfortunately, all of his maneuvering would be wasted effort if Alexandra Poe didn't show up.

But as he started to check his watch again, the door behind him opened, and one of the receptionists stuck his head in. "Sir? Your visitors are parking now."

THE STONEWELL COMPOUND was in a forested area about four miles outside of DC, down an unmarked road that was easy to miss if you didn't know where you were going. Fortunately, McElroy's coordinates had been very precise and Alex had no trouble finding the place.

A quarter of a mile in, a guardhouse stood in the middle of the road, flanked on either side by a gated fence that disappeared into the woods. Topping the fence were large coils of razor wire.

As Alex pulled her Jeep to a halt, a uniformed man stepped out of the guardhouse. This wasn't some fifty-year-old, potbellied rent-a-cop just doing time, however. He couldn't have been more than thirty, with the build and demeanor of a human bull.

He leaned down and looked inside the Jeep as she lowered the window.

"Ms. Poe, Mr. Jones. Welcome to Stonewell."

Alex and Deuce nodded.

"Put this on your dash," the guard said, handing her a piece of paper through the window. He looked out at the road beyond the gate. "Continue on for four tenths of a mile, then make a right, and that'll take you to the parking area next to the main building. Your assigned spot is number seventy-two.

Please make sure you use only that number. When you arrive, stay in your car until someone comes out to get you."

Alex raised an eyebrow, but didn't say anything.

The man took a step back, reached behind him, and pushed something just inside the guardhouse door. The gate began rolling out of the way. "Have a good day."

Alex was tempted to give him a salute, but didn't. Instead she hit the gas and started forward again, knowing what Deuce would say before he even opened his mouth.

"Stay in the car, huh? I've got a better idea. How about we turn around right now and head back home? It's not too late, you know."

"Shut it, Deuce."

"I haven't been here two minutes and I'm already getting bad vibes."

"Just close your eyes and go to your happy place. I'm not turning around."

"You'll wish you had. Mark my words."

Alex shot him a glance. "I'm gonna mark your face, you don't shut the hell up."

The turn was precisely where the guard had told them it would be. A hundred yards in, the forest opened up into a large parking area in front of a wide, two-story building, its façade little more than a wall of dark glass. An array of antennas and satellite dishes graced the roof.

Alex found slot number seventy-two and pulled into it. Killing the engine, she glanced over at the building's main entrance and saw three men heading their way.

"At least they're not keeping us waiting," Deuce said.

One of the men was wearing the same type of uniform as the guard at the gate, and looked every bit as capable. The other two were Cooper and McElroy.

Alex and Deuce popped their doors and climbed out.

"Right on time," McElroy said, smiling. He walked over to Deuce and held out a hand. "Mr. Jones, good to meet you. I'm Jason McElroy. Welcome to the Stonewell team."

Deuced looked at the hand, then shook it with far less

enthusiasm than McElroy.

"This is my associate, Shane Cooper," McElroy said. "He'll be working with both of you on this project."

After Cooper and Deuce shook, the uniformed man removed two lanyards from his pocket, each with a plastic ID badge attached. "Please wear these at all times," he said, handing them to Alex and Deuce. "They'll grant you access as your clearance allows."

Deuce slipped the lanyard over his head. "And what does our clearance allow? The commissary and the restrooms?"

"Mr. McElroy will make that determination."

"Will I have to take some kind of oath first?"

Alex shot him a look. "Deuce, lighten up. We're all on the same side here."

"I just want to get the rules straight," he said. He grabbed his badge and waved it at the man in uniform. "What if I lose this thing?"

"Don't," the man told him, his face stone.

Deuce, however, wasn't intimidated by authority, nor, Alex knew, was he a huge fan of corporate rules. But before he could say anything else, she put a hand on his forearm and squeezed. "Play nice, big guy."

"I'm just asking a question."

"There'll be plenty of time for questions. How about if we get inside first?"

She saw the other three men exchange a look. McElroy said, "That sounds like a very good idea. Why don't you both follow me?"

JUDGING BY THE wall of glass outside, Alex had been expecting some kind of swanky lobby with cushy chairs and a Barbie doll receptionist. But the lobby was not a lobby at all, just a long white corridor intersected by other hallways and lined with several doors.

McElroy led them through the maze and into a large conference room. A long glass table surrounded by more than a dozen black leather chairs took up the middle of the space.

On the walls were several framed photographs. On first glance they looked like vacation shots from around the world, but Alex knew that the gray-haired man in the photos was Stonewell founder and Chairman of the Board Thomas Greer. In each shot he was with someone different—a US president, a prime minister, a powerful political figure.

"Have a seat," McElroy said, motioning to the chairs.

Deuce dropped into one of them and spun it around. "Hey, cushy."

Alex rolled her eyes. One minute he was playing hardball, the next he was acting like the class cutup. She wished he'd make up his mind.

She sank into the chair next to him as McElroy said, "All right, first things first. Contract?"

Alex pulled the contract out of her pocket, unfolded it, and placed it on the table. "I could use that pen now."

McElroy happily provided it, and she signed at the bottom of the page.

"Excellent," he said, then set it next to one of the three folders that were lying on the table. He slid the nearest one to Deuce. "And this is yours."

Deuce eyed it dubiously for a moment, before taking out the contract and giving it a quick scan. "Same as Alex's?"

"Yes," McElroy said. "Exactly the same."

"What do you think, Alex? Should I sign it?"

She sighed and spun the pen toward him. "Deuce, if you don't quit acting like a jackass, I'll kick your butt out of here before *they* have a chance to. Now sign the damn thing and shut the hell up."

"All right, all right," he said. He picked up the pen and signed. "Happy now?"

McElroy smiled. "Thank you, Mr. Jones."

"Deuce. Call me Deuce."

"All right, Deuce." McElroy put his contract on top of Alex's, then picked up the remaining two folders and put one in front of each of them.

Alex opened hers and found a small stack of documents.

"What's this?"

"Just a formality," he told her.

She looked through the papers. There was a medical questionnaire, something about next of kin, and several other informational forms. "We already signed our contracts."

Another McElroy smile. "Yes, you did. These are simply documents that all contract employees fill out before they're allowed to work for Stonewell."

"So if we don't fill them out," Deuce said, "we don't get the job?"

Alex couldn't help but notice the hopeful tone in her partner's voice.

McElroy spread his hands. "I don't see why that would even be an issue. Just look through the forms. If there's anything either of you have a problem with, we can talk about it."

Alex returned her gaze to the top document. She liked her privacy as much as Deuce did, and any other time she might have decided his instincts were right—that it was time to walk. But considering what was at stake, she couldn't do that.

She picked up the pen and started to fill in the blanks.

"She took my pen," Deuce said.

McElroy produced another, and Deuce started in on his stack.

They were only halfway through when McElroy's cell phone rang and he stepped outside to take the call. When he came back in, he said, "You'll have to excuse me for a bit. Cooper will take you around, and I'll catch up with you at the briefing."

As he turned to leave, Alex got to her feet. "Wait a minute. Aren't you forgetting something?"

"I don't think so. Why?"

"You said that after we signed our contracts, you'd tell me where the woman is."

He nodded. "And I will. All your questions will be answered at the briefing."

Before she could protest further, he was out the door.

Annoyed, Alex sank into her chair and went back to the forms. It took another five minutes before she finally closed her folder.

Deuce was still scribbling away when he turned to her. "Who'd you put for your emergency contact?"

"You," she said.

He grinned. "And I'm putting you. Sure gonna suck for them if we both die."

He finished his last sheet, closed his folder, and slid it next to Alex's.

She looked at Cooper. "Now what?"

"Now we get you certified."

"For what?"

"Weapons."

"Are you serious?"

A shrug. "Company policy."

Alex felt anger rising. "Come on, Shane, what is this bullshit? Am I being jerked around or what?"

"No more than any other recruit. I told you, it's company policy."

Grinning, Deuce said, "So do we get to shoot?"

"That *is* the general idea," Cooper said.

"Hell, if you'd told me that earlier, I would have filled these things out a lot faster. Let's rock and roll."

THEY USED ONE of several all-white golf carts parked behind the main building to drive out to the range, Cooper behind the wheel.

As they drove, Alex looked out at the maze of roadways and clusters of buildings, which reminded her of a trip she and Danny took with their parents to Universal City, back before all the shit came down. This facility had the feel of a Hollywood backlot. "How big is this place?"

"Couple hundred acres," Cooper said. "Give or take."

Deuce frowned. "What do you need all the room for?"

"Research and development. Training. That kind of

stuff."

As they passed the last cluster of buildings, they came upon an elaborate obstacle course to the right that looked as if it had been plucked directly out of a war-torn, Middle Eastern city, complete with bombed-out buildings and makeshift hidey holes.

"Jesus," Deuce murmured. "This is like a mercenary's wet dream."

"Or a combat vet's nightmare," Alex told him.

They heard intermittent gunfire long before the firing range came into view—a pair of shooters, maybe three at most. The firing range itself was in a rectangular clearing surrounded by twenty-foot-high mounds of dirt meant to catch any stray bullets. It was long, eight hundred meters at least, with half the firing line covered to protect shooters from the sun and elements, and half not. Behind the firing line was a long, thin building that Alex assumed served as the armory.

Once out of the cart, they passed through a gate into the range. The shooters were down at the other end under the roof. There were three targets set up down range, two at fifty meters, and the last at three hundred.

Another shot echoed off the embankment. Though there was no way to see exactly where it had hit, Alex did notice the far target jerk with the impact of the bullet.

As they turned down the wide concrete walkway that ran between the building and the firing line, a man who was standing at the far end watching the shooters looked over and started walking toward them.

He was tanned and toned, with cropped hair and a purposeful walk that bespoke yet another military alum. Stonewell seemed to be crawling with them.

"Coop," the man said. "These them?"

"Yes, sir." Cooper motioned to his two companions. "Alexandra Poe. Deuce Jones." With a glance at them, he said, "And this is Carl Dugan. First sergeant, retired. He's the range master."

Alex had a momentary urge to jump to attention, but it

passed quickly and she held out her hand. "Mr. Dugan," she said.

He gave her a once-over, then took her hand as a smug little smile creased the left side of his face. "Ms. Poe."

Alex knew immediately what that smile meant. There had been guys like him in her unit in Baghdad, guys who thought she belonged at home making snacks for the boys, or down on her knees worshipping the great god Johnson.

When Dugan shook Deuce's hand, most of his disdain had disappeared. He focused back on Cooper. "Standard checkout, right?"

"Right," Cooper said.

Dugan turned to Alex. "So, ladies first? Happy to give you a little lesson, if you like."

Alex stared at him, expressionless. "Deuce will go first."

Dugan smiled again. "Whatever you'd prefer, ma'am."

The standard check involved shooting a Beretta 92A1 9mm pistol at a target twenty-five meters out, and an M16A4 military-grade rifle at a target two hundred meters down range. To pass, the shooter had to hit within the outer boundaries of the target eight out of ten shots.

Dugan led them down to one of the empty lanes under the roof, then retrieved the weapons and ammunition from the armory.

"You load," he told Deuce after he set the pistol and box of 9mm ammo on the counter.

Deuce popped the mag, filled it, and jammed it back in. While he was doing this, Dugan clipped a target to the auto-positioning wires, programmed in the required distance, and set the target on its way. He handed out adjustable earmuffs, and clear shooting glasses.

"You want to take a few practice shots?" he asked Deuce.

"Sure."

"Have at it."

Deuce stepped up to the line, pulled on his earmuffs, and raised the pistol. He held his position for several seconds, then let off five quick shots.

"More?" Dugan asked.

"No, I'm good."

Dugan brought the target in and changed it for a fresh one. Alex was happy to see that Deuce had landed all five shots within the large circle. Once the new target was in place, Deuce took aim again. This time he shot in bursts of two, until he finished the needed ten.

The target whizzed back. Nine shots within the circle, the tenth just barely outside.

"Dammit," Deuce said. "Can I try again?"

"Nine's passing," Cooper told him.

"Yeah, but ten's better."

"Let's just keep moving, shall we?"

Deuce took longer between shots with the rifle. This time he got credit for all ten.

"All right, you pass," Dugan said. "Congratulations. Though you could use some work on tightening things up."

Deuce grunted dismissively, but Dugan ignored him and gestured to Alex. "All right, ma'am, your turn."

Alex switched places with Deuce, snatched up the nine, and reloaded. Once the target was twenty-five meters out, she moved into position and aimed down the barrel.

Dugan came up beside her. "Take as many practice shots as you want, ma'am."

"That won't be necessary," she said.

"You sure? Don't forget, it's eight out of ten or you fail."

She looked at him. "I'll take my chances."

That rueful smile came out again. "Just trying to be helpful."

Alex eyed the target and immediately slipped into the zone, waiting for that moment when instinct and training became one—just as her father had taught her when she was thirteen years old. Then she pulled the trigger in steady succession—*bam, bam, bam, bam, bam*—until she finished her tenth shot.

Dugan was still smiling as he pushed the button to

retrieve the target, but his condescending expression disappeared the moment he got a good look at what she had done.

Not only had she placed all ten shots within the large circle, every single one of them was contained within the much smaller circle in the center.

"I'd call that a pass," Cooper said.

Dugan, looking considerably less cocksure than he had a moment ago, mounted a new target and sent it rushing down the range.

"It's a combined test," he said. "Still gotta pass the rifle."

Alex picked up the M16. Though it had been years since she'd held one, its heft was familiar. She sighted down the range, and let off a single shot. Even at this distance, she could tell that while it was in the smaller circle, it had hit slightly off center. She compensated for the discrepancy with the sight, and shot off another round. This one was near perfect.

Eight shots later, she was done.

Once the target was back, Dugan looked at it, then at her. "I take it this isn't your first time out."

Alex removed the magazine from the rifle and popped the remaining bullet from the chamber. "I've had my share of practice. But most of the targets were shooting back."

"She was also brigade champion for two years running," Cooper told him. "Did I forget to mention that?"

Dugan leveled his gaze at Cooper. Without looking at Alex, he said, "You pass." He folded up the target and walked back to the armory.

Deuce watched him go. "Guy's kind of a prick, isn't he?"

"Pretty much," Cooper said.

Despite herself, Alex was smiling now. "I have to admit that was worth the trip. What's up next?"

Cooper gestured toward the exit. "Time for your briefing."

SEVEN

THEY WENT TO a different building, about a quarter of the size of the previous one. It looked more like a cement bunker, and was tucked away in the trees, accessible only via a narrow path.

Inside, Cooper took them down to a room in the sub-basement two levels below ground, where McElroy and a young woman were waiting.

Though it was clearly a meeting room, it was nothing like the one they'd gathered in earlier. If the Stonewell property was, as Deuce had so delicately put it, a mercenary's wet dream, then the room they had just entered would undoubtedly produce a similar sense of euphoria for someone obsessed with technology.

One entire wall seemed to be a monitor screen that could be divided multiple ways into sub-screens of various sizes. At the moment, a large portion was dedicated to a looping animation of the Stonewell Associates logo, while charts and graphs filled up rectangles along the sides and partially across the bottom.

The conference table was made of wood, and inset in front of each chair was a screen where more data could be displayed. By the way the young woman was tapping away at her screen, Alex realized each had touch control, too. Finally, there were computer stations along the shorter, far wall, each with an oversize monitor.

"So?" McElroy said to Cooper as soon as they entered. "Pass or no pass?"

Deuce looked indignant. "Really, dude?"

"Pass," Cooper said. "Both."

McElroy smiled. "Excellent. But I can't say I'm surprised."

"That's more like it," Deuce told him.

"Is anyone hungry or thirsty? There are drinks in the fridge behind you, and some small sandwiches there on the counter. Feel free."

Deuce grinned and headed for the counter. "I could use a bite. Alex, you want something?"

But Alex was barely listening. Now that they were about to get down to business, her mind was once again on her father, and the real reason she was here.

"Alex?"

"What I want," she said, locking gazes with McElroy, "is to know where Fadilah El-Hashim is. You've dangled that carrot long enough."

McElroy nodded and took a seat. "Then perhaps we should get started."

The young woman touched the screen in front of her and the lights immediately dimmed. On the wall, the logo animation faded, as a map of the Black Sea took its place.

"Seriously?" Deuce said. He was standing in front of the now darkened table of food, an empty plate in his hand.

Ignoring him, McElroy launched into his presentation. "As I mentioned yesterday, Ms. El-Hashim is in Ukraine. Specifically, Crimea."

Crimea was a bulbous peninsula in the Black Sea that was connected to the rest of Ukraine by a comparatively narrow spit of land. A yellow dot appeared on screen, along the north end of the peninsula, then the map zoomed in.

At first it looked like the dot was right on top of a small town labeled Slavne, but as the image continued to enlarge and more details emerged, the dot began moving southward out of the village, until it stopped at a point roughly halfway between Slavne and a town called Ryljejevka. The map switched from graphic representation to satellite view, and the dot faded until it was a barely ghosted circle surrounding a group of seven buildings.

Central in the group were three identical rectangular structures lined up side by side. South of them, on the other side of a gap that Alex judged to be about fifty yards wide, was another building similar to the others, but set at a ninety-degree angle. Running from each end of this building, all the way around the other three buildings, was a thin line that could only be a wall. Beyond the north end of the enclosure was a fifth, smaller building. It was walled off like a pimple on the larger fortress.

The remaining two structures were outside the walls. One looked like it could be a house, while the other an office building, or storage facility, or—what Alex thought most likely—barracks.

"Slavne Prison," McElroy said.

Alex sat up. "I'm sorry. Prison?"

"Please, Ms. Poe, if you'll just let me—"

"That's where this woman is? In *prison*?"

McElroy hesitated before saying, "Yes, but—"

"What the hell?" Deuce said. He had managed to pile a couple of sandwiches on his plate and had stopped halfway back to his chair. "How are we supposed to get to her there?"

"If you'll bear with me, I'm going to cover that."

But Alex was already ahead of him. It didn't take much brainpower to figure out McElroy's plan. "This is a women's prison, isn't it? You want me to go in. *That's* why you need me."

Before McElroy could reply, Deuce dropped his plate to the table, spilling one of the sandwiches off the side. "Whoa. Absolutely not," he said. "This is not even close to a good idea. Alex, we're done. Let's get the hell out of here."

"You've already signed contracts," McElroy said.

"So sue us," Deuce told him, crossing for the door, not looking back until he got there. But Alex remained in her seat. "Alex? Come on."

She didn't move. She knew Deuce was right, that they should leave, but she kept thinking about that photograph of her father and El-Hashim. Kept visualizing it, thinking about all the years that had passed since she and Danny had last seen him.

"Alex," Deuce said. "Hello? Let's go."

She still didn't move.

Deuce frowned deeply now, then crossed to her chair and leaned in close. "You cannot possibly be considering this."

"It won't hurt to listen to what he has to say."

Deuce gaped. "It's a *prison*, Alex. A prison in a former Soviet country. Are you—" He paused and glanced at the others. "Can I speak to my partner alone for a moment?"

McElroy exhaled an exasperated breath. "Please make it quick." He, Cooper, and the technician left the room.

The moment Alex and her partner were alone, Deuce said, "What are you thinking?"

"You know why I'm here. This woman, she spoke to my father."

"Good for her," Deuce said. "But right now she's locked up in a goddamn Ukrainian prison out in the middle of nowhere. You think you're just gonna slip in there and walk her out? I don't know exactly how these dickheads think they're gonna pull this off, but whatever their plan is, you and I both know it could go south about a thousand different ways."

She nodded. "I'm sorry, Deuce. I shouldn't have involved you in this."

"What the hell are you talking about? It's a *woman's* prison. I'm not the one who'll be walking into the line of fire. That'll be all you. If something happens while you're inside, I'm not going to be there to help. Father or no father, I'm not gonna let that happen."

Alex knew he was only speaking out of concern for her—out of love, when it came down to it—but Deuce could never fully understand the sense of loss she'd felt concerning her parents. If there was a chance to ease her pain—and Danny's, too—she had to consider it.

"I'm staying, Deuce. I want to at least hear what McElroy has to say."

Deuce studied her for a long moment, then sank into the seat next to her. "Jesus Christ," he said, staring at the ceiling for several more seconds. "Okay, here's the deal. We listen to their plan. But if it's as batshit crazy as we both know it's bound to be, we blow this place."

Alex could only answer him with a smile. This was a promise she couldn't make and Deuce knew it.

He sighed heavily. "Fine." Reluctantly, he rose again, hesitating like he wanted to say more, but whatever it was, he kept it to himself. He went to the door, opened it, and headed back to his seat without another word.

McElroy stuck his head in. "Are we a go?"

Alex nodded. "Let's continue."

Once everyone was back in place, McElroy pointed at the satellite image of Slavne Prison.

"As you so astutely pointed out," he said, "the facility houses only female prisoners. What I was going to tell you before the interruption was that it's a low-security facility that's used both for women convicted of nonviolent crime and women awaiting trial."

Deuce gestured to the image. "You call that low security?"

"I know it looks intimidating, but it's been there since well before World War Two. At that time, yes, it was intended for higher-risk inmates, but over the years they've built better, more modern facilities for those purposes."

"I'm sure it's just like Club Med," Deuce said.

McElroy frowned at him. "May I go on?"

Deuce didn't object.

"Slavne Prison is designed to hold just under fifteen hundred inmates, all housed in one of these three buildings." With a laser pointer, he circled the three identical buildings within the big wall. "The amount of prisoners changes daily depending on trials. Sometimes they're actually overcrowded, but currently they're running at about eighty-seven percent of capacity." He moved the light to the perpendicular building below them. "This is the administration building. It's also where the infirmary is. Here and here"—the light touched on two points along the edge of the admin building—"are the only two intended ways in and out of the facility."

"Are there any unintended?" Alex asked.

Ignoring the comment, McElroy touched on the two buildings outside the wall. "These are housing facilities for guards and other staff." He moved the pointer to the building with its own wall on the other side of the prison. "And this is isolation, where they keep problem prisoners."

"And where, exactly, is El-Hashim?"

He pointed at the middle of the three parallel buildings. "Here, on the second floor." He glanced at his assistant. "Barbara? Schematics."

The map shrank down until it was the size of one of the smaller rectangles, then moved to an empty slot along the bottom. Replacing it in the larger screen was an architectural drawing of one of the prison buildings.

"Push in on the cell," McElroy ordered.

The whole image swung to the side, revealing it as a three-dimensional file, then traveled through the outside wall into the main corridor that ran through the center of the second floor. There, it pivoted, showing one of the doors.

"The cells have a three-digit numbering system. The first number indicates building, the final two the actual cell. This is cell number 259. El-Hashim seldom leaves it."

"How the hell do you know that?" Deuce asked.

"We have someone on the inside. An informant."

"And does this informant keep a constant eye on—"

"Can we get to the meat here?" Alex said, cutting Deuce off. "The bottom line is that I'm supposed to go in, right?"

"Yes."

"As what? A visitor?"

"Prisoner."

Alex had known what he was going to say, but hearing it didn't make it sound any less crazy.

"See?" Deuce said. "I told you."

But Alex's attention was still on McElroy. "Okay, so

that's how I get in. Now how do I get out?"

"Our informer."

"Who is?"

"Code name Traz," McElroy said. "Someone very well placed."

"So why doesn't he or she deal with El-Hashim?"

McElroy shook his head. "We're not talking about an operative, and it isn't someone who has El-Hashim's ear. The contact is extremely concerned about being found out by prison officials."

"Then why cooperate at all?"

"We have something Traz wants."

"Which is?"

"I'm afraid that's classified," McElroy said. "All that matters is that this contact is our eyes and ears. And once you're inside and you've convinced El-Hashim to leave, Traz will facilitate the escape."

"Why all the mystery?" Deuce asked. "Who is this person?"

McElroy shook his head. "One of the conditions Traz insisted on was that his or her identity remain a secret in case something goes wrong before Alex gets to the facility. Once she's inside, Traz will reach out."

"So, in other words," Deuce said, "Alex goes in completely blind." He looked at Alex. "You get that, right?"

"I get it. But if I were in this Traz's position, I'd ask for exactly the same guarantee. You would, too."

She sensed Deuce's resistance, but he kept his mouth shut. What could he say? He knew she was right.

A small smile of satisfaction creased McElroy's face, but Alex moved quickly to kill it. "Just because I can understand the reasoning doesn't mean I don't need some safety assurances of my own."

"Of course. You're wondering if any of our intel is trustworthy."

"Gee, it's like you're reading my mind."

McElroy turned. "Cooper, can you tell Ms. Fazakas to

join us?"

Cooper got up and exited the room. Moments later he returned with a dark-haired woman who was a good four inches shorter than Alex and looked Eastern European, maybe in her late thirties to mid-forties.

"Ms. Poe," McElroy said. "This is Ms. Fazakas. Ms. Fazakas, Alexandra Poe."

The woman nodded hello, then reluctantly took Alex's offered hand and shook.

"Ms. Fazakas spent the better part of two years in Slavne Prison. After we're through here, she'll give you a thorough briefing, but suffice it to say the contact at the prison is known to her, and was the one who helped Ms. Fazakas get out."

Alex eyed the woman. She realized now that Fazakas was probably younger than she looked. Whether it was the time in prison or life before that, something had taken its toll on her. She looked worn, tired, and, if Alex was right, a little fearful.

Alex eyed her. "You think this Traz can do it again with me?"

"Escaping a prison isn't an easy thing," Fazakas said. "But if Traz says it is possible again, then I assume yes."

"So how did you get out?"

The woman hesitated. "The prison has high walls and several guards, but security is lax at times. I was able to get out in a hidden compartment on a delivery truck. I doubt you will be going the same way, though."

"Why not?"

"The compartment was barely large enough for me. As I understand it, there will be two of you."

Alex looked at McElroy. "Do you know how we're getting out?"

He hesitated. "Ms. Poe, as I mentioned before, Traz is very concerned about something going wrong, and has insisted the information not be shared with anyone on the actual mission, and I have to agree. If you are caught, it will be better if you have no knowledge of the escape route. That way, if we need to send someone in to rescue *you*, it will still be open to us."

"That is bullshit," Deuce said. "You expect Alex to walk into that prison and not know exactly how she's getting out?"

McElroy ignored him and looked directly at Alex. "I'm asking for your trust. Everything is in place for when you will need it. And unlike when Ms. Fazakas escaped, you will have help on the outside." He motioned at Cooper and Deuce.

Deuce opened his mouth to say something again, but Alex put a hand on his shoulder, stopping him. She understood compartmentalizing information. She'd been in the army, after all. And as much as she might have liked to have a clearer picture, she couldn't disagree with McElroy's logic.

"Let's assume I accept, and that there's an adequate exit plan," she said. "Can you at least explain how I'm getting in?"

"That's the easy part. You'll be arrested."

She raised an eyebrow. "And then what? Wait around until they finally decide to send me to Slavne?"

"Of course not. We have planned out every aspect of the mission. Your transfer to Slavne Prison is already arranged. You'll be sent there the same day you're picked up."

"Oh, the power of corruption," Deuce muttered.

McElroy shot him a look. "It does come in handy sometimes. Most of the time, in fact."

It was nearly half a minute before Alex spoke again. "So you have me in, and you have me out. I still see one big problem."

"Only one?" Deuce said.

Alex ignored him. "Why me? Why in the world would El-Hashim listen to me?"

"Because the two of you already have a shared connection," McElroy said.

"My father?"

McElroy nodded.

"Even if I used that, why would she believe me?"

"You'll be imprisoned under a false name. As soon as the opportunity presents itself, tell her who you really are. She isn't completely cut off from the outside world, and will have ways of confirming your identity. Once she does, play up that you're there on your father's behalf to help her escape."

"You don't even want me to point out the number of potential holes in that story," Deuce said.

McElroy greeted the comment with a grunt. "Not if we keep it simple." He focused back on Alex. "If asked, you know nothing about your father's activities or his relationship with El-Hashim. You're doing this because he asked you to, and nothing more."

Could it work? Alex wondered. Maybe. But it seemed so—

You go see Dad. Danny, smiling and happy and hopeful. Then in words he hadn't spoken, but still in his voice: *Bring him home, Aleck. Bring Dad home.*

She closed her eyes, resting her forehead on her hand, her father's face from the surveillance photos front and center in her mind.

When she finally looked up again, she said, "All right, let's start at the beginning. Tell me exactly how we're gonna do this."

MCELROY REMAINED IN the conference room alone after everyone else had left.

The briefing couldn't have gone better.

Alex was in. As was, although reluctantly, her partner Deuce.

There had been a few dicey points during the discussion, but that was to be expected. It wasn't an easy mission, by a long shot. But McElroy had been able to keep the conversation on track. He had even been able to smooth over the fact that he couldn't tell them exactly how they were getting out of the prison. He hadn't lied when he said Traz didn't want anyone on the ground in Crimea to know the route in case they were captured and questioned. The insider had been very clear about that.

But McElroy had implied that he, himself, had been told. That was not exactly true. Traz's fear extended to *everyone* involved on Stonewell's side. And while McElroy would have preferred to know the details, the condition was one he was willing to live with in view of the potential reward.

That was why he was in charge to make the difficult choices. And in this case, it had definitely paid off. The mission was on, and he knew without a doubt that the abduction of El-Hashim would reap the information he needed to locate and finally capture Raven.

Yes. It couldn't have gone better.

EIGHT

Bern, Switzerland

THIS WAS NOT their usual day for a meeting, nor their usual time. But emergencies happened, and this one, the woman thought, couldn't be more urgent.

She sat quietly on the left side of a rectangular conference table as her colleagues filed into the room and took their seats. Three men, all with well-known faces, each one seasoned by circumstance, and a bit haggard after a number of sleepless nights.

The woman hadn't slept much, either. Not since she had received the news. She was no stranger to the complexities of their situation, having spent the last five decades in the trenches with some of the most powerful men and women in the world, but this particular complication could destroy all of that hard work in an instant.

At the center of the table was a speakerphone with an encrypted connection, allowing the fifth member of their assembly to attend remotely. The connection was crystal clear, and she could hear him quietly breathing on the line.

As they settled into their chairs, the oldest of the men said, "All right, so where do we stand?"

To the world outside, he was a prominent banker. Cautious, conservative, trustworthy. But the more appropriate description was *greedy*. For it was greed that had brought them all together in the first place—a flaw, or perhaps strength, that the woman was more than willing to admit to. After all, wasn't it greed of one kind or another that drove most human beings?

"Nothing's changed," she said. "My source tells me the

Ukrainian authorities still have no idea who they have in custody."

The banker nodded. "What guarantee do we have it'll stay that way?"

"None, I'm afraid. Leaks are inevitable. It's really only a matter of time."

"That's pure speculation," the voice on the speakerphone said. At fifty-one, he was the youngest—and least seasoned—member of the committee. "And even if she's compromised, I doubt she'll say anything."

The banker nodded in agreement. "He has a point. El-Hashim has been an extremely loyal and efficient operative. She knows what's expected of her, and she'll carry it out."

"What she knows is too much," the woman said. "I don't doubt her loyalty for a moment, and I'm sure she'll do everything she can to remain silent. But if the Ukrainians find out who she really is—and speculation or not, I believe they will—they're bound to turn her over to the British or the Russians or, God forbid, the Americans."

The mood around the table grew darker at the prospect.

"Once that happens, gentlemen, she'll be out of our reach. And loyal or not, she's only human. If they can't get her to talk, they'll outsource the job, and sooner or later she'll tell them everything she knows."

Silence. Darker than ever now.

"We all know why we're here today," the woman continued. "We all know what has to be done. There really isn't much more to discuss."

The man directly across from her leaned back, letting his gaze take in the rest of the assembly. He was the de facto leader here, a well-dressed man in his mid-seventies known as a financial advisor to presidents and kings. "She's right," he said. "We should put the motion to a vote."

Nods all around.

"All right, then. On the matter of immediate termination, what say you?"

"Yea."

"Yea."

"Yea."

There was nothing from the speakerphone, and for a moment the woman thought they had lost their connection. Then the voice said, "Yea."

The man across the table pushed himself upright and rose. "My vote is yea also. The motion is passed." He looked at the woman. "You'll handle this?"

"Of course," she said. "Everything has been arranged. I just need to give the go-ahead."

The man looked around the room. "Does anyone else have anything they'd like to add?"

Everyone remained silent.

"Good. Then we're adjourned."

There were no goodbyes, no talk of exchange rates or bond yields or pending loans. The speakerphone disconnected, the other two men rose from their chairs, and they all walked out of the room, leaving the woman to do what needed to be done.

She sat there a moment, feeling no remorse, no hesitance. And why should she? This, like most things in her life, was merely business.

What she felt was relief.

Setting her briefcase on the table, she retrieved one of the three mobile phones she carried. A burner, like the others, obtained specifically in case she needed to make this call. Once she was finished, the phone would be destroyed.

She punched in a number, waited. Then a voice said, "Yes?"

"Authentication: theta omega seven theta two two tau alpha nine."

"Recognized."

"We're a go," she said. "Send her."

"Understood."

The line went dead.

NINE

THEY FLEW EAST on one of Stonewell's private jets. Alex tried to sleep for the first few hours, but finally gave up and stared out the window into the darkness.

She had to admit that the plan, as laid out by McElroy with details filled in by Fazakas, was well thought out. That didn't mean it would be easy or even successful. More like risky and beyond dangerous.

And yet, possible.

El-Hashim had better know something about my father. Because if she doesn't, I'm going to make McElroy's life a living—

"Thirsty?"

She twisted around, startled by the voice.

Cooper was standing in the aisle next to her seat, a small bottle in his hand. "I assume you still like orange juice."

"Yeah," she said. "Thanks."

She took the bottle from him and unsealed the top, as he gestured toward the empty seat across the aisle from her. "You mind?"

She shook her head.

He plopped down, and set the small duffel bag he was carrying on his lap. From inside, he removed a blue booklet and handed it to her. "Your new identity."

It was a passport. Canadian. Roughed up a bit to not look new.

She opened it and found the picture that had been taken after the briefing staring back at her. The name next to the picture was Powell, Maureen.

She flipped through the pages and saw that Maureen had made trips to Mexico and the UK.

"It's completely valid," he said. "If anyone runs it, they'll find you."

She stuffed it into her pocket.

Next out of the duffel came a white envelope, which he tossed to her.

"Cash. Enough to get you where you're going. The local currency is the hryvnia. It's good in both the Ukraine and the Autonomous Republic of Crimea."

"What about Romania?" The plan was to cross from there on land into Ukraine.

"There's a few lei in there, too. But you won't be there very long."

She checked the envelope, and nodded.

"You're clear on everything?" he asked.

"Yeah," she said.

"Any questions?"

Just a million, she thought, but said, "I think I'm good."

"Deuce and I will be no more than a couple miles away from you at all times."

"I know," she said.

Cooper was trying to put her at ease, but it wasn't exactly comforting. Once Alex was behind the prison's walls, she'd be on her own until she got out again.

"Look, Alex," Cooper said, as if sensing her concern. "If at any point you want to call things off, even if you're already inside, then do it. Don't worry about the target, just get yourself out."

"Yeah, McElroy would love that."

"I'll worry about that asshole. You just worry about you."

"Not very corporate of you."

"I'm not a very corporate kind of guy."

"And yet, here you are working for them. How long now?"

He hesitated. "Three years."

"Three years. Wow."

"I had to land somewhere after I got out."

Just the hint of his time in the army was enough to quiet them.

It was nearly a full minute before he said, "I, um, I wish it had gone differently."

"Don't," she said quickly.

"You don't know how many times I've thought about it, what I could have done."

"Let's not talk about this."

He turned to face her. "The thing is, as much as I wish it hadn't happened the way it did, I did the only thing I could."

She turned to the window and looked out at the night sky again, trying not to think about that day, trying not to think about anything at all.

"Alex, please."

She didn't move.

After several more minutes, she heard him get up and head toward the back of the plane.

She closed her eyes, the tension easing from her shoulders.

He was right. She had undoubtedly thought about it as much as he had, if not more, and she knew in her head there was nothing he could have done differently.

Her heart, though, was having a hard time buying it, because it was her heart that had taken the blow that day.

Stop thinking about it.

But she'd already started.

IT HAD BEEN a simple resupply convoy, their platoon a tactical movement team escorting the vehicles—in this case, a handful of fuel trucks.

Once they got them to Baghdad, they were scheduled for a day off. Everyone was looking forward to that. Just one day when they didn't have to worry about IEDs or snipers.

Hot. Dry. Sand pitting their skin even as they sat inside their MRAP Cougars. The platoon was divided among eight of the armored fighting vehicles, which were then peppered throughout the convoy. Alex was in a vehicle near the rear, manning the roof-mounted gun turret.

She saw the flash of the explosion a split second before the sound ripped down the road past her vehicle.

"Halt! Halt! Halt!" a voice yelled over the radio unnecessarily.

While the fuel trucks had all slammed to a stop, the Cougars moved into positions where they could get a better look around. The MRAP Alex was in rocked as it drove off the road into an empty lot. From the turret, she could see that the Cougar at the head of the convoy was sitting at an angle, blackened by fire.

But the MRAP was a tough machine that had stood up more times than not to IEDs without killing its occupants, a far cry from the army's early days in Iraq, so Alex was confident her friends inside were okay.

Most IEDs were set off remotely by an individual hiding somewhere nearby, but the platoon couldn't discount the possibility of a full-on ambush, so Alex swung around, searching for movement.

The second explosion came from the middle of the convoy, sending the cab of a fuel truck fifteen feet into the air.

A third explosion toppled another truck on its side, spilling its cargo onto the road, where it immediately caught fire in a loud *whoosh*.

"Everyone, get moving! Now! Now! Now! Keep going."

The orders were transmitted by Cooper, the convoy commander. It was obvious they had fallen into a massive trap, and who knew how many more explosive devices were waiting to be set off.

Engines roared and gears grinded as the convoy started moving again.

The next explosion sent shrapnel flying through the air, dinging up the back of one of the fuel trucks and cracking a window on one of the MRAPs, but not disabling it.

Alex's Cougar hung back to cover the rear as the convoy

shoved its way around the two trucks that had taken direct hits. The only vehicle that seemed to be having problems was the MRAP involved in the initial explosion. While Sanchez, the vehicle's driver, reported that his men were okay, he couldn't get the engine running.

As soon as the rest of the convoy had cleared Sanchez's vehicle, Bryant, the man in charge of Alex's Cougar, said over the radio, "Poe, keep a keen eye."

He then turned their MRAP toward Sanchez's.

"Sanchez," Bryant said as they neared the disabled vehicle. "We can squeeze you all in here with us."

"Just go," Sanchez said. "I'll get this working."

"Are you sure?"

"Yeah, yeah," Sanchez said.

"Okay. We'll watch your back until you're running again."

Bryant ordered the remaining four men in his vehicle to check on the soldiers who had been in the two destroyed fuel trucks.

Alex, hyperalert for any sign of danger, kept her gaze moving back and forth across the road as her squad mates climbed out and carefully made their way over to the now useless hulks. She had no doubt this would go down as one of the scariest moments of her army career.

The check was quick and far from satisfactory.

"Dead," Wilson reported. "All of them. Should we bring the bodies?"

Bryant relayed the information and question to Cooper.

"The birds are on their way. They'll pick them up," Cooper said. "Sanchez, status."

There was a delay, then Sanchez came on the radio. "I think I've got…"

With a sudden roar, the engine of the other vehicle came back to life.

"Back in business," Sanchez said.

"Good! Get a move on," Cooper ordered. "Both of you."

For Sanchez to move, Alex's Cougar had to get out of

the way, so Bryant took the lead and headed after the convoy. Alex looked over her shoulder until she was sure Sanchez was following them before she focused back on the road.

That was why she only heard the explosion and didn't see it.

The impact sent her vehicle flying, until it dropped back down several feet away. She slammed against the gun, her chest screaming in pain from the impact.

"What the hell was that?" Bryant asked.

Wincing, Alex turned and looked behind them. Sanchez's MRAP was lying on its side, flames engulfing the hood.

"Sanchez is hit!" she said, breathing hard.

Without thinking, she scrambled out of the turret and dropped over the side of the Cougar onto the ground. Ignoring her bruised chest, she raced toward the other vehicle.

"Poe, stop!" Bryant ordered. "Get back here!"

She ripped her radio earpiece out and ran on without hesitating.

The bomb had been waiting on the side of the road, disguised as who knew what at this point—a soda can, a rock, a discarded shoe. The only things Alex knew were that the blast had been more powerful than any of the previous explosions, and that her vehicle had driven right past the device seconds before it went off.

She stopped near the front, out of reach of the flames, and looked through the windshield. She could see only one person—Riggins, crumpled against the passenger side door, at the bottom of the tipped truck. Sanchez had to be in there somewhere, too, but she couldn't see him.

Using the undercarriage, she climbed up until she was standing on the driver's side that was now facing the sky. She could feel the heat coming from the flames that still burned across the hood as she sidestepped over to the door and tried to pull it open. But it wouldn't budge. She got down on all fours, then, cupping her hands at the sides of her face, she looked through the window into the cab.

From her new vantage point, she could see that Riggins's head was cocked at an impossible angle, his neck broken. She took two quick, deep breaths, feeling them burn in her bruised chest, then looked around for Sanchez, and found him partially strapped in his seat. His face was smashed into the steering wheel, his eyes open and dead.

She took another breath. Riggins and Sanchez were gone, but there were others in the truck who might still need her help. She scrambled back to the ground and sprinted to the rear of the MRAP.

The metal door that would drop down like a ramp when opened was sealed shut. She pounded on it.

"Hey! Hey, open up! It's me, Poe!"

Nothing happened.

"Can you hear me?"

"Poe?" The voice was muffled and weak.

"Yeah! Yeah! Who is that?"

"Mill...wood," the man on the other side answered.

"How bad are you hurt?"

A pause. "Bad."

She cursed under her breath. "What about the others?"

Another pause, this one longer. "Boyd and Drew are dead, I think. Chambers looks like he's still...breathing."

"You need to release the door. I can't get to you otherwise."

"Don't know if I...can."

"Try, goddammit!"

She could hear something clatter against the door, then what sounded like a grunt.

"Millwood! Are you all right?"

A scrape, but no other response.

As she raised her hand to pound against the door again, she caught movement out of the corner of her eye. She twisted around, reaching for the gun she wasn't carrying.

"Dammit, Poe! What do you think you're doing?"

Cooper.

"Get the hell back to your vehicle," he ordered. "We've

got to get out of here!"

"Millwood's inside. He's still alive. Chambers, too."

Before Cooper could reply, automatic gunfire broke out a couple hundred yards away. By the sound of it, they both knew it wasn't coming from someone in their platoon. Almost instantly an MRAP returned fire.

Cooper lost focus for a moment, frozen in place. He then depressed his transmit button. "Copy that. Get them moving. Bryant, swing around here and pick us up." He listened for a moment, then said, "Do it." He focused back on Alex. "You're sure they're alive in there?"

"I talked to Millwood just a moment ago."

He grimaced for half a second, then moved toward the door. "Let's get this open."

Together, they tried to pry the door loose as the sound of gunfire grew dangerously closer, but the damn thing wouldn't budge.

"Millwood! You've got to help us," Alex yelled.

No sound from inside.

"Millwood!"

Bryant's Cougar barreled around the corner and braked to a hard stop.

"Millwood!"

There was the *ping-ping-ping* of bullets striking the metal of the downed MRAP. Alex and Cooper ducked.

"Come on," Cooper said. "We've got to go!"

"They're still in there!"

"We're dead if we don't move now!"

He grabbed her by the arms and pulled her toward the other Cougar.

She twisted side to side, trying to get free, but he held on tight.

"No! We can't leave them!"

More bullets, streaking down the far side of Sanchez's MRAP.

As Cooper got Alex to the back of Bryant's vehicle, someone inside lowered the door. The second they were on board, the door shut again.

Ping-ping-ping-ping. This time the shots were hitting their truck.

"Go! Go! Go!" Cooper yelled at Bryant.

The Cougar began moving away quickly. Alex, free now from Cooper's grasp, pressed herself up against the side window and looked back through the protective slats at Sanchez's wrecked MRAP.

"Air support is coming," Cooper said. "They'll get 'em."

"Oh, God!" Alex said.

The back of the other MRAP had started to swing open.

"They're trying to get out! We have to go back!"

Cooper rushed to the window, then yelled to Bryant, "Turn around!"

Bryant had just started to turn the wheel, when a pickup truck with a machine gun mounted on back circled around Sanchez's vehicle and stopped near the widening rear doorway. The gun swung around and pointed through the opening. Alex and Cooper saw flashes of gunfire as attackers flooded the interior of Sanchez's vehicle with bullets.

Horrified, Alex pushed back from the window and grabbed at the hatch to the turret. As soon as it was open, she pulled herself up and pivoted the gun around, aiming it at the pickup.

Running on pure adrenaline, she let loose a steady burst of gunfire, riddling the truck and its occupants with holes.

When she was done, there was little of the vehicle left untouched.

ALEX HAD BLAMED Cooper for the deaths of their colleagues, and had requested a transfer out of their platoon, which was denied.

She had known, even then, that Cooper had given the only orders he could, and by doing so had saved her life.

But that hadn't brought Millwood and Chambers back.

Nor had it quelled the feelings of self-doubt that had plagued her ever since.

Why hadn't she reacted faster?

Why hadn't Cooper let her stay just a moment longer? Long enough to get that door open and pull Millwood and Chambers to safety? And what about Sanchez and Drew and Boyd and all the others?

Why were they gone, too?

Why *their* lives instead of hers?

There weren't any real answers to these questions, of course. Fate had taken her colleagues—her friends. And there was little that she, or Cooper, could have done about it.

It wasn't until the Stonewell jet came in sight of the Iberian Peninsula that Alex was finally able to close her eyes and fall asleep.

TEN

Galati, Romania

THEY LANDED AN hour before dawn at a small private airfield just outside Galati. An Immigration and Customs official met them on the tarmac, stamped their passports, and welcomed them to the country.

Once those formalities were complete, Cooper excused himself and jogged over to a building that served as the airfield's terminal. Alex and Deuce used the time to stretch muscles that had been cramped by hours of flight.

Deuce eyed the dark countryside. "So, this is where Dracula's from, right?"

Alex shook her head. "That's north of here. Probably a couple hundred miles."

"Oh," Deuce said. He looked around some more. "That's probably good, huh?"

"You do know Dracula's fictional, right?"

"Sure. But it's always good to be safe."

There were times when Alex didn't know if Deuce was messing with her or just being Deuce. It was part of his charm—when it wasn't annoying.

A few minutes later, Cooper returned via a baggage van driven by a member of the airport crew.

"We've got to get you to your ride," he said to Alex.

She picked up the bag she'd been given by Stonewell. The well-worn, faded green backpack and the nondescript clothes she was wearing helped reinforce the just-another-summer-backpacker-making-her-way-through-Europe cover.

"Let's go," she said.

Cooper opened the back door of the baggage van, and

both Alex and Deuce climbed on board.

"Take the passenger seat," he told her. There were no chairs in the back, only the hard metal floor.

She was about to argue, but decided, *Screw it.* Things were going to get very unpleasant for her pretty. damn soon. Might as well take advantage of what comfort she could now.

She looked out the windshield as they drove into Galati, noting her surroundings as she always did. It took only a few minutes before that old feeling returned to her, that sense of elsewhere that always hit her when she was out of the States—not a bad feeling, not a good one. Just different, brought on by the sense of age in the buildings and the land and the people themselves.

The city was in the process of waking and traffic was light. A few cars, some bikes, and a handful of pedestrians. While above, the stars were quickly receding, daylight pushing ever forward across the sky.

When they reached the edge of the Danube, the city abruptly stopped. They drove parallel to the river for several blocks, then the van braked to a halt.

"This is you," Cooper said to Alex.

He opened the door and they climbed out. He then looked at his phone for a moment.

"Okay," he said. "There." He pointed toward a building down the street. "That's Hotel Vega." He glanced at his watch. "Your bus will arrive in forty minutes. The receptionist in the hotel is holding a ticket for you."

Alex took a deep breath, and nodded.

"If something happens before you're able to get to Crimea, call the number we gave you, then hunker down until we can come get you."

"Right," she said. "Got it."

"If everything goes to hell once you reach the peninsula, get to the safe point. We'll be checking it twice every day. At ten a.m. and p.m."

She nodded again.

"Any questions?"

The only questions she had were for herself. Was she crazy? Was trying to track down her father worth the risk she was taking? She looked at Deuce and he had an expression on his face that told her it wasn't too late to back out. That said he *wanted* her to back out.

"No," she said to Cooper. "I'm good."

"You sure?" Deuce said, eyeing her intently.

"I'm sure." She smiled. "And don't worry. I won't do anything stupid if you don't."

"Look where we're standing, Alex. We've already failed that test."

For a moment, none of them spoke, then Deuce opened his arms and she hugged him.

"We can go home right now," he whispered.

"I'll be okay."

"I can't watch your back in there."

"I know."

"So don't you dare get yourself hurt."

"It's not part of my plan."

He grimaced, shaking his head as he let her loose. "It never is."

Cooper held out a hand. "No matter what happens, we won't leave you in there."

She stiffened slightly as they shook, the memory of Millwood and Chambers still a raw nerve. "Good to know," she said, then donned her pack and adjusted the straps. "I guess I'll see you on the other side."

With a quick wave, she turned and started walking toward the hotel.

In unplanned unison, Cooper and Deuce called out, "Alex."

She turned and looked at one, then the other, eyebrows raised.

The men glanced at each other, then Deuce blurted out, "Be careful."

She gave him a smile, then looked at Cooper.

"That's, um, actually what I was going to say, too," he

told her.

"I'll do my best," she said.

Without another word, she headed down the road.

ELEVEN

DESPITE WHAT OTHERS might have believed, Alex was only fluent in English. She did, however, have an excellent grasp of her mother's native Farsi, and a more than adequate, conversational knowledge of French—also thanks to her mother. But beyond those, she knew only a handful of phrases in Arabic, from her time in Iraq, and a few in German that were best not spoken in public. The last, compliments of Emerick.

None of those could help her now. She had zero knowledge of Romanian, a fact that was reinforced the moment the receptionist at the Hotel Vega greeted her.

"*Cu ce vă pot ajuta?*"

"I'm sorry," Alex said, offering her an apologetic smile. "I don't understand."

A light seemed to go on in the face of the woman across the counter. "Ah. England?"

"Canada, actually. You speak English?"

"Little bit. May I help you?"

"I think you have a bus ticket waiting for me to pick up."

The woman's brow creased as she bit her lip, uncertain. "Bus ticket. You have for me."

"No," Alex said, tapping her own chest with a forefinger. "For me. You have one for me."

Still looking confused, the young woman mumbled something unintelligible. A second receptionist, who was helping another guest, leaned toward her and whispered something in Romanian.

Again, the spark of realization. "Okay, yes," the first receptionist said, smiling. "Bus. Yes. Name you?"

"Maureen Powell."

"Again, please?"

Instead of repeating herself, Alex pulled out her Canadian passport and opened it to the information page. A moment later, she was in possession of the ticket that would take her into Ukraine.

The receptionist pointed toward the door. "Bus come..." She paused, searching for the right words, then turned to the other receptionist for help.

Her colleague looked at Alex, and said, "Bus arrive twenty minutes. Can sit and wait."

"Thank you," Alex said.

She used a bit of her Romanian currency to purchase a pastry and a bottle of water from a small shop in the lobby, then took a seat. It wasn't long before others started drifting in with their bags. A few arrived from outside, but most seemed to have been staying at the hotel. They all looked to be in their early twenties. While a few were toting suitcases, most had backpacks like Alex.

The bus arrived ten minutes late, but it didn't take long to get their bags stowed away and everyone on board. Alex sat next to a Dutch girl named Heike who was touring with two others, Romee and Anika, sitting in the next row up. Heike was apparently in the mood to talk—in nearly accent-free English—so Alex nodded politely and threw in a few words here and there as the bus passed through the city and into the countryside.

It wasn't long, however, before they stopped at the border crossing into Moldova. Alex's passport performed as advertised, raising no red flags with the immigration officials. Once everyone on the bus was cleared, they were off again, only to stop less than two kilometers farther on at the Moldovan border with Ukraine.

Passport checks again, this time with a thorough inspection of the bus's luggage compartments. One of the passengers who'd been sitting near the back was hauled into a room by two unsmiling officials. They all had to wait over half an hour until the door opened again and the young man returned, looking both scared and relieved. The word circling around the bus later was that the guards had accused him of trying to smuggle drugs into the country, but had been unable to find anything to back that up.

With the exception of a few places where they passed along the Black Sea, the road was lined with farmland nearly all the way to Odessa. Twice they made stops, letting a few of the backpackers off at each.

They finally entered Odessa just after three p.m., and reached their final destination, the Bristol Hotel, fifteen minutes later. As they'd neared the city, Heike had asked Alex how long she was planning to stay there. Alex had made the mistake of saying she would be catching a train out of town that very evening, because it turned out that Heike and her friends were heading to the train station as well.

Not wanting to look like a jerk, Alex agreed to share a cab ride with them.

The cabbie didn't look too happy as the four girls squeezed themselves and their gear into his car. Several times during the ride, he spit out something in Ukrainian that was undoubtedly meant to express his displeasure. Feeling a bit guilty, Alex slipped him double his fare when they disembarked at the Odessa-Glavnaya station. The act gained her a frown and a grunt that she assumed was thanks.

The Dutch girls were headed to Moscow. Unfortunately, the Moscow train had left two hours earlier. The best they could do was catch an overnight to Kiev, and get on another train there.

Alex's train to Simferopol, the capital of Crimea, was scheduled to leave at midnight, an hour after the girls' train departed for Kiev. She so wanted to say goodbye right there at the ticket counter, but when Heike invited her to join them for dinner, Alex said yes. She was playing a role, after all, and summer backpackers were in large part a social group.

The trouble happened a few hours later. If Alex had really been someone else, she could have walked away and let the girls deal with it on their own.

Unfortunately, role or no role, she was still Alexandra Poe.

THEY WERE IN an area right off the main central portion of the station, sitting on the floor. The other girls were passing around their cameras, showing off the pictures they'd taken that day. Romee had not fully closed one of the zippers on her backpack, leaving an opening just wide enough for a small, emaciated teenager to slip his hand inside before they even realized it was happening.

Alex had her back to the guy, so she first noticed that something was up when Anika jumped to her feet, yelling, "Hey! Hey!"

Alex whirled around. "What?"

Anika pointed at the guy running away. "He took something from Romee's pack!"

As Alex jumped up, Romee pulled the zipper all the way open. "My passport! He has my passport!"

Alex jumped over the bags and raced down the hall. Waiting passengers surprised first by the running boy, then by Alex, jumped out of the way. A few shouted in anger.

Ahead, the kid pushed through a group of people who hadn't seen him coming, then shoved open a door and ran outside.

"Move, move, move!" Alex shouted. She weaved through them, burst through the doorway, and found herself standing before a row of train platforms. Several were filled with passenger cars waiting to leave the station, while others sat unused.

The boy, apparently deciding that speed was better than deception, had run straight down the platform directly in front of Alex. There was a train on one side and none on the other. The boy was sticking to the empty side where few people were walking.

Alex kicked it into high gear. She may have been six or seven years older than the kid, but those years had been productive ones when it came to improving her physical abilities, so she immediately began closing the gap between them.

The gray and red brick platform curved slightly to the left before descending to the level of the tracks and disappearing. Halfway down, the kid looked over his shoulder and nearly stumbled when he saw Alex still behind him. He caught himself and began pumping his arms harder, but it was clear he was already going as fast as he could.

Somewhere back toward the station, Alex heard a whistle and knew the police were on their way. She didn't bother to check.

At the far platform a train started pulling away, its clickety-clack growing faster and faster as it gained speed.

"Stop!" Alex shouted as she closed to within fifty feet of the boy.

He shot another look back, this time without losing his balance, then raced to the end of the platform and onto the ground between two of the tracks.

Shit.

Alex pounded down after him.

With the platforms gone, the tracks closed in on each other, giving the sense that the train now leaving the station was heading right at them. The illusion must have been enough to scare the boy. He angled his path to the right, hopping over the nearby rails, and getting farther away from the moving locomotive.

"Stop!" she shouted again. In case he didn't understand, she tried, "Halt!" but she was wasting her breath.

There was another whistle, this one much deeper and more powerful than the earlier police whistle. It was also coming from in front of them, not behind. Alex looked past the boy at the tracks ahead. Less than a quarter mile down, coming around a bend to the right, a train was heading toward the station, and appeared to be on the same tracks that she and the kid had just hopped over.

The boy seemed to notice this, too, and moved again to

the right, jumping over the next set of tracks. But as he went over the final rail, his toe caught the top, sending him flying through the air, his arms outstretched in front of him as if he were Superman.

With a thud and a loud groan, he hit the ground less than a foot in front of the next set of tracks. Any farther and he would have cracked his skull on the rail. As it was, his right arm had smacked hard against the steel.

"Ah, ah, ah!" He cried in pain, grabbing his arm.

Alex reached him a few seconds later, putting a hand on his back. "Don't move."

He tried to shake her off. "Let go."

At least he spoke English.

"I'm not trying to hurt you," she said. "I just want to see where you're injured."

Reluctantly, he let her look him over. His forearm was definitely broken. It lay bent on the ground as if it had a second elbow. She gave him credit for not passing out from the pain. As she finished checking him, she noticed he was still clutching Romee's red passport, and what appeared to be a small, zippered pouch with a floral design.

"Were these worth it?" She ripped them from his hand and slipped them into her pocket.

The train whistled again, and as she looked up, she realized they'd both been wrong. It wasn't on the other track, but on the one the kid's arm was now lying across.

"Sorry," she said, then grabbed his shoulders and lifted him up.

Clutching his broken limb, he screamed. Alex ignored the howl, and half carried, half dragged the boy over the tracks, back to where the platform stopped.

The train passed by with another blow of its whistle as she was setting the thief down. Seconds later, two police officers arrived. They paused for a moment, catching their breath, before talking to Alex in Ukrainian.

"Sorry," she said. "I don't understand."

They tried again, but she shrugged and shook her head,

so they turned their attention to the boy, barking at him in their native language.

Struggling through his pain, the kid said something that made both officers look at Alex, then the one closest to her grabbed her arm.

"Hey!" she cried. "What do you think you're doing?"

He whirled her around and started patting her down, stopping at the pocket where she'd put Romee's pouch and passport. He pointed at the bulge and said something sharp and abrupt.

She shook her head. "Uh-uh. No way."

He pointed again, and repeated his words more forcefully.

She pressed her lips tightly together, and pulled out Romee's things. She didn't want to, but she let him take the items from her. He opened the passport, looked at the picture, then at her, and back at the picture.

She didn't have to understand Ukrainian to know what he meant when he spoke again.

"Yeah, I know," she told him. "Not me. That belongs to my friend." She pointed at the kid. "He took it."

The cop ignored her and unzipped the pouch, revealing the tip of a wad of cash.

His eyes widened slightly and he said something to the boy, who responded quickly and nodded emphatically. The cop turned to Alex, repeated almost the same words to her, while holding out the pouch and gesturing to the boy.

"No, it's *not* his," she said, then pointed to herself. "It's mine. Well, my friend's. It's definitely not his."

Looking annoyed, the cop studied her a moment before he turned to his partner. A quick conference resulted in the first one helping the boy to his feet as his partner grabbed Alex's arm again.

The officers escorted Alex and the boy back toward the station. Heike and Romee were waiting right outside the doors. The two girls ran over as Alex and the others neared the end of the platform.

"Are you all right?" Heike asked.

Alex nodded. "Fine."

Heike looked at the boy. "My God, what happened to him?"

"He didn't watch where he was going."

The cop holding the boy spoke abruptly, waving the girls out of his way.

Seeing the passport in his hand, Romee said, "Is that mine?"

"Yeah," Alex told her.

Romee pointed at the passport, and said to the cop, "Give that to me."

The cops stopped, and the one holding the passport opened it to look at the picture.

"He's got your money, too," Alex said.

"My money?"

"A little zippered pouch. Flowers on the outside?"

Romee stiffened and her face paled. She said something under her breath in Dutch, then whispered to Heike. Heike's eyes grew big as her friend spoke, and her expression turned angry. Romee cowered a bit, saying something in a tone that could only be pleading.

"What?" Alex asked, afraid of the answer.

Heike stared at her friend for a moment longer, then turned to Alex. "Do they speak English?"

"No, but Mr. Quick Fingers over there does a little, at least."

Heike looked confused for a moment, then seemed to understand who Alex meant. She leaned in so no one else could hear. "Did they look inside?"

"Just enough to see the cash. Why? What's in there?"

"Not here," Heike whispered.

While they were talking, the cop compared the passport photo to Romee. Finally, he pointed at the two girls and gestured for them to come along.

Pantomiming as she spoke, Romee said, "I don't want to cause trouble for the boy. Just give me my things and we forget everything."

Son of a bitch, Alex thought.

She realized now what was going on.

Somewhere in that pouch was hash or marijuana or something similar. Whatever it was, it would land them all in a whole boatload of trouble. Which meant her mission was about to end before it even started.

Shit.

The police officer repeated his gestures, this time emphasizing it with words. He shoved the passport and pouch into his pocket, and grabbed Romee's arm with his free hand. The other cop latched on to Heike and they continued on their way.

They were quite a sight for all the waiting passengers. Alex would have laughed at the irony if she could have. There would be no problem getting thrown into prison now. Unfortunately, given that she was still hundreds of miles from Crimea, it wouldn't be the *right* prison.

How the hell would she get out of this?

The police took them into a small three-room office down a back hallway of the station. They put the girls in one room and shut the door. Alex could hear them moving around in the outer room for a few minutes, then it grew quiet. She guessed they were getting the boy some medical attention.

She looked at Romee, and said in a low voice, "What the hell's in that pouch?"

Romee hesitated. "Marijuana."

Jesus. "How much?"

"Very little. Not even enough to make smoke, um, joint, yes?"

Alex closed her eyes and counted to ten. Did this idiot not understand anything? In some countries, even a trace amount could get you a dozen years in prison.

Alex wasn't up on the latest Ukrainian laws, but she knew they had to be a hell of a lot harsher than those in the Netherlands, where you could legally buy pot at the corner coffee shop.

"They probably won't even find it," Romee said.

Alex opened her eyes again. "The moment they pull your money out, they'll see it."

"No. It's in the lining. There's a hole at the bottom, closed with a safety pin. If they don't open the pin, they won't find it."

"How much do you want to bet on that happening?"

Alex checked her watch. It was 9:50, two hours and change until her train left. A train she couldn't miss. Dammit. She should have just let the guy run.

Voices in the outer office again, three separate ones this time. While Alex recognized two as belonging to the cops, the third was definitely not the boy's. It was female.

Several minutes passed, then the door to their room opened. The main cop stood in the doorway, pointed at Alex, and gestured for her to follow him. She pushed herself off the desk she was leaning against and headed out. The other two girls started to fall in step behind her, but the cop barked at them and shook his head.

As soon as Alex was out, he shut the door.

The other cop was standing near the woman. She was a bit older than both men, perhaps in her forties, with a stern face that wasn't helped by her pulled-back hair.

The cop led Alex to the third room, the smallest of the lot. He jutted his chin at the lone empty chair. Alex took the hint and sat.

As the stern-faced woman stepped inside, the cop closed the door, leaving his partner outside on guard duty. He and the woman stared at Alex for a long moment without saying anything.

Finally, Alex held out her hands. "Can I help you?"

The woman smiled humorlessly. "Your name, please."

Alex was relieved that she spoke English. "Maureen Powell."

"May I have your passport?"

Alex pulled her passport out of her pocket and handed it over. The woman examined it, then handed it to the man.

"Canadian, I see," she said.

"Yes."

"And you are in Ukraine for…?"

"Holiday."

"Your entry stamp is from today. Good way to start trip, yes?"

"Not exactly."

That smile again. "Please, tell us exactly what happened."

Alex proceeded to describe the events as she'd witnessed them. She paused every now and then so that the woman could translate her response to the police officer. She was honest and straightforward, leaving nothing out.

"So you were trying to get back items for friend?"

"That's correct."

"I see." A pause. "How long have you known friend?"

"We just met today."

"Today?" the woman said, surprised. "You very nice to someone known to you only a few hours."

"That kid tried to steal something. I don't like it when someone takes something that's not theirs. I don't care if I've just met the victim or known her all my life."

A sneer grew on the woman's face. "So you are good person."

"Maybe. Does it matter? Look, you've got the guy. He obviously had Romee's passport and bag. Is there a problem?"

"He say he not know why you chase him. He say items you say he take, you have, not him."

"Of course he does. Just talk to my friends. They saw him take it. There's probably another half a dozen people wandering around the station who saw him do it. Do you guys have cameras? It has to be on video, too."

"Talk your friends next."

"But you talked to the kid first, huh? And you believe him?" Alex shook her head. "You know what? As far as I'm concerned, you can keep what he took. I've got a train to catch." She rose to her feet.

"Please. Sit back down."

"I really don't have time to hang around here any longer."

"You will leave when we say it's okay."

"You've got no reason to keep me here."

"There is matter of boy's broken arm."

"What about it?"

"He says you pushed him."

"Excuse me? I wasn't even close enough to touch him, let alone push. The kid tripped over the rail. I bet if you went back there, you could see scuff marks and figure it out all on your own."

"If this is case, he would not have trip if you had not chased him, no?"

Now Alex was getting pissed. "And I wouldn't have chased him if he hadn't *stolen* my friend's passport and pouch. Tell me, what would you have done if it had been your friend?"

They went back and forth like this for several minutes, before they returned Alex to the other room and exchanged her with Romee. It was now almost ten thirty. The time until Alex's train departed was growing dangerously short. And unless they were all released in the next twenty minutes or so, the Dutch girls were definitely going to miss theirs. Of course, they didn't have an appointment to be arrested the next day in Crimea. It would be only an inconvenience for them, while for Alex it would mean losing out on the opportunity to get a lead on her father.

After Romee, it was Heike's turn.

Romee took a chair as far from Alex as she could, occasionally looking over, meek and wary.

"Did they…did they ask you about the pouch?" the girl finally asked.

Alex waited a moment before she answered. "No."

"They didn't say anything to me, either," Romee said quickly. "I don't think they found—"

"Shut up," Alex said.

"Sorry. I was just…I'm…" Romee's shoulders drooped. "What's going to happen to us?"

Alex decided it was best not to answer that question.

It was almost eleven when Heike was ushered back in.

As soon as the three were alone, Romee asked Heike a question in Dutch.

"I don't know," Heike said in English. It was clear she was still angry with her friend, and wanted to include Alex. "They didn't tell me anything."

Alex heard the main door to the outer office open, then new voices. She cursed under her breath. Just what she needed. Additional authorities to slow things down even more. She had been toying with a last-ditch plan to make a run for it the next time the door to their makeshift cell opened. She was more than confident she could get away from the two bozos who'd been holding them, and somehow get on that train and leave town. It would mean leaving without her passport and her backpack, which, hopefully, Anika was still watching. The backpack was unimportant, but the lack of a passport would be a problem. Still, it would be better to be headed to Crimea than stuck here on a potential drug charge. But if the cops now had friends, that escape plan was not nearly as viable.

The voices outside grew heated until a bark of finality silenced the room. When the conversation resumed, the tones were quieter and more contrite.

Footsteps approached the door to the girls' room. When the door opened, the two original cops were standing there, looking unhappy. One of them blurted out something while the other waved for the girls to come out.

Not needing a second invitation, they filed into the larger room. There were three new men there now, two uniformed cops probably in their twenties, and a middle-aged man in a suit.

The older man barked something at the original officers. There was a second's hesitation, then passports were produced and returned to the girls.

"What about my money purse?" Romee asked.

The older man shot a look across the room at the translator. The woman was standing in the corner, looking as if she wanted to be anywhere else. The man asked her a question, she answered, then he looked at the two arresting officers and barked again.

The taller one pulled Romee's pouch out of his pocket and handed it to her.

The suited man started talking to the girls. When he finished, he glanced at the translator again.

"Colonel Hubenko apologizes for your...inconvenience. He hopes you will not let this keep you from enjoying rest of stay in Ukraine."

The colonel said something else.

"If you need anything, please let him know," the woman translated.

"We're free to go?" Romee said.

"Yes."

"We've missed our train," Heike said. "Tell him we've missed our train. We were supposed to go to Kiev tonight."

The translator talked with the colonel for a moment, then said, "We will put you in hotel near train station tonight, compliments of the Ukrainian police. In morning, Colonel Hubenko himself will make sure you are on first train out, private compartment. Is this okay?"

Heike and Romee shared a look.

"Yeah, that will be fine," Heike said.

"For three, yes?" the woman asked.

"Yes. Our friend is waiting in the station with our bags. She's probably scared to death."

"Your friend?" the woman said.

"Yes."

The translator looked at Alex. "What about you?"

"I still have time to catch my train."

The woman translated everything to the colonel, who took a moment to yell at the two cops again. Alex was pretty sure she knew what the problem was this time. The cops hadn't even thought to see if there was anyone else traveling with the girls. The lack of luggage should have been a glaring clue. The colonel was not happy.

They found Anika with their bags right where they had left her. The relief on her face was immense. As she hugged her two friends, Alex strapped on her backpack.

"Hopefully the rest of your trip isn't quite as adventurous," Alex said.

Heike pulled away from her friends and eyed Alex gratefully. "We didn't thank you for chasing that boy."

"Almost wish I hadn't," Alex said, smiling. "You guys take care."

After hugs and goodbyes, Alex navigated through the station and out the door to her platform. The train to Simferopol was already in the station, waiting.

As she neared her car, a voice said, "Next time you get arrested, make sure it's when you're supposed to."

Cooper was standing on the other side of a large baggage trolley piled high with suitcases.

Alex stopped. "Technically, I wasn't under arrest."

"Technically," he said, smirking, "it isn't easy to find a police colonel I can bribe on such short notice. You should consider yourself lucky."

"Thank you."

"Try not to let it happen again, huh?" He smiled.

"I'll do my best."

He touched his forehead as if tipping a hat. "Safe journey." With that, he headed down the platform toward the station.

"Here's hoping," Alex said to herself, then climbed aboard the train.

TWELVE

Crimea

SHE ARRIVED IN Simferopol without further incident, a few minutes before noon the next day.

The plan was for her to be arrested at 3:30 p.m. outside the domestic terminal at the city's airport. Having a little time to kill, she grabbed some food. Since it was likely the last good meal she'd have for a while, she left nothing on her plate.

After paying her bill, she found a cab outside and climbed in.

"Airport," she told the driver.

He looked at her for a second in the mirror before his eyes widened. "*Aeroport.*"

"Yes, *aeroport,*" she said, nodding.

She leaned against the seat, and stared out the window as the city passed by, but her mind was elsewhere. This was her last chance to walk away, to say forget it. All she had to do was tell the cabbie to stop and let her out. But she didn't move. *Couldn't* move.

She had no choice.

While Alex was devastated by her mother's death, her father had reacted with the same stoic fortitude he always displayed. Alex had begun to wonder if he was secretly glad her mother was gone. Then one night, when she couldn't sleep, she went out to the kitchen to get some water. The light was on in the den, so she assumed her father was up. He often worked late, after all. She didn't want to talk to him, but there was no way to get to the kitchen without passing the office's door.

Steeling herself, she continued down the hall, hoping he wouldn't notice her. As she glanced inside the den, however, she saw he wasn't there, and his desk, which was usually clean and tidy, was now covered with squares of paper.

No, not paper, she realized, as her curiosity propelled her into the room.

Photographs.

She couldn't help but pick one up. A snapshot of her mother, cradling a very young Danny.

Alex touched the image, her mother's hair dark and thick, her creamy brown skin so perfect.

God, she was beautiful.

While Alex had inherited the hair, she had always wished she'd gotten her mother's darker skin, too. And even half her beauty.

She set the picture down and scanned the others. They were all of her mother.

One by one, she looked at each, the tears growing in her eyes with every memory.

She wasn't sure how long her father had been standing behind her, but at some point she heard him take in a breath.

She turned with a start. "I'm...I'm sorry," she said.

Without saying a word, her father put his arms around her and pulled her to him. She cried for what seemed like days. She thought maybe he'd cried, too. And as her tears petered out, so did her strength, and she fell asleep standing there, leaning against him.

When she woke the next morning, it had almost felt like a dream. But she knew from that moment forward that her father was grieving also, and that made getting through each day easier. Her relief, however, lasted only until the morning he left the house and never returned.

There had been no goodbyes, no "I have to go away for a while."

He was simply there one day and not the next.

The army had said he'd gone AWOL, that he had sold secrets to some foreign organization. Her father? A traitor?

Not a chance. He was a good soldier, a great one. Next to his own family, serving his country was the most important thing to him. He was no more a traitor than the commander of the joint chiefs himself.

As the years went by, she held on to that thought even as her anger at him began to blossom.

So many questions only he could answer.

And now, here she was, riding in the back of a cab in the Autonomous Republic of Crimea, one step closer to getting those answers.

When the cab reached the airport and pulled to the curb, Alex didn't enter either of the terminals. Instead she made her way over to the small plaza between the buildings.

It was 3:30 p.m. Her instructions were to find a red-roofed building, something that wasn't hard to do. It came into view, just beyond the plaza's diamond-shaped flower beds, the moment she turned the corner. Words in large Cyrillic type were displayed on white beams across the apex of the roof—an advertisement or perhaps an identifier of what was inside. The door to the building was to the right of center, flanked by a pair of windows.

Alex walked casually toward the door. Twenty feet before she reached it, a voice yelled out.

Though she didn't understand the words, she recognized it as the very same thing the cop at the Odessa train station had shouted at her.

She stopped and looked around, expecting to see the officer who had been bribed to take her into custody, but instead of one cop, there were five. All had pistols pointed in her direction.

She immediately raised her hands in the air. "No need for that. I'm unarmed."

"Down on ground," the one on the far left shouted.

She dropped to the ground, her pack heavy on her back.

"Arms, legs out!"

She assumed a spread-eagle position. Apparently her contact had decided to make her capture seem more realistic than planned, and had involved some of his friends. As long as she got where she needed to go, that's all that really mattered.

One of the men—she couldn't see which—approached her, and used a knife to cut the straps to her backpack so he could pull it off.

"Hey! That wasn't necessary," she said. She didn't really care about the bag, but a knife that close to her skin was not something she was fond of.

The man dropped the backpack beside her, knelt down, cuffed her wrists behind her, and began a body search. As his hand slipped over her hip and between her legs, she squeezed her thighs together. "What do you think you're doing?"

Putting on a show was one thing, but she was not about to put up with bullshit like this. She shifted her hips, moving from his touch. He grabbed her and dug his fingers into her thigh.

That did it.

In a sudden twist, she wrapped her legs around him and pulled him to the ground, rolling him onto his back. With an *oomph* he collapsed, and she dug a knee into one of his kidneys. "Don't you *ever* do that again. To anyone!"

"Step away!" one of the other cops yelled at her in English.

She gave a parting shove of her knee to the downed cop and stood up, arms still cuffed behind her back.

"I'm cooperating," she said. "That son of a bitch just wanted a little more than I'm willing to give."

"You funny woman, huh?" the English speaker said as he stepped closer to her.

By now quite a crowd had gathered, and what was supposed to have been a simple—and subtle—arrest was turning into a scene.

"Do you see me laughing?" she asked.

The cop said something to the guy on the ground, who grunted a response, and slowly rose to his feet. Alex eyed him warily as he gave her a once-over before leaning down and picking up her pack.

"You come no problem?" the English speaker asked her.

"Just tell me where to go."

"Car waiting."

They formed a rough circle around her, and pushed their way through the crowd to the road that ran in front of the terminals. There, three police cars were parked bumper to bumper. Alex was led to the one in the middle. The cop in front of her opened the backdoor, while the one behind grabbed the top of her head. He pushed her down and through the opening, but not before making sure the top of her head smacked against the doorframe.

She winced as she fell into the seat, and felt blood start to trickle down her scalp. The pain of the blow grew like a wave. She gritted her teeth and shut her eyes to ride it out. Once she opened them again, the car was already pulling away from the airport.

There were two cops in the car with her. The one who'd opened the door was sitting behind the wheel, and the English speaker was looking back at her from the passenger seat.

"Apologies," he said. "But appearances must be kept up."

So this was her contact. She glanced at the driver then back to the other man.

He shook his head. "Only me. He not understand English."

Tempering her response so the driver wouldn't wonder what was going on, she said, "And your friend back there. The one with the wandering hands. Was that for appearances, too?"

There was a flash in the man's eyes. Anger? Annoyance? It was hard to tell. "You should be very careful how you speak to me. You are in Crimean system now. I can be friend, or I can make problem."

Apparently he was a touchy bastard. And an arrogant one as well. But as much as she might've liked to slap the attitude right out of him, she knew he was right. She was at his mercy.

He could easily forget he'd been paid to make all this happen.

That was the kind of trouble that could lead to her being "lost" in his beloved Crimean system.

Never to be found again.

THEY ARRIVED AT a big block of a building that screamed municipality. Columns and gray stone and wide stairs leading inside, it could have been picked up and plopped down in almost any country and looked at home.

They parked behind the building and took her in through a basement door. The English speaker said something to his friends, then headed down an intersecting hallway on his own.

The four who were left escorted Alex to an empty, windowless room that was clearly a holding cell. There she was left, her wrists still cuffed.

Minutes passed. Five. Ten.

When the door opened again, a single cop entered, only it wasn't the English speaker. It was the son of a bitch with the wandering hands.

Oh, joy.

He was carrying a knotted sock full of coins or rocks or something equally hard and heavy. A sap, or this guy's version of one, anyway. By the look in his eyes, he was anxious to test it out on her skull.

"You've got to be kidding me," she said. "Did you learn nothing?"

He was only a year or two younger than Alex, and had that look of indignant self-importance that was so common among people her age who hadn't yet tasted real life.

Alex had never been cursed with that disease. Her real life began when her mother died, and continued on through Iraq and the occasional Maryland mean street. She was sure this idiot was used to getting his way, and after failing to feel her up, he now wanted to reestablish his perceived dominance to save face with his buddies.

He took two steps forward, testing her, but she didn't back off. He slapped the sock against the palm of his free hand, trying to intimidate her.

Without warning, she dropped her head and rushed him, targeting his nose. He turned just enough that she ended up slamming into his cheek instead. She could feel the cut on her head open up again, but gave it no further thought.

The jerk staggered to the side, the side of his face red from the impact. Before he could do anything else, she kicked sideways and caught him in the abdomen right below his sternum.

He doubled over, coughing, and dropped the makeshift sap to the ground. She hooked it with her foot and hurled it across the room, out of reach.

She took a couple steps back, keeping her eye on the cop the whole time. He coughed once more, then began panting as he caught his breath. As soon as he was more in control, he tilted his head up and looked at her. There was fire in his eyes, an anger several times stronger than it had been when he'd entered the room.

The roar began, barely noticeable, at the back of his throat, then flew out of his mouth as he launched himself at her.

Alex had the fleeting thought that she needed to be careful not to hurt him too much, as it might negate whatever deal Stonewell had worked out to get her into Slavne Prison. Cops worldwide were rabid when it came to protecting their own, even when one of their own was a complete shit.

She dodged to the side, trying to get out of his way, but his shoulder still glanced against her rib. In a way, it was a good thing. The blow spun him sideways, and kept him from smashing headfirst into the wall and breaking his neck. It did not, however, keep his other shoulder from crashing into the cement and dislocating.

The cop crumpled to the floor in a howl of pain.

Alex rushed to the door, and started kicking it. "We need help in here! Hey! Anyone there? Help!"

When she heard several pairs of feet running toward the holding cell, she backed away and moved up against the wall to look as harmless as possible.

The door flew open and three cops rushed in. After a quick look at her, they noticed their colleague lying against the far wall. Two of them went to him, while the other approached Alex.

He said something to her in Ukrainian, his tone harsh.

"Don't look at me," she said calmly. "He did that himself."

The guy rattled off at her again.

This time she just shrugged and looked past him at the others. They had helped their friend back to his feet, and were trying to find a way to get him out of the room without disturbing his damaged shoulder.

The cop standing in front of Alex said something to the others, and ran out of the room. He returned with his English-speaking colleague right after the injured man was led outside.

"What happened?" the cop asked, not looking happy.

"Your friend decided he wanted a little revenge."

"But he was on the ground."

"Again," she added for him.

"Yes, again."

"What can I say? He's an idiot. Look, my hands are cuffed behind my back. He comes at me with a weapon and all I can do is—"

"Weapon? What weapon?"

She looked around, spotted the sap in the corner, and nodded toward it.

He walked over and picked it up. From the look on his face, she knew this wasn't the first time he'd seen it.

He shouted something toward the door, then turned to Alex. "I will be back. Someone bring you towel now, for you clean up." He left.

The promised towel showed up a few minutes later, but because of the cuffs, the cop who brought it had to wipe the blood from her face and hair. She had forgotten about the cut on her head and the towel was a red mess when he finished.

He left for a moment, then returned with a piece of gauze that he clumsily taped over the wound.

When the English speaker came back, he looked her over, gave her a nod, and said, "Come."

He was her only escort as he led her up a darkened stairway to an office on the second floor. The room was crammed with books and stacks of paper, with an oversized wooden desk dominating the center. There were three chairs—one for the old man sitting on the other side of the desk, and two, currently empty, for visitors. The cop motioned her into the far chair, and took the one beside her.

The old man behind the desk was wearing a black judge's robe over a white-collared shirt and light blue tie. Hanging from a blue and yellow ribbon around his neck was a gold, multipointed starburst medal. The only hair he had were two tufts of white above each ear.

Since the moment they'd walked in, his gaze had followed Alex. Now his eyes were locked with hers. She wasn't sure how she was supposed to act, so she decided to match him stare for stare. In theory, he was also in Stonewell's pocket.

Finally he smiled and leaned back in his chair as he broke eye contact. He clasped his hands in front of his chest, his elbow resting on the arms of his chair.

"Welcome to Simferopol, Maureen Powell. I am Justice Gurka." His voice was surprisingly devoid of any Ukrainian accent, and sounded more like he'd come from London than the former Soviet republic.

"Thanks," she said. "I heard it was a friendly place. Haven't been disappointed."

A condescending smile. "Most people don't get arrested so soon after entering our country."

"So it's my fault."

"Does it really matter?" The judge leaned forward again and opened a large ledger in front of him. "You have been charged with violence against a person or persons and possession of a deadly weapon." This was part of a prearranged story that connected the weapon in question—a knife planted in Alex's backpack—to a recent stabbing in the city. The severity of the crime would give her a certain cachet in prison that she could use to her advantage if necessary. "Unfortunately," the judge went on, "I will not be able to schedule your trial for several months. Which means that unless you can produce bail in an amount I have yet to determine, you will be a guest of the Crimean judicial system."

"Looks like I'm shit out of luck," she said. "Unless that bail is under a few hundred bucks."

"Well, then, that settles that." He wrote something in the ledger. "As much as I would like to house you in one of our local jail facilities, they are not meant for stays more than a few days."

True or not, at least he was sticking to the script. "I understand."

"We will have to transfer you to one of our local prisons. Yalta, I think. It will be better suited to your needs."

"Wait. Yalta?"

"There's a women's facility just outside of the city. You'll have a nice ocean breeze, clean air. You'll enjoy it."

The judge closed the ledger, and the cop stood up, ready to leave. But Alex remained in her seat.

"I think you and I should have a private conversation," she said to the judge.

"That would be highly irregular."

"Wouldn't you say this whole situation is irregular?"

The judge regarded her for several seconds, then looked at the cop. "Please step outside." The cop hesitated, but the judge smiled and said, "She's handcuffed, and I'm behind my desk. There's little she can do before you'd be able to get back in here."

I wouldn't be so sure about that, Alex thought, and could see the cop was thinking the very same thing. But he nodded and stepped outside, closing the door behind him.

"So, Ms. Powell, you have a problem with my orders?"

"We both know Yalta isn't where I'm supposed to go."

"Do we?"

If it hadn't been for the knowing look in his eye, Alex might have begun to wonder if she'd been taken to the wrong judge.

"What do you want?" she asked.

"Want?"

"That's what this is about, isn't it?"

"Are you trying to bribe me, Ms. Powell? I can hardly be bought for 'a few hundred bucks,' as you say."

"I'm sure they already gave you much more than that."

The judge steepled his fingers and tapped them against his upper lip, letting out a low, quick laugh. "I'm afraid, my dear, that I find the…"—he paused, smiling as he leaned forward—"the *gift* your colleagues were kind enough to provide me isn't quite as generous as it could have been."

You son of a bitch, she thought, but kept her tone neutral. "So you want more."

Turning his palms up, he shrugged. "I'm only one man in a very powerful and unforgiving system, and I'm taking on a lot of risk. It seems only fair that—"

"Save it. You want more, I'm not the one you need to talk to."

"No, but you can relay the message."

"I'm not in contact with my colleagues."

"Easily remedied."

The judge opened one of the desk drawers and pulled out a mobile phone. Disposable, most likely. Definitely not traceable back to him. He held it out to her, but she didn't take it.

He frowned. "I assume you know what number to dial."

When she finally moved, she snatched the device from his hand, making it clear she was annoyed. Moving the phone below desk level so the judge couldn't see the keypad, she punched in the emergency number she had memorized before leaving DC.

It rang twice before it clicked and a female voice said,

"Yes?"

"Omega twenty-four slash four," she said.

"One moment."

The silence lasted for nearly half a minute, then another click.

"Poe?"

McElroy.

"How you doing, Jason?"

"What the hell's going on? Shouldn't you be on your way to prison by now?"

"Just a little hiccup."

"You got yourself in trouble *again*?"

Her eyes narrowed. Of course he'd heard about Odessa. "Actually this trouble isn't mine. It's yours." She told him about the judge's request.

"That son of a bitch," McElroy murmured.

"I thought the very same thing."

"Where are you now?"

"Sitting in his office."

"He's there *with* you?"

"Right in front of me."

"All right. Good. You tell him that—"

"I don't think so," she said, feeling tired and sore and more pissed off by the moment. "That's your job, not mine."

She set the phone down and slid it across the desk.

"It's for you," she told him.

The judge let it sit where it was. "I'd prefer that you handle the details."

"Like I told him, that's not my job. You want more, you ask for it."

The superior smile he'd been wearing disappeared.

He hesitated, then picked up the phone. "Hello?...Yes, I'm afraid the situation has...That's right...Oh, I wouldn't dare be so presumptuous. I think you can come up with a suitable number." The pause that followed was longer than the previous ones. By the time it ended, the judge was smiling again. "Yes, I believe that will do quite well. Very generous of you, thank you." His gaze flicked to Alex. "Not to worry, I'll make certain she's on her way the moment the money is transferred. It's been a pleasure doing business with you."

As soon as he ended the call, he opened the back of the phone, removed the SIM card, and broke it in half. He opened the ledger in front of him again and called out, "Kaskiv!"

The door flew open and the English speaker reentered.

"I've just checked with Yalta, and apparently they are unable to take a new prisoner at this time. I believe there is room for her at Slavne. I have a call in to them now. As soon as I hear back and get the okay, she can be on her way. Please take her back to her cell."

"Yes, sir."

Alex rose and moved toward the door.

"Ms. Powell," the judge said.

She looked back at him.

His smile had widened. "I do hope you'll enjoy your time in our country."

THIRTEEN

SHE WAS TRANSPORTED in the back of a Soviet-era sedan that she was sure wasn't long for the world. The entire drive to the prison was lined with farms and the occasional small village.

Nearly two hours after they had left the Crimean capital, her driver, a boyish cop who couldn't have been on the job for more than a few months, turned left off the country road onto a narrow, tree-lined street.

Alex had a weird sense of déjà vu as they entered a wooded area, and approached a guardhouse that sat in front of an imposing gate about a hundred yards in. It reminded her of the entrance to the Stonewell facility.

Here, however, the gate was flanked on either side by not one fence, but two. The parallel barriers stood twenty feet high, the no-man's-land between them wide enough to make it impossible for someone to jump from the top of one to the other. So while an escapee might get over the first fence, she'd never reach the top of the second before being seen, and probably shot.

Alex's driver stopped next to the gate and lowered his window. The guard who stepped out of the building leaned down and looked into the car. His gaze lingered on Alex, a sneer digging into his cheek. He and the driver spoke for a moment, then he returned to the hut and the giant gate in front of them swung open.

There was a small rise in the road ahead, so Alex didn't get her first view of Slavne Prison until they reached the crest. Satellite pictures were one thing, but seeing it in person brought only one thought to mind.

Hellhole.

If a group of buildings could exhale misery, those in front of her were doing just that. Gray and grimy and foreboding, the walls that surrounded the prison proper rose a good three stories into the sky. Centered along the front was the boxy and equally depressing administration building. The few windows that existed were small and dirty. Alex spotted a few places where other windows had once been, but had since been bricked over. Beyond the prison wall, she could barely see the tops of the identical buildings inside.

The road they were on led to a parking area right in front of the admin entrance. Just before the lot, another road branched off to the left, allowing access to the two buildings not within the prison walls. The two-story rectangular box was clearly a barrack. No doubt it was where the guards who didn't have places in town stayed when they were off duty. The house, Alex guessed, was where the equivalent of a prison warden must have lived. It was only slightly less morose than the other structures.

Three uniformed guards were standing outside the administration door. As Alex's driver pulled into an empty spot near them, they walked over. The driver made a motion for her to stay where she was, then climbed out.

She almost laughed. Where would she go? She was once again wearing handcuffs, her wrists in front of her this time, and there were no inside handles on either of the sedan's rear doors.

After a quick conversation with the guards, her escort returned, fetched some papers from the front seat, and gave them to one of the other men. The documents were examined, heads nodded, and the back door of the sedan was finally opened.

One of the guards grabbed her bicep and yanked her out. Alex avoided catching her feet on the doorframe lip by the width of a hair, but couldn't avoid stumbling as he pulled her away from the car.

The guard who'd been given the papers walked up to her,

and looked down at the sheet again.

"Ma-uh-reen Poh-well?"

"Yes. Maureen Powell. That's me."

The guard launched into what sounded like a memorized speech, and when he finished, he asked a question, then stared at her. When she didn't respond, he repeated the question.

After another silent moment, the young cop who'd driven her said something to the guard in a tentative voice. Alex was pretty sure he was explaining she only spoke English. The guard barked at the cop, then nodded sideways at the sedan. Looking frightened, the cop stepped back, mumbled a few words in reply, and hightailed it back to his vehicle.

Once the cop was gone, the guard repeated his question.

Why couldn't they just cut the bullshit and take her inside?

"I'm sorry," she said. "I don't understand."

Her answer, however, didn't seem to please her new friend. He moved in close, their noses only inches apart, and shouted the question this time.

She almost told him that turning up the volume wouldn't make any difference, but she bit back the response. He might not understand her, but he'd likely recognize the tone. Best not to piss off everyone just yet.

Instead, she took the opposite tact. She furrowed her brow and put a quiver in her voice as she said, "I-I'm sorry. I don't know what you want."

He shouted again, but not the same question. Alex allowed herself to jerk back in surprise, even considered trying to produce a tear or two, then simply lowered her head in a show of deference.

Either this did the trick or the idiot had grown bored with her. He stepped back, spat a few words at the other guards, and headed toward the building entrance. The two remaining guards grabbed her, one on each arm, and guided her inside.

Unable to help herself, Alex took a deep breath right before they entered, her body craving one last lungful of free air. It wasn't until the door closed behind her that she actually began to feel the fear she'd been feigning a moment earlier.

She was really here. She was really in prison. And if Stonewell screwed up somehow, she might be here for a very long time.

She tried to focus on a memory, anything that might remind her why she was here. But she could only hear a voice, echoing through her head.

Deuce's, of course. Who else?

This was a bad idea, it said.

No, shit, she thought.

THE DRAB PRISON reception room was nothing like the lobby of a normal office building. It was only about fifteen feet long by ten wide, with no pictures on the walls or tables full of magazines. No tables at all, for that matter. There were only six chairs, broken up into two rows, their legs bolted firmly to the floor.

The only way out of here, other than the door they'd just entered, was a mechanically operated, barred door on the opposite wall. Next to this was a thick Plexiglas window that looked into a guard station. There was a metal speaker box on the wall below the window. Next to the grill was a single button.

The guard with the papers walked up to the box, pushed the button, and said something. The response from the guard inside came through the speaker, tinny and overamplified.

A loud *ca-chunk* filled the room, and the barred door swung open.

Alex felt her pulse quicken as she was led through the doorway. She didn't have to fake a jump of surprise when the door clacked shut behind them.

They were now in a long hallway that ran vertically along the spine of the building. After turning left, they went halfway down the hall before entering a windowless room, with a front counter area and what appeared to be a storage section in back beyond an open doorway. There were two people behind the counter—a female guard, and a woman in a gray, formless, calf-length dress.

Alex's escort and the guard exchanged words. The woman in the dress shuffled into the back, and returned a moment later holding some folded gray material. The guard took it from her, opened it up, and tossed it to Alex.

Alex caught it with her cuffed hands, not surprised to see that it was a dress exactly like the one worn by the woman.

Prison garb.

Lovely.

One of her escorts grabbed her hands and removed the cuffs, only scratching her wrist a few times in the process. He pointed at the dress, then at her.

She looked around. "You want me to change *here?*"

He pointed at her and the dress again.

"I don't understand," Alex told him. "You actually want me to—"

"Yes," a voice said, and they all looked at the prisoner who had fetched Alex's new clothes. "Change here. Nowhere else."

Alex's escort snapped at the woman, but whatever response she gave seemed to satisfy him. He turned to Alex again, and pointed at her more emphatically, gesturing to the dress.

Still, Alex hesitated.

"Do you want them to hurt you?" the woman asked.

"No," Alex said.

"Then put on dress. So what, they see you? They will see you every day."

Alex looked around the room, then turned so her back was to the guards, and unbuttoned her shirt. She thought she heard one of them snicker, but she didn't look back. When she started to pull the dress over her head, one of the guards shouted something at her.

Alex paused and glanced over at the prisoner.

"Your brassiere, cannot have. They think could be weapon."

With the dress piled on top of her shoulders, Alex unhooked her bra and did a quick dance of getting it off as she pulled the scratchy dress down to minimize her exposure. This time it wasn't a snicker, but an outright laugh. She ignored it as she undid her pants and pulled them off.

"What do I do with these?" Alex asked, holding up her clothes.

"Give to me. We keep here."

Alex handed her shirt, bra, and pants to the woman.

Their task completed, the guards grabbed Alex again and manhandled her toward the door.

"Good luck," the prisoner called out.

Alex seriously doubted there was such a thing as luck in a place like this.

Several steps later, she found herself in the prison infirmary, where she was given an examination by a man she assumed was the facility's doctor. When he came to the blood-soaked gauze still taped to the top of her head, he removed it, looked at the wound, and retrieved a set of electric shears.

At first, she was sure he was about to cut off all her hair, but he stuck to the area around the wound. When he was finished, he put in a couple of stitches, covered it with a new bandage, then poked her upper arm with a syringe, and gave her a shot of what she assumed were antibiotics. He dismissed her with a wave, and the guards grabbed her and escorted her outside.

This time they went up a set of stairs to a waiting area on the third floor where a woman sat behind a desk, typing something into her computer. There were plenty of chairs here, but the guards kept Alex on her feet while they waited for who knew what. It was at least five minutes before the woman's phone rang. When she finished the call, she looked at the guards and nodded.

Tightening their grips on Alex's arms, they marched her through a doorway beyond the woman's desk.

The room they entered was larger than some apartments

Alex had lived in. There was a desk at the far end, while the area closer to the door was largely devoted to a couch and a set of matching chairs. This was the first thing Alex had seen since arriving here that didn't seem aimed at destroying souls.

The only person in the room was a man standing straight-backed next to the couch. He was large, with broad shoulders and a barrel chest. By the creases on his face and the color of his hair, Alex thought he was about fifty-five, but he looked as if he could handle himself quite well in a fight with someone half that age.

This, she decided, must be the warden. If she needed further proof, the fact that her guards stood at attention once they'd all moved into the room sealed the deal.

The warden walked over and stopped in front of her. Lifting his chin, he looked down at her as if trying to classify what species she was. He unclasped his hands behind his back and swung them around. In one was a small blue booklet—a Canadian passport.

Maureen Powell's Canadian passport.

The warden took his time looking it over before closing it again.

"Can-a-da," he said.

Not knowing how else to reply, she nodded. "Yes."

He smiled and gave her a thumbs-up. "Wayne Gretzky."

"Yeah. Right. Wayne Gretzky."

"Justin Bieber."

She nodded and returned his thumbs-up. "Wayne Gretzky."

"Wayne Gretzky." His smile lasted a few more seconds, before he folded his arms over his wide chest. "You...no problem. Yes?"

"No problem."

The smile returned. "Good. You no problem, me no problem."

"Deal." She could tell he didn't understand the word, so she said, "Yes. Good."

With a nod, he put his hands behind his back and headed

across the room toward his desk. Apparently it was the signal that their meeting was over, as Alex was immediately hustled out of the room.

Back on ground level, they took her through two sets of barred checkpoints before reaching a heavy-looking metal door. When one of the guards opened it, Alex wasn't surprised to find the prison yard on the other side. Walking back into the sunshine, she noticed at least two dozen women wearing the same type of gray dress she was. At least, the dresses had started out the same. Many had been modified— refitted, shortened a bit—while others were simply faded and torn from overuse.

The prisoners noticed her, too, each stopping what they were doing to stare at her. Alex wondered if any of these women was Traz, her inside contact, but for all she knew, Traz could be one of the guards. There was no way to tell until Stonewell's inside source was ready to make his or her presence known.

The guards led her across a mix of grass and dirt, toward the three buildings in the center of the walled-off yard. Each of the wide buildings was four stories high, built of the same stone that made up the walls, with entry doors painted the same faded white as the one she'd passed through moments before.

As they drew nearer, their course veered toward the structure on the far right, building number one. That was a disappointment. According to McElroy, El-Hashim was in building number two, the middle one, but there wasn't much Alex could do about that at the moment.

Mounted next to the door of Building One was a dilapidated metal box. The guard in the lead pulled out a key and used it to unlock the cover. Inside was a phone that looked like something out of 1940s Berlin. He picked it up, spoke a few words, and before he could return the receiver to its cradle, there was a metal groan followed by a *pop*, and the door swung open.

The smell was the first thing to hit her as they entered. A

jumble of body odor and spoiling food and human waste permeated the narrow green hallway. The smell seemed to be leaking out of the walls themselves. She blinked several times, and had to work hard not to gag.

Then there was the sound, which was almost as bad as the smell. Everywhere cackles and shouts and cries. The noise became even louder as they crossed into the first block.

Cells lined both sides of the concrete walkway, each with a number above. While most of the barred doors were open and the cells beyond empty, a few were closed with three, four, even five prisoners looking out from inside. The moment the occupants caught sight of Alex, they began to howl and scream. They banged plates and cups against the bars and underlined the racket with piercing whistles.

The noise crescendoed as Alex and her guards moved from one block to the next. At the back end of the first floor was a tired-looking wooden staircase. Alex scowled as she was led onto it. She had seen another stairwell at the front of the building, but apparently the guards had wanted to show her off to as many prisoners as possible. A scare tactic that probably worked on ninety-five percent of the people they brought through.

They passed the second floor and went all the way up to the third. There, they proceeded to the block in the middle and stopped in front of cell 185. It was one of those with the door closed. Inside were three prisoners. While they had been yelling it up like the others when Alex first stepped into their block, they were silent now, staring warily out at her.

The lead guard turned to a camera mounted in the ceiling and gave it a wave. Almost immediately, a loud buzz cut through the din. The guard grabbed one of the bars and pulled the cell door open.

Standing aside, he said something to Alex and pointed inside.

Knowing she could show no weakness, she walked straight in as if she'd been living there for years. The buzz sounded again, the door closed behind her—

—and there she was.

Home.

There were four beds in the room, split between two bunks butted head to toe along the same wall. Though none looked particularly comfortable, all four appeared to be claimed, which meant someone was hoarding space. Having no idea which was the extra, Alex decided to claim the one she wanted—the bottom bunk, nearest the front of the cell.

As she swept the belongings atop it to the floor, the largest of her three cellmates yelled out and shoved Alex's shoulder. Instead of fighting back, Alex pushed the complainer to the side and sat down on the mattress.

The woman yelled again, grabbed Alex's arm, and yanked it. Alex let her shoulder roll forward, then snapped back, jerking the woman toward her. She planted her free hand on the woman's clavicle and gave it a small, upward nudge right before her attacker reached the bed. The change in trajectory was more than enough to send her new roommate's forehead crashing into the frame of the upper bunk.

The woman staggered backward, stunned, blood trickling down the bridge of her nose. Alex popped to her feet, knowing she needed to finish this before the other two women decided to join in. Grabbing her rival by the hair, she dragged the woman kicking and screaming to the other lower bunk and pushed her onto the mattress.

Without a word, she returned to her own bunk, climbed on, and stretched out.

The other two women were pressed against the wall near the bars, watching her with a mix of fear and awe.

"Problem?" Alex asked.

The mousier of the two shook her head. "No," she said. "No problem." Her accent was more German than Ukrainian.

"Good." Alex squirmed around until she was comfortable. "I assume you wouldn't mind if I took a little nap?"

"Of course not," Mousy said.

"I'd advise you to make sure your buddy there doesn't try to take advantage while I'm out. I'm hell full of mean if someone wakes me up before I'm ready."

Mousy hesitated. "Yes. Yes, I will let her know."

"I appreciate it."

Alex closed her eyes, and though she hadn't planned to fall asleep, she did.

FOURTEEN

COOPER LOWERED HIS binoculars. "Well, she's in," he said.

Deuce lowered his own set a moment later, frowning. "Yep."

They were lying on the crest of a hill, overlooking the prison from half a mile away. They had just watched Alex being escorted into the building.

"You'd better let the boss man know," Deuce said.

Cooper nodded, pulled out his phone, and fired off a text:

INSERTION COMPLETE

The reply came back within seconds.

ACKNOWLEDGED

"So what now?" Deuce asked.

"Now we wait."

AS SHE HAD done on each of the three previous days since her arrival, the assassin took careful note of any new arriving prisoners, just in case El-Hashim had been able to smuggle in more help.

The woman had already surrounded herself with three bodyguards. And while the assassin knew she could take care of them with very little effort, the time it would take could be problematic. Any delay might give El-Hashim a chance to escape or, worse, get the attention of the guards who might stop the assassin before she reached her target.

No matter *how* she proceeded, failure was not an option.

She had to be a hundred percent sure that this assignment concluded with the death of El-Hashim, and that the assassin herself wasn't caught in the process.

As on the previous days, none of the new prisoners made a beeline for the cellblock where El-Hashim had holed up, so it was still just the three bodyguards. In fact, the only unusual thing about this day's arrivals was a woman who appeared to be from North America.

The assassin mentally filed away the woman's face, along with the others she'd noted that day, just in case any of them popped back up on her radar. Information was key to her job, and she never missed an opportunity to gather what she could.

Her task completed for the day, she set her mind back on the more important matter at hand.

The demise of Fadilah El-Hashim.

FIFTEEN

WHEN THE BUZZER sounded, Alex came awake, her muscles tense.

For a split second, she wondered why a mattress was hanging a few feet above her. Then she remembered. She wasn't home. This wasn't her bedroom.

This was prison.

And the sound she'd heard hadn't been an alarm.

Her cellmates were shuffling past her bunk, giving her wary looks as they headed for the cell door. Alex twisted around and saw it was open.

"What's going on?" she asked Mousy.

The girl looked at her as if she'd rather not answer, but said meekly, "Night check." A pause. "If you don't want problem, you'll come, too."

Alex crawled out of her bunk and followed the others into the common area in the middle of their cellblock. All the other doors were also open, the inmates forming two parallel lines, each facing the cells they'd just left.

Alex's cellmates fell into the line side by side, spreading themselves out just enough so that there was no room for her. They were probably hoping she'd go down to the end of the line, where she'd undoubtedly be disciplined for being out of position. Instead, she forced her way between Mousy and the woman she'd taken the bunk from.

"Thanks," she said with a smile.

Her sparring partner muttered something under her breath that Alex didn't need translated to understand. She ignored it.

All conversation and movement in the room suddenly

stopped. Silence reigned for nearly a minute, until the block door opened and five male guards piled in.

Their gender didn't surprise Alex. She knew that, even in the US, the majority of prison guards were male, and not necessarily restricted to inmate processing when it came to female prisoners. Back home, many women inmates were left to the unchecked mercy of their male captors, and it obviously wasn't any different in Ukraine.

In fact, it was probably much worse.

While one guard remained by the door, the others divided in half, one pair walking up each row. They read from a list—names or numbers, Alex wasn't sure which—and each time a different inmate would say something that sounded like "talk" or "tack."

When they reached Alex, they stopped. The man holding the paper ran a finger down the list, and said something to his partner. They both looked at the list again, the second man pointing at something near the bottom.

The man with the paper read what was there, and they both looked at Alex.

"What?" she asked.

"It's your number," Mousy whispered. "Just say yes."

"Okay. Yes."

The guard closest to her narrowed his eyes, a small oval birthmark on his cheek stretching slightly.

"*Tak*," Mousy whispered. "Just say *tak.*"

"*Tak*," Alex repeated.

The guard stared at her a moment longer, smirked, then he and his colleague moved to the next person in line.

When they were far enough away, Alex whispered, "Thanks," but Mousy didn't acknowledge her.

Once the guards reached the end of the lines, one of them barked an order, and the prisoners headed back to their cells.

Within minutes, all but a couple of the lights in the central area went out. Alex crawled into her bed, and stared at the bunk above her as she tried to quell a sudden sense of claustrophobia.

Fadilah El-Hashim. Find her. Get her out.
Get me *out.*

BREAKFAST THE NEXT morning was in a large, gray room in the basement of Building One. Alex fell into line behind her cellmates and followed their lead, grabbing a bowl and spoon before accepting a ladle full of porridge that nearly matched the shade of the walls.

When she took a seat next to Mousy at a table in the middle of the room, the woman gave her a dirty look but didn't tell her to go away.

The initial taste of the porridge was enough to reinforce Alex's desire to get this whole thing over with as quickly as possible. The goop was like liquid cardboard flavored with spoiled milk. She powered through, however, knowing she needed to keep her energy level at its highest.

Being the first at the table to finish, she asked Mousy, "What do I do with my bowl?"

Mousy glanced over, and put another spoonful of porridge in her mouth without answering.

Alex had to fight hard not to roll her eyes. "I'm just asking a question. Would you rather I stay here and wait for you?"

Before Mousy could respond, a brown-haired girl with a faded black eye sitting across the table said, "There." She nodded past Alex, so Alex turned to see what she meant. "Hole in the wall. You put on the shelf."

The hole was a glassless window with a counter sticking through it that had several bowls already piled on it.

"Thanks," Alex said as she started to rise, but then she paused. "Where am I supposed to go after that?"

The girl laughed. "Oh, right. First day. It is always like this."

Alex looked at her, surprised, then realized she'd seen the woman before. "You're the woman who gave me the dress."

A grin. "Frida."

"I'm sorry?"

"My name. It is Frida."

"I'm Maureen," Alex told her. She nearly reached out to offer the girl her hand, but stopped herself because she didn't know what the norm was here.

The girl made no move to shake, and instead said, "One hour yard time. So go outside. After, assigned duty."

"Assigned duty? I don't know what that is."

"They give to you. No worry."

Alex stood the rest of the way up. "Thanks, Frida."

"You're welcome," the girl said, adding, "Maureen."

TURNED OUT THERE was only one direction Alex could have gone after leaving the cafeteria. She took the stairs back to the ground floor, and found a barred door had been closed across the hallway to the cellblocks. The only one open led outside.

As she stepped through the doorway, she had to raise a hand to shield her eyes from the bright, hot sunlight. A few feet out, she stopped and let her body soak in some rays as she took in several deep breaths of fresh air. Finally she forced herself to set about familiarizing herself with the prison yard.

She'd already been exposed to the area between the cellblock and admin buildings, so she circled around Building One to get a look at the backside. Grass and dirt dominated this part of the yard, too. The only exception was an area close to the wall on her far left that appeared to be set up for sporting activities. She decided to wander in that direction to get a better look.

There were only a few dozen other inmates outside so far. Most seemed to be keeping to themselves, while some were paired off in twos and threes. Wanting to stay as far under the radar as possible, Alex chose a path that kept her well away from any of the others.

As she reached the area near the wall, she found bars and beams for exercising, and a concrete pad with a volleyball net strung across the middle. The net wasn't in the greatest shape, and had at least one hole big enough to fit a ball through.

She scanned the prison wall to the back of the yard, past the corner guard tower, then along the rear portion of the enclosure. Not far down, she paused her gaze on a door built into the wall. It was painted a light gray that blended well with the stone surrounding it, making it hard to see. Judging by its location, it had to be an entrance to the small walled-off area that enclosed the isolated building.

She continued her study of the wall, but found no other points of interest. It was all just stone and guard towers and barbed wire.

Back at the cellblock buildings more and more women were piling outside. Larger groups were forming, and the buzz of conversation increased. Soon the place would be crowded.

Alex moved over to the chin-up bar, lowered herself onto the ground, and leaned against the post to watch her fellow prisoners, trying to get a feel for the dynamics here. The majority of the women were Caucasian, maybe eighty percent, and those who weren't looked more Mediterranean—Italian, Greek, Turkish, perhaps even Arab. No more than a dozen were of African descent.

A group of women standing near Building Two caught her eye. They wore the same gray dresses as everyone else, but their heads and most of their faces were covered by cloth, also gray.

Hijabs, Alex realized. She was surprised that the prison officials allowed the women to wear religious head scarves.

Alex watched them intently, wondering if one of them could be her target. El-Hashim had a worn similar hijab in all of the photographs Alex had seen.

She softly clicked her tongue against the roof of her mouth. ID-ing the target was her number one priority, but how would she go about it?

The easiest solution, of course, would be to find El-Hashim's prison cell and get a look inside. If she was there, it was done. If she wasn't, that would increase the likelihood that she was standing with the group of scarf-wearing women right now.

Two fifty-nine. That was the cell number McElroy had said.

She recalled the map he'd shown her. Building Two, center block.

The problem was, since the cellblocks of Building One were currently sealed off, it was a fair guess that those in Building Two would be, too.

How long would that last? To the end of yard time? Or longer?

Frida had told her that after yard time was assigned duty, but would that entail allowing the prisoners back to their cells first? Could it be that some of the assigned duties were *in* the cellblocks?

One option would be to spend the day observing how everything worked, then take her chance at that point. But doing that would negate a card she could play today and, quite possibly, only today, especially if her hunch was right and the cellblocks would be opened up again very soon.

She weighed her choices, but the decision was an easy one. Rising back to her feet, she began walking toward the central buildings so that she'd be in position once yard time was over.

As the new kid, she garnered a lot of looks while she worked her way through the crowd. She was passing the entrance to Building One when someone touched her arm. She jerked it back, tensed, ready for a fight.

"Relax," Frida said. "Only me."

Alex smiled. "Sorry."

"Not problem. So what you think?"

"It's no Disneyland."

Frida laughed. "I could not say. I have never been to Disneyland. It is good?"

"The happiest place on Earth," Alex said. She looked around, knowing she didn't have much time to get into position. "I need to find a toilet, so I'll catch you around, huh?"

As she started to walk away, Frida said, "I can show you where."

Keeping the frustration from her voice, Alex smiled. "Thanks. That would be great."

Frida led her back through the open door to Building One. Instead of going left down the hallway, however, she turned right. There was a door five feet back, dead-ending the corridor.

"Here we are," she said.

Alex had dismissed the door as an entrance to a closet or storage area. What it led into, though, was a narrow room with a row of toilets against one wall and a long, metal trough sink along the other. There were no dividers between the toilets, privacy not a luxury in a place like this.

Frida walked over to the nearest toilet, hiked up her dress, and sat down. From the hem around the garment's arm, she removed a cigarette and a match.

Alex wanted to get out of there, but she didn't want to raise any suspicions. So while Frida lit her cigarette, Alex sat on the adjacent toilet.

The smell of tobacco filled the air as Frida took her first drag, then held it out to Alex, butt first.

"I don't smoke."

Frida shrugged, took another puff. "Why are you in here?" she asked.

It took Alex a beat to realize she was talking about prison in general, not this particular room. "Assault. Or whatever the equivalent is here."

"A…salt. I don't know this word."

"The police say I attacked someone with a knife."

"Is this person dead?"

"If they were, I'm pretty sure I'd be here for murder instead."

Frida considered her for a moment. "Did you do it?"

Alex purposely looked away. "What does it matter? They'll find me guilty if they want to."

"You have not gone to judge yet?" Frida asked.

"Not yet."

"Many people here because waiting for same."

"What did *you* do?"

"They say I try to leave country with few ounces of pot."

"And did you?"

"Try but not succeed." She took another drag.

"How'd you get that black eye?"

Frida unconsciously touched the fading bruise. "I hear in movie once. I walk into hand."

"Fist," Alex corrected her.

"Yes. I walk into fist. This is prison. It happens sometimes."

Somewhere outside, a loud horn sounded.

Alex stiffened. "Yard time's over?"

"You learn fast."

Shit. Alex flushed the toilet and stood up. "I probably should go see what my assigned duty is. See you later, I guess."

"Check with guard near main building. He will tell you."

"Thanks again."

Alex hurried outside, but instead of heading across the field to the administration building, she circled back around to Building Two. There was a group of women approaching the door. She fell in behind them.

And sure enough, access to the cellblocks was open again.

THE LAYOUT OF Building Two was exactly like that of Building One, and Alex found the front stairs right where she'd expected them. She glanced around to make sure no one was paying her any attention, then headed up to the second floor.

Keeping her gaze on the floor, she walked with purpose into block one of the second floor. She could hear a couple people talking to her right, and some movement ahead and to the left, but no one seemed to take notice of her.

She immediately noticed something different when she

entered block two. While there were voices here, too, all activity seemed to be coming from a single cell toward the far end on the right.

She checked the numbers—241 through 250 on the left, and 251 through 260 on the right. The noise was coming from 259.

El-Hashim's cell.

Alex slowed her pace, but kept on a course that would take her through the next door into block four. As she got closer to the occupied cell, the voices began to fall silent.

Tilting her head just a bit, she shot a sideways glance into the cell as she passed. There were four women inside. While one was turned away, the other three were staring out at her. Like the group of women who had been outside, these were all wearing head scarves that revealed only their eyes.

As Alex approached the end of the block, one of the women called out what sounded like a question, but Alex kept walking. As she passed through the door into block three, the question was repeated.

She picked up her pace and walked all the way into the back stairwell, where she stepped to the side and tucked against the wall.

Fadilah El-Hashim had to be one of the women back in 259, most likely the one who had turned away as Alex walked by. And judging by the way the other three cellmates had looked and acted, they were serving as El-Hashim's protection. Two of them had been giants, both tall and wide, while the other was about the same size as El-Hashim.

Alex grimaced. Getting anywhere near the woman was going to be difficult.

A buzzer sounded throughout the floor. Alex could hear inmates leaving their cells and making their way toward the exit.

Take the stairs down or try for one more look?

She didn't want to raise El-Hashim's curiosity, but she also didn't know if she'd get another chance to recon the area before making her direct approach.

One more look, then.

She exited the stairwell, and hurried over to the loosely forming line of inmates leaving block three.

As she passed through the door back into block two, Alex picked up her pace so that she was almost abreast of the woman in front of her, and could use the inmate to partially block her from view from El-Hashim's cell.

Once she was parallel to the cell, she glanced over. The four women were still there, but none were looking out. She studied them as quickly as she could so that she'd be able to recognize them even with their faces covered.

Another three steps and the cell was behind her, El-Hashim and her friends out of sight. Alex was just starting to relax when a voice boomed, "Po-well!"

She craned her neck, looking ahead at the doorway between blocks two and one, and spotted one of the guards who had taken her to her cell last night, the one with the birthmark. He ran over and grabbed her by the forearm, yanking her out of line.

The words that spewed from his mouth were angry and loud. She didn't understand them, but she knew they had ruined her smooth exit. Back at El-Hashim's cell, the woman's three protectors were stepping into the common area to see what was going on. They stared at her as if memorizing her face.

Way to go, Alex. Way to go.

SIXTEEN

HER ASSIGNED DUTY turned out to be cleanup crew for Building One's kitchen—washing dishes, cleaning a bathroom she hadn't even realized was down there, washing more dishes once lunch was served, and making sure everything was clean before dinner prep began. Thankfully, her job didn't extend into the dinner shift, and she was able to partake in a portion of the afternoon yard time the rest of the prisoners were already enjoying.

When she'd been in the yard that morning, she'd mainly spent her time getting a sense of the place, so now, as much as she would have liked to just find a quiet spot and rest, she used this second venture outside to delve more into details—memorizing distances, sight lines, doorways, and the like.

She'd been at it for twenty minutes when she realized she hadn't seen Frida. She was happy to not have the distraction, but was surprised the girl hadn't tracked her down. As she strolled around behind the central buildings, she found out why.

There was a group of around thirty women gathered in a semicircle against the back of Building Two. Some of the women jeered while others were laughing, their attention focused on someone in the center.

As Alex got closer, she realized they weren't gathered around just one person, but at least two. Through the crowd, she could see glimpses of two bodies, and could hear one of their voices, loud and menacing.

A slap, then another, followed by a cry. The loud voice railed again.

Alex kept walking by, not wanting to get pulled into

something, even tangentially, that might interfere with her plans, but then a different voice called out, the voice that had cried moments before.

"Alex!"

Frida.

Alex tried not to look over, but she couldn't help herself. A few of the women had parted and were looking back in her direction. Through the gap of the semicircle, Alex could see Frida twisting around, trying to get out of the grasp of another, much larger woman.

"Alex, please!"

The woman yanked Frida's hair and slapped her in the face.

Dammit.

When she didn't move right away, those who had twisted around to look at her closed the gap again, and refocused on the action in front of them.

She heard flesh hitting flesh, another cry of pain.

Dammit, dammit, dammit!

Lips pressed tightly together, Alex raced into the crowd. A murmur went through the onlookers as she pushed her way past them into the center.

"Let her go!" she shouted once she was clear.

The woman holding Frida snorted and pushed her to her knees, grabbing Frida by the hair. Alex sensed the woman was about to slam a fist into Frida's face, so she took two quick steps forward and shoved the woman in the chest.

The attacker lost her grip on Frida's hair and staggered back, almost all the way to the wall. The buzz of the other prisoners cranked up a notch as Alex took Frida's hand and helped the girl back to her feet.

"Come on," she said.

They'd barely turned to leave when Alex heard the other woman coming at her.

Shoving Frida toward a small break in the crowd, she said, "Run!" and ducked down just as the other woman reached her.

The nape of her neck tingled as the woman's fist flew past her, less than an inch above her flesh. But momentum's a bitch, and while the woman's arm passed harmlessly through the air, the rest of her body kept coming. With a thud, her hip whacked into Alex's shoulder, sending Alex toppling sideways toward the ground.

Cheers rang out as the woman stumbled over her but remained standing. She whirled around, undoubtedly expecting to take advantage of the fact that Alex was down, but Alex had rolled with the fall and was already on her feet again.

They circled each other, the woman big and strong and mean. There were probably few who had ever tried fighting back, and fewer still who had won.

But Alex was willing to bet the woman had never met a prisoner like her.

The woman's face scrunched in fury; she yelled and charged. Her arms were stretched to either side, as if making herself look bigger might somehow intimidate Alex into immediate submission.

Alex waited until the last possible second before she moved to the side and grabbed the woman by the head. With a violent jerk, she yanked her forward, and the woman's arm slapped into Alex's side, fingers scrambling to grab a handful of dress. But the newly added momentum whisked her past before she could. She stumbled, fell in a heap, and tumbled into the wall behind them.

She lay there, stunned for a moment, then her eyes found Alex's, hate oozing from every inch of her body. Slow and deliberate, she climbed back to her feet.

"You don't want to do this," Alex said. "Trust me."

But the woman's gaze didn't waver. Even if she understood Alex, it appeared she wasn't going to listen. As she took a step forward, something glittered through the air and landed at her feet.

Son of a bitch.

It was a knife. And not a random piece of metal twisted

into a homemade shank, but a real, honest-to-goodness knife—four inches of blade with a nice, comfortable hilt to grab on to.

Before the woman even started to lean down to pick it up, Alex raced forward. She knew it was too late to stop the woman from getting her hands on the weapon, but it wasn't too late to jam a knee into her opponent's face.

With a howl of pain, the woman grabbed her nose with her free hand as she staggered back a few feet. There was no trickle of blood. It was a downpour, rushing out of her nose and over her lips and chin.

Her eyes were truly on fire now as her gaze zeroed in once more on Alex.

Knife leading the way, she charged, swiping the blade through the air as she neared. Alex thought she'd given herself enough time to get out of the way, but as she dodged to the side, the tip of the knife sliced a shallow groove across her forearm.

She knew better than to allow the pain to influence her emotions, though. Fighting was about control, and the one who maintained control the best would win ninety-nine times out of a hundred.

The woman, bolstered by her success, came at Alex again, this time literally for the kill, Alex was sure.

The blade rose as the woman prepared to slash it at Alex's neck. Not a bad target, but the execution was the problem.

As soon as the arm rose, Alex dived under it, getting behind her attacker. Before the woman could turn to try again, Alex grabbed the arm with the knife and yanked it backward as hard as she could.

Which was pretty damn hard.

The pop could be heard even over the cheers of the onlookers.

The woman sucked in a surprised, gut-wrenching breath, then dropped to the ground a quivering mess, her arm lying unnaturally at her side.

The crowd went silent.

A whistle blew, then another, the guards finally deciding it was time to come break things up. The knife had fallen onto the ground near Alex's feet, and she quickly kicked it over so that it was lying next to the woman. The last thing she needed was another weapons beef.

The onlookers parted so the guards could get through, some wandering off, the show over. Two of the guards rushed over to Alex, while three others went to the woman on the ground.

Alex noticed that one of the guards had discovered the knife, but instead of showing it to his friends, he quietly slipped it into his pocket.

Another guard yelled at Alex, and she thought it was probably a question.

"She's the one who attacked me," she said, pointing at the woman on the ground. "I was only defending myself."

The guard barked something at her, then grabbed Alex's bicep on the arm that had been cut.

She winced and tried to pull away. "Careful, dammit."

The guard seemed to notice the cut for the first time, which didn't say much about his observational skills, considering she was bleeding all over the place. He quickly looked around, searching for the cause, then said something to the guards over by the woman. They looked around their area. The one who'd stowed the knife shook his head and shrugged.

Interesting, Alex thought.

Apparently this bitch had a friend.

The guard grabbed Alex again, this time by the other arm. But before he and his partner could walk her out of the circle, Frida stepped in their way. The guard shouted at her, then she spoke, just a few words that were obviously difficult for her to pronounce. One of the other guards grabbed Frida and the five of them cut through the crowd, headed toward the administration building.

Though everyone stared at them as they crossed the yard, there was one inmate in particular who caught Alex's attention. Medium-sized and steely-eyed and wearing a hijab. Though the rest of her face was covered with a scarf, Alex was sure it was one of women who had been with El-Hashim in her cell.

And she seemed very interested in Alex.

FIFTEEN HUNDRED DOLLARS a day, Alex thought as the doctor sewed up her cut. Stonewell was getting one hell of a deal.

The infirmary examination room was broken up into several individual stations. Each of the women involved in the altercation had been taken into her own, curtains drawn for privacy.

Not complete privacy, of course. Alex was willing to bet that Frida and the other woman were enjoying the company of one of the guards, like she was. Hers had been kind enough to keep staring at her as she removed her torn and bloodied dress and given it to a nurse, who had whisked it away.

So far, a new garment had yet to materialize, and this asshole seemed to be having a helluva good time staring at Alex's breasts. If he didn't start showing her a little respect very soon, she might have to knock that grin off his face.

The doctor tugged on the needle and poked it into her skin again. He said something unintelligible and it took her a moment to realize he had spoken in thickly accented English, the word "pain" the only thing she understood.

He was asking if it hurt.

"Just a little," she said, knowing that her "little" was probably a lot to some people.

He seemed to be trying to decipher her response, so she held her thumb and forefinger about a quarter inch apart.

"Little," she said.

"Ahhh."

He nodded, offering her a doctorly smile. After he finished closing off the wound, he examined the other scrapes and bruises she'd received, then ducked around the curtain and left without another word.

Sitting there on the cold, uncomfortable table in only a thin pair of panties, with a guard about two threads of spittle away from full-on drool, Alex felt the urge to fold her arms and cover herself, despite the wound that would make such a task difficult. But then she decided, *Screw it.* She wasn't going to act like some shy schoolgirl because this asshole couldn't take his eyes off her.

It wasn't as if he'd ever see or get any more than this.

Not from her. Not ever.

So enjoy the show, numbnuts.

Finally, a different nurse returned and handed her a dress identical to the one she'd been wearing, only clean. The guard's disappointment was palpable as Alex eyed him defiantly and slipped it on.

From the infirmary, she was taken to see the warden. Frida was already there, sitting in one of the chairs outside his office, and Alex was pushed onto the seat next to her.

"You all right?" Alex asked.

Frida nodded. "Thank you."

It was the first time they'd had a chance to talk since the fight.

"So how did it start?"

"You think this was first time?"

"Your black eye from before. The same woman?"

Another nod.

"What's her problem?"

"I do not know. A month ago she just decide to beat me. I had never even talked to her before. It was like she chooses me..." Frida demonstrated pointing at several people before stopping on one.

"Randomly," Alex suggested. "Without any reason."

"Yes. No reason."

"Well, she's not going to pick on you for a while."

"But when she gets better? Then what?"

Alex could say that she would help, but given she wasn't planning on being around very long, it would be a hollow promise. Instead she asked, "Why didn't you just walk away when the guards showed up? They didn't know you were involved."

A half smile. "If you come by yourself, they probably not believe you. But they know Kalyna has hurt me before, so better if I tell them what happened."

"Kalyna? That's her name?"

Frida nodded.

"You didn't have to do that for me," Alex said.

"You help me, I help you."

It was an admirable philosophy, but one that might ultimately cause Frida more trouble.

A few minutes later, they were ushered into the warden's office together. In her halting, slow Ukraine, Frida gave her version of the events, and did the best she could to act as an interpreter for Alex. At the end, the warden rattled on for over a minute, then brushed his hand in the air, dismissing them.

"What was that all about?" Alex whispered when they were out of the office.

"He is not punishing you since you are so new, and..." She paused. "And you might not understanding the...rules? Rules like 'do this,' 'do this,' 'do this,' yes?"

"Like laws. Guidelines."

"Yes, same. You not understanding rules of fighting."

"I think I understand the rules of fighting just fine. I believe I just beat the crap out of your friend Kalyna."

Frida smiled. "I mean rules that there is no fighting here."

"Uh-huh," Alex said. "And, tell me, does anyone ever follow that rule?"

Frida's smile faltered. "Not really."

"Well, knock me over with a feather."

ALEX AND FRIDA separated after they entered Building One, Frida staying on the ground floor while Alex took the stairs up to level three. Passing through the cellblocks, she couldn't help but notice that the other prisoners grew quiet as she walked by.

So much for keeping a low profile.

Her cellmates were all there when she walked in. Like the others, they also stopped talking and simply stared at her as she stretched out on her mattress.

"What?" she said.

In a panic, they turned away as if she wasn't even in the room.

All right. Be that way.

She tried to make herself comfortable, turning first one way then the other. As she started to flip onto her side, something scratched her calf. She winced, climbed out, and felt around the bunk, thinking something might have gotten between the blanket and mattress.

There was nothing there.

Frowning, she lay back down. And felt it again.

This time, it was clear the scratch had come not from the bed, but her new dress. Specifically, the hem. At one spot, it was stiff.

She twisted the dress around as best she could for a better look. Surprisingly, it appeared as if the hem had been cut and resewn—hastily, by the looks of it. But that wasn't what was stiff. The hem was about an inch wide, and within it, right where it had been redone, was what felt like a piece of paper.

Alex ran a finger across the seam and found a loose thread. It put up little resistance as she gave it a gentle tug and worked it out.

After checking her roommates and confirming they were doing everything they could not to look in her direction, she fished out the piece of paper. It had been folded twice, which accounted for why it had felt so stiff.

She quietly unfolded it.

It was a note. In English.

Home concerned about timeline. Increase speed as much as possible. When ready to leave, request new dress. Until then, no more fights.

The only person it could be from was Traz, the inside contact, who apparently worked in the administration building. That made sense, given that Traz was supposed to help her get out.

But who was it?

Request new dress. Someone who worked in the storage room? The female guard? Or it could have been any of the medical staff—the nurse who'd taken her bloodied dress away, the one who'd brought her a new one, hell, even the doctor.

The only thing she knew for sure was that it had been someone who had gotten a few minutes alone with the garment before it was brought to her. Unfortunately, she wasn't in the position to conduct a full-scale investigation.

She read the note again. She had a pretty good idea why McElroy would want her to speed up the schedule—that bastard judge back in Simferopol. He'd already fleeced them for more cash once, and chances were good he'd try again, threatening to expose her as a "foreign agent." So McElroy would want her done and gone before anything else blew up.

Whether or not this was his reasoning, she was completely in agreement. Prison life was not suiting her at all, and the sooner she was out, the better.

Of course the question she couldn't answer was how the hell to make that happen.

SEVENTEEN

"NICE JOB ON Kalyna."

Alex looked over her shoulder. The dusty-blonde woman who had just fallen in behind her in the dinner line was lean and tall and, surprisingly, in possession of an accent very similar to Alex's.

"Sorry. Don't know what you're talking about."

"Really? Apparently every else does, because they're all talking about it. And I was a witness. Saw the whole damn thing. Not the first time you've ever been in a fight, is it?"

Alex shrugged. "I'd rather not get into it."

The line moved forward, allowing both women to set their trays on the counter.

"Sure, I get it," the blonde said. She held out her hand. "I'm Rachel. Rachel Norman."

Alex hesitated, then shook her hand. "Maureen Powell."

"You know, when I got here a few days ago, I thought I was gonna be the only one from the States. Can't tell you how good it is to meet someone from home."

"You're still the only one," Alex said. "I'm Canadian."

"Oh." Rachel appeared to be momentarily caught off guard, then she smiled. "Close enough, I guess. At least we both know how to string a couple sentences together without tying our tongues in a knot. I'm getting pretty tired of trying to decipher every other word that's thrown in my direction."

While it was nice to hear a voice from home, Alex had neither the desire nor the time to make friends. She'd already gotten too close to doing that with Frida.

"So…where?" Rachel asked.

Alex realized she'd missed something the blonde had

said. "I'm sorry?"

"Where in Canada? I've been to Toronto once. And Vancouver when I was a kid."

"Winnipeg."

"Where the hell's that?"

"Right in the middle."

"Sounds cold. Me, I'm from San Diego. You ever been?"

Alex had, but she shook her head, and moved forward with the line.

"Pacific Beach, Mission Beach...oh, and the Gaslamp district. Man, I miss it."

Alex glanced at her and was about to grunt, "Uh-huh," when she noticed a large woman wearing a hijab enter the room.

Alex recognized her height and body shape. No question, it was one of the women who'd been with El-Hashim in her cell. Which was weird; this wasn't her building. She seemed to be searching for someone, because her eyes suddenly locked on to something, and she headed quickly across the room, disappearing into the kitchen.

As Alex lay in her bunk prior to dinner, she had formulated an action plan for the evening. After she finished eating and before everyone was locked up for the night, she would pay El-Hashim's cellblock another visit. At worst she might be able to gain some more intel, and at best, she might find herself in a position to make contact.

Having one fewer member of El-Hashim's entourage in play might facilitate that very situation.

"So what did they put you in here for?" Rachel asked. "They popped me as an accessory for a stolen car. The guy I was hanging out with took it, and I didn't even know—"

"I'm sorry," Alex said, stepping out of line. "I forgot something. It was nice meeting you."

Returning her tray and dish to the stack at the head of the line, she exited the cafeteria as quickly as possible.

THE SUN WAS still an hour from setting as she stepped into

the near-empty prison yard. Painfully aware of how visible she was, she stayed close to the buildings, in hopes they would mask her presence. It seemed to have worked, as she was able to slip into Building Two without raising any alarms.

There, she took the stairs down to the cafeteria. Though McElroy's information indicated El-Hashim seldom left her room, seldom was not never, so the woman could be downstairs for dinner.

Alex paused just outside the doorway so as not to be seen, and scanned the dining room. Neither El-Hashim nor her protection detail was there.

Alex went back to the stairs and took them to the second floor. The first block was completely empty, but as she entered the second, she could hear noise coming from cell 259—at least two voices, talking low. She hugged the wall, moved all the way to the cell doors on the right. Keeping just as tight to them, she made her way toward the voices and stopped just short of El-Hashim's cell.

There had been no interruption in the conversation, no indication they'd heard Alex's approach. This close, she could clearly hear what they were saying, and surprisingly, could even understand them for the most part, as they were speaking French.

"…for the best, I think," one of them was saying.

"Not sitting in this pit would be for the best," another replied, not sounding happy. "I need to leave this place."

"Yes, but that isn't an option right now. A few more days, a week at most, and you should be out again. But until then—"

"Until then, Marie, we have *this* to deal with, too!"

There was no question in Alex's mind the unhappy one was El-Hashim. What was interesting was that it seemed something more than just sitting in prison was upsetting her.

Perhaps this wasn't the best time to make an approach, Alex realized.

As she turned to retreat to the block entrance, a new voice spoke up in the cell.

A male voice.

What the hell?

"I know this news is distressing," he said in halting French. "But it is better to know than not."

His tone was familiar, but the French was throwing Alex off, so she was having a hard time placing it.

"You tell me that my life is in danger, but you don't tell me from whom," El-Hashim said. "It would be better if you had a name!"

"If I knew," he told her, "the problem would be removed."

"Is it a prisoner? A guard? Someone else on staff? Do you know that much, at least?"

Silence.

"Whoever it is," Marie said, "there's no reason for you sit in this cell and wait to be attacked. I think we should take him up on his offer."

There was another moment of silence before El-Hashim spoke. "All right. Fine. We'll do as you suggest."

"Excellent," the man said. "I'll make the arrangements. You'll be out of here in less than an hour."

Alex heard the shuffle of his shoes on cement, and stiffened. With this guy on the move, there was no way she'd make it back to the other block without being seen.

She turned quickly, and scanned the cells along the wall.

The door to each was open. Thinking it would be a bad idea to hide in the cell right next to El-Hashim's, she scrambled for the next one over and moved inside. As she dropped to the floor and slipped under the front bunk, she heard the man's steps entering the common area.

Lying on her stomach, her chin propped on the cement, she looked out through the bars. A second later the man came into view—a guard she was sure she'd never seen before.

She was thinking she must have been wrong about recognizing the voice when another set of steps echoed through the common area, and a second man walked into view.

The warden.

Son of a bitch.

So El-Hashim had the most powerful person in Slavne Prison in her pocket. No wonder the Stonewell contact was being extra cautious.

As soon as Alex was sure the two men were off the block, she started to crawl out from under the bed, but froze again when she heard someone else enter the common area.

It was the woman who'd been visiting the cafeteria in Building One. She walked quickly through the outer room and over to cell 259. A moment later, voices drifted down from El-Hashim's cell, not quite as clear from this distance.

"…list…"

"Don't…for any…"

"…finished."

Alex scooted out of her hiding spot, tiptoed to the door, and carefully peeked around it.

The common area was clear. They were all inside their cell.

It was now or never.

She left the cell and quietly retraced her steps to the cellblock doorway. She was within seconds of the exit, when a voice behind her shouted in Arabic. It was a word she had learned while stationed in Iraq, and she knew exactly what it meant:

Stop!

Rather than comply, Alex took off, running through the doorway and into the next block. Behind her she could hear the pounding of footsteps, someone in hot pursuit.

Alex bore down, speeding through block one and into the stairwell, then took the steps two at a time, hurrying down to the first floor. As she leaped off the last step, she nearly ran into a group of inmates who had just entered the stairway. They jumped out of the way, and yelled at her as she rushed by.

"Sorry," she said, as she rounded the corner into the hallway leading to the building's exit.

A few seconds later, she heard more shouts behind her that she assumed meant her pursuer was still following.

The door to the outside was propped open now. She sprinted over the threshold and into the yard. The outdoor area was no longer empty, as many prisoners were taking advantage of a few minutes of fresh air before the buildings were locked up for the night. Alex ran to the corner of Building Two, then turned into the open space between it and Building One.

"Hey, what's the hurry?"

Rachel was leaning against the wall.

Alex made a snap decision, put on the brakes, and quickly moved over to her.

"We've been here awhile," Alex said.

"All right," Rachel said, intrigued. "You want to give me a little—"

Before she could finish her sentence, one of El-Hashim's protectors ran across the opening between the buildings. When she noticed Alex and Rachel, she immediately changed course and headed toward them.

As soon as the woman was in range, she grabbed the front of Alex's dress. "Why you there?"

"Hey, let go," Alex said. "What do you think you're doing?"

"Why you there?" the woman yelled.

"Why was I where?"

"Outside cell."

"I don't know what you're talking about. When was this?"

"Liar! Outside cell just now."

"Just now?" Alex looked at her as if she were crazy. "I've been right here since I finished dinner."

There was a hint of uncertainty in the woman's eyes. Since everyone wore the same gray dress, and Alex was not the only dark-haired woman in the prison, the only way El-Hashim's colleague could be sure she had the right person was if she'd seen Alex's face.

And it was clear by her reaction that she hadn't.

"Leave my friend alone," Rachel said.

"You outside cell," the woman said to Alex again, only this time her tone wasn't quite as sharp.

"I don't know what to tell you," Alex said. "Not me."

"Yeah, we've been right here for, like, twenty minutes," Rachel added.

"Here? Twenty minutes?"

"Well, we started off down there," Rachel said, pointing at a spot a dozen feet away. "But we ended up here."

"Not you running?" the woman asked Alex.

"Running where?"

She pointed at Building Two. "Out of building."

"That would be *no*," Alex said, looking at the woman's fist still grasping her dress. "So, do you mind?"

The woman glared at her through the slit in her hijab. She leaned forward and said to Alex, "Don't come near us again."

"Whatever."

With a final, cold look, the woman walked away.

As soon as they were alone, Rachel said, "That was fun."

Alex was already pushing herself off the wall. "Thanks for backing me up." She started to walk away.

"Hey, aren't you going to tell me what that was all about?"

"Just a misunderstanding, that's all."

"Some misunderstanding. She was ready to take your head off."

Alex gave her a quick smile. "Thanks again."

She headed back into the main yard in front of the buildings, and moved in near a cluster of prisoners, close enough to seem part of their group without actually having to join them.

She'd learned one interesting thing during her excursion. While El-Hashim and her friends were clearly trying to portray themselves as Arabs, their accents all seemed to be European instead of Middle Eastern. Were they Arab or not?

It wasn't a question she'd be able to answer right now. Besides, she had more important things to worry about at the moment.

She focused her attention on the administration building. If she was right, the warden, or someone representing him, would be making a return trip to Building Two.

I'll make the arrangements.

You'll be out of here in less than an hour.

If Alex hadn't overheard the earlier part of the conversation, she would have assumed the warden was planning to remove El-Hashim from the prison altogether. And if that were the case, the Stonewell project would be dead in the water. But taking into consideration what El-Hashim and Marie had said just prior to that, it seemed pretty clear that they would not be leaving, even though El-Hashim's life was apparently in danger.

So what was the warden planning?

The main door to the administration building finally opened and out walked the man of the hour, followed by a squad of six guards. This was not about to go unnoticed by the other prisoners. All conversations stopped as the inmates watched the procession march past them and enter Building Two.

A moment later, the horn blared, telling everyone it was time to go back inside.

Shit.

Alex was sure El-Hashim would be with those guards when they came out again. She needed to know where they were going to take her.

Apparently evening yard time was ending early, because the other prisoners were making unhappy noises like they were being shortchanged. This was obviously a move on the warden's part, to get them all out of the yard while he and his guards did whatever they were planning to do.

Alex knew if she lost track of El-Hashim's whereabouts, it would be as if the woman were removed from the prison entirely.

Slowly heading back toward her building, Alex kicked at the ground, looking for a stone that had an edge to it. She was less than thirty feet from Building One's entrance when she spotted one that would hopefully do the trick.

She stumbled and allowed herself to fall to the ground, then grabbed the stone and immediately set to work, doing her best to ignore the pain.

A shout in Ukrainian, aimed in her direction.

She peeked over her shoulder and could see a guard heading her way.

"Come on, come on," she said under her breath, continuing to work the stone.

Another shout, only a dozen feet away.

She knew he was telling her to get up, but she couldn't. She had to finish.

When he poked at her back with the toe of his boot, she felt two of the stitches come apart from the wound in her arm. She pulled at the cut until blood started to flow out, then groaned theatrically and rolled onto her back.

"I need the doctor," she cried, showing her wound to the guard.

He leaned in close, let out an exasperated breath, and helped her to her feet.

"Careful it doesn't get infected," she said, then looked back toward her building. Rachel was standing near the door with a mischievous look on her face. One that said she had seen the whole thing, and was impressed.

With a wave, she went inside.

Wonderful. She'll be asking me questions until my ears *start to bleed.*

As she was escorted across the yard to the administration building, Alex periodically glanced back at Building Two to see if the warden had reemerged, but by the time they reached the door, there had been no sign of him.

So inside they went, through the checkpoint, down the hall, and up the stairs. She had to resist the urge to try to get the guard to hurry up. She knew there were windows in the infirmary that looked out onto the yard, but until she got there, she was blind to the outside.

Cradling her arm, she moved with the guard down the second-floor hallway, and rushed into the infirmary the moment he opened the door. While the guard explained the situation to the nurse on duty, Alex got as close to the windows as she could without letting on what she was up to.

At first, she thought the yard was empty, but then she noticed movement to the left.

Ten...no, eleven people walking toward the back wall of the yard.

There was no doubt in her mind that seven of them were the warden and his six guards. The remaining four were wearing gray prison dress and had hijabs covering their heads. Unless this was some kind of elaborate decoy, El-Hashim and her people were being escorted toward the door in the far wall. The door that led to the isolation building.

This wasn't good.

"Po-well."

She turned and saw a youngish man in a doctor's coat standing nearby. He wasn't the one who had treated her before, but she remembered seeing him help someone else.

"Arm, please."

She moved to him and held out her arm. He used a gauze pad to blot away some of the blood, and gave the wound a closer look.

"What happen?" he asked.

"I fell," she said. She pantomimed tripping.

He looked at the wound again and didn't seem convinced, but he didn't ask her a second time.

"Come," he said, as he turned toward the examination area.

Alex chanced another look out the window. The small parade was passing through the isolation-area doorway.

"Please," the doctor said. "Come."

As Alex followed, she realized that the guard and the reception nurse were no longer around. The doctor pointed at one of the examination tables, and, as she sat down, he pulled the curtain closed around them.

He said, "Do you not think easier to make new cut than open this one again?"

"What?" she said, surprised. His English was a hell of a lot better than it had been a moment before.

"You did this yourself, yes?"

She shook her head and said, "Why would you say that?"

"Look." He turned her arm so they could both see the torn sutures. "If you fell as guard say, maybe one stitch break and come loose. You have two, and they are both *cut*. Look? You can see it."

She didn't glance down, and instead kept her face neutral. "I'm sorry. I don't—"

"You are lucky I working tonight. If Dr. Timko, he report you to warden. After getting into fight today, the warden have had no choice but to punish you. Then where you be?"

"Traz?" she said, her voice low.

"Who else you think?"

"Are we safe talking like this?"

"Infirmary cameras cannot see behind curtain, and not have microphones."

"What about the nurse? The guard? They could come back."

"Irina is my partner. She is occupying guard while we talk."

"Partner? You mean…you're both Traz?"

"Why not?"

It had never occurred to her Traz would be two people. She shrugged and said, "Why are you talking to me now?"

He frowned. "I thought you come to talk to me, yes?"

"I came here so I could see what was going on in the yard."

The frown deepened. She told him she had just witnessed the prisoner he knew as A'isha Najem—the prisoner she was interested in—being moved.

"You are sure?" he asked when she finished, suddenly concerned.

"Absolutely."

"A moment, please."

He ducked around the end of the curtain and left.

Once his footsteps faded away, the only sound she could hear was the *click-click-click* of a clock on the wall ticking off the seconds.

She knew a lot of the inmates would've loved to be in her position right now—alone in the infirmary. Even though there were cameras outside this curtain, plenty of escape attempts had been started from considerably more difficult locations.

The doctor returned after several minutes, his steps moving rapidly across the tiled floor. When he ducked around the curtain, she could see he looked worried.

"You are right," he said. "They take A'isha Najem and her cellmates to isolation."

"Do you know why?"

"The official reason is disciplinary."

"Is there any way for me to get to her?"

"You mean go to isolation?"

"Yes."

He looked away for a moment. "Well, I guess there is, but it's…"

When he didn't finish, she said, "Difficult?"

"Yes."

"I've flown five thousand miles to *purposely* be put in a prison, and help break someone out who very likely won't want to come with me. Define difficult?"

Alex and the doctor talked for several more minutes, then she scribbled a quick message for Cooper and Deuce, and gave it to the doctor, whose name she discovered was Teterya. The note made no mention of pulling the plug on the mission.

She wasn't about to go through all of this for nothing.

EIGHTEEN

THE ASSASSIN SPENT much of the night thinking about what she had seen before the horn went off.

She had tailed the North American woman during the dinner hour, saw her enter Building Two, and followed her up to the second level. She had waited in the shadows of the doorway between the blocks, and watched the woman approach El-Hashim's cell then pause just outside of it to listen.

That was when the assassin knew the North American woman was not one of El-Hashim's associates.

Not wanting to risk being caught, the assassin had headed back downstairs and outside. There she had witnessed the woman exit Building Two in a hurry, followed soon by one of El-Hashim's bodyguards, and the confrontation that occurred.

So who was this woman? And what was she up to?

More importantly, how might she affect the mission?

The assassin would find the answers.

She always did.

VANKO LEONCHUK HAD worked as a guard at Slavne Prison for three years. Before getting the job, he wouldn't have believed the things women were capable of doing to themselves and each other. They were almost as bad as men. He'd seen drug overdoses, suicides, more fights than he could count, and five straight-out murders.

His sensitivities to such things had dulled quickly, so when he saw that the new prisoner's arm was bleeding from the wound she'd received earlier that day, his only thought was to wonder if this was going to make him late for the barracks' card game.

She said something to him in her native tongue. German? English? He wasn't sure which, but he knew what she wanted, and what he had to do.

Annoyed, he escorted her into the administration building and up to the infirmary. When he opened the door, she rushed inside. He followed, hoping this wouldn't take very long, but then he spotted the nurse on duty, and his whole mood changed.

Irina was an excellent example of genetics gone right. Round hips; nice, succulent ass; flat stomach; and breasts that just begged to be kissed. Her face wasn't bad, either, but Vanko wasn't much of a face man.

He could imagine what she'd be like in bed.

Unfortunately, imagine was all he'd been able to do. Since she'd come to work at the prison, he'd asked her out at least four times. And each time, he had been met with a quick but polite rejection. She never told him why, but he assumed there was a boyfriend in the picture somewhere.

So Vanko had finally stopped asking her. The lusting, though, didn't go away. Maybe if she hadn't been so polite in her refusal, he could have gotten angry about it and moved on. Women really knew how to toy with a man, and there was something about this one that refused to let him go.

Now, here she was, looking as ripe and tasty as ever, smiling up at him as he approached her desk. "Vanko, how are you?"

"Good, thank you. And you?"

"Good, also." Another smile, then she looked around him at the prisoner who wandered over near the windows. "A problem?"

"She was the one in that fight earlier. It looks like her wound has reopened."

Irina seemed surprised at the mention of the fight. She looked at the woman again before saying, "Let me get someone to examine her."

When she returned, Dr. Symon Teterya was with her.

"What's going on?" the doctor asked.

Vanko told him, then said, "She doesn't speak Ukrainian."

"What does she speak?"

"I don't know."

"Well, then, what's her name?"

Vanko didn't like the attitude Dr. Teterya was giving him, but that wasn't surprising. In Vanko's view, the doctor had always acted superior to the guards. Of course, the real reason Vanko disliked him was that he got to work directly with Irina. Vanko wouldn't admit it to anyone, but there was more than a little jealousy coloring his opinion of the man.

"I don't remember her name. She's a new prisoner. Came in yesterday."

"Do you at least know what cell she's in?"

Of course Vanko knew which cell. He knew everyone's cell. "One eighty-five."

Dr. Teterya nodded at Irina, who typed the number into her computer. In a low voice, she said, "Maureen Powell. Canada."

"English, then, most likely," the doctor said. He strode across the room to the woman.

Vanko couldn't be sure, but he thought Dr. Teterya shared a quick look with Irina before he left. Vanko immediately forgot about it, however, when Irina said, "I could really use a cup of tea. How about you? Would you like to join me?"

His gaze flicked toward the doctor and the prisoner. Teterya was examining the wound. "I should stay here."

It was protocol, after all.

"Dr. Teterya will be fine. She won't be a problem."

Vanko glanced at the other two again. Problem or not, having a cup of tea with Irina would be as close as he had ever come to a date with her. Besides, the break room was just down the hall. He could be back here in seconds if there was trouble.

Irina rounded her desk and started walking toward the door. "If you'd rather, I could bring you back a cup."

"No. I'll…I'll come with you."

She smiled. "Good."

VANKO HAD TO work very hard not to stare at Irina's chest as they sat at the small break room table and drank their tea. This was the longest he'd ever been alone with her.

They talked about things two people who worked at the same place always talked about—their coworkers and bosses. It was funny. Irina was actually letting *him* do most of the talking, and seemed genuinely interested in what he had to say. He didn't mind. It gave him a chance to puff his feathers a bit, and let her get to know him a little better. Maybe if he renewed his attempts to get her to go out with him, the answer would be different this time.

He was telling her about a prison yard fight he'd broken up the other day—adding a few flourishes, of course—when Irina jerked and pulled a phone out of her pocket.

She took a quick look at the screen and said, "They're finished."

A text from the doctor, Vanko thought, ending their break together. Yet another reason to hate the guy.

After they returned to the infirmary, and Vanko took charge of Powell again, his friend Danya Sosna—another guard—arrived with a prisoner in tow who was clutching her stomach. He and Danya exchanged a quick greeting, then Vanko and Powell left as Dr. Teterya led his new patient to the back.

When they entered Building One, Vanko couldn't help but notice the looks Powell was getting from the other inmates. Powell had obviously made a mark on the rest of the population—and so soon, too. He'd seen it happen before, and knew she was either destined to be someone the others won't mess with in the years ahead, or dead before the end of the month.

After locking her in, he headed for the exit, and his

thoughts turned from Powell back to Irina. Just a few more minutes in that break room and he would have asked her out again. He knew she would say yes this time, and could instantly picture their date—a decent dinner, heavy on the alcohol, then a cheap room in town where the night could really begin.

Goddamn Dr. Teterya.

Vanko checked his watch as he entered the yard. His shift had officially ended ten minutes ago. Not as bad as it could have been. He might not be at the barracks for the beginning of the game, but he could join in as soon as he got there and wouldn't miss much.

Irina. Drinks. A hotel room.

The thoughts danced with each other as he crossed the yard and reentered the administration building. After passing through the checkpoint, he looked at his watch again.

Maybe I can spare just a little more time.

Instead of going to the locker room and changing out of his uniform, he headed back to the infirmary. As he exited the stairwell onto the second floor, he almost ran into Danya and his prisoner.

"Finished already?" Vanko said.

"I think she's faking it," Danya told him. He gave the girl a shake. "Aren't you?"

"No," she said. She wasn't holding her stomach like before, but she didn't look particularly well, either.

"Isn't your shift done?" Danya asked Vanko.

"Yeah. Just have one more thing to do."

Danya smiled knowingly and glanced back at the infirmary. "Still pursuing the impossible, I see."

Vanko blushed slightly. "Nothing is impossible."

Danya laughed, and pushed his charge past Vanko. "I wish you luck, my friend."

"Thank you."

Unfortunately, Danya's doubt had taken some of the steam out of Vanko's mission, and Vanko was no longer certain Irina would say yes. Giving himself a quick pep talk, he took a deep breath, and headed down the hall.

When he opened the door to the infirmary, he was surprised to find no one there. He walked over to Irina's empty desk and looked back into the examination area. It, too, was deserted.

He wondered if she might be in the break room, and was about to go check, when he heard a low voice coming from the other side of the examination room. He couldn't make out what was being said, but it sounded like Irina.

Entering the examination area, Vanko walked toward the sound. There was another room beyond this that he had never been inside. The door that closed it off had a square window inset at eye level, but while Vanko could hear Irina's voice, he couldn't see her.

Probably on the phone.

He took a few more steps forward, and craned his neck to see if he could get a glimpse of her through the door's window. Instead, what he saw was Dr. Teterya.

Curious now, he moved in until he was able to see Irina standing next to the doctor. They seemed to be looking at a piece of paper the doctor was holding.

"That's all there is?" Irina asked.

Dr. Teterya nodded.

"Okay," Irina said, "I'll deliver it when I get off at four."

She took the paper from him and started to fold it.

"I should do it," he told her. "It could be dangerous."

"No. I'm off three hours before you. It makes more sense for me to do it." Her voice softened. "Besides, the only dangerous part is here at the prison. I'll be fine."

Vanko was confused. They were doing something dangerous? Something that was more dangerous *here*? And what did this piece of paper have to do with it? A little backchannel prison business, perhaps?

If he had turned and walked away at that moment, he would have left it at that. If Irina and Dr. Teterya had found a way to earn a few extra bucks, who was he to get in their way?

Everyone did it at some point, didn't they?

He certainly had. The television in his parents' house had been fully paid for by a few errands he'd run for some of the prisoners.

But Vanko hadn't turned away. It hadn't even crossed his mind. So he was looking directly at Irina through that small window when she put a hand on Dr. Teterya's cheek and kissed him passionately on the lips.

Now Vanko not only wanted to look away, but also tear his eyes out—to unsee what he had just seen. But he watched as the doctor pulled her into an embrace they had undoubtedly shared many times before.

"You must call me as soon as you've dropped it off," Teterya said when they finally parted. "I want to know you are all right."

"I told you, I'll be fine."

"You'll call me. Promise."

"All right, I'll call you."

Vanko backed quickly away from the door, his whole body numb.

He had once thought that if Irina had been cruel to him, it would've been easier for him to move on. Well, she was definitely being cruel now, even if she didn't realize it. He froze, an image in his mind of the tea they'd had together.

He cursed to himself. She had only been *pretending* to be interested in him, leading him on for some reason.

But what?

The moment Dr. Teterya had texted her, their tea had ended.

And that could mean only one thing.

She had suggested the tea to get him out of the infirmary.

Which meant that whatever their little business deal was, it must've involved the prisoner Powell. So had Powell purposely reinjured her arm so she could be taken to the infirmary to meet with Teterya and Irina?

Anger began to boil inside Vanko, melting the ice that had numbed him.

167

He had been played. First by Powell, then by his lovely Irina.

He was a stooge, an unknowing errand boy.

And he did *not* like it.

As he whipped around to head for the exit, his hand bumped a clipboard sitting on a tray. It was but a few centimeters above the floor when he grabbed it, preventing it from clattering against the tile. He shot a look behind him, wondering if the doctor or Irina had heard anything, but the door remained closed.

He carefully put the clipboard back and left.

IRINA EXITED THE administration building at twelve minutes after four a.m., climbed into her car, and drove out of the prison parking lot.

As soon as she was out of sight, Vanko dropped his car into gear and followed.

After clearing the main gate, Irina turned east at the highway. Vanko, who months earlier had learned the details of Irina's life, knew that her small flat was to the west, in Slavne itself.

Well, isn't this interesting, he thought as he got onto the highway several seconds behind her.

She stayed on the road only a few kilometers before turning onto a small lane. Vanko had driven this stretch of the highway thousands of times in his life, but he had never once gone down that narrow road. In fact, it was so insignificant, he couldn't remember ever noticing it.

He pulled to the side of the highway before reaching the turnoff, and considered what he should do. While his headlights wouldn't have seemed out of place on the main road, Irina would surely take note of them on the much-less-traveled lane. But he really wanted to know what she was up to. She had fucked with his life, so he was more than ready to do the same with hers.

He switched his lights off and examined the road, then smiled. The night was just bright enough that, if he didn't go too fast, he'd be able to see what he was doing.

He eased the accelerator and drove forward again, hitting the brake as he got to where Irina had turned. Red light radiated from the back of his car onto the trees that flanked the lane's entrance. He immediately pulled his foot off the brake, realizing he'd have to stick to his hand brake or simply let the car roll to a stop.

He turned down the road, and drove almost a kilometer before finally spotting her car again. It wasn't on the road, but parked about fifty meters ahead off to the side. He jammed on the hand brake, hoping he hadn't given himself away. When his car stopped moving, he studied Irina's vehicle and realized it was empty.

Where the hell had she gone?

Unless someone else had picked her up, she was on foot. Which meant he needed to be, too. But he couldn't just park along the road as she had. He might not be able to get back to his car in time, and she'd spot him as she drove away.

He made a quick assessment of the area around him, and picked out a wide opening between several bushes where he thought his car would fit. Taking it slow, he drove off the road, squeezed through the gap, and rolled to a stop.

Once the engine was off, he carefully opened his door to avoid any loud noise, and stepped out of his car. He decided to stay off the road, thinking that would cut down on his chances of bumping into her in the dark, and headed south.

When he finally found her, she was facing a tree, her back to him. He couldn't see what she was doing, so he moved several feet to his right in hopes of getting a better view. As soon as he repositioned, however, Irina turned and headed back to her car.

Motionless, he watched her walk within twenty feet of his hiding place. He held his breath, sure she would see him, but she passed by without a glance in his direction.

He looked back at the tree, and could now clearly see a box attached to it.

He had assumed she was going to deliver the piece of

paper she'd gotten from the doctor directly into someone's hands, so it took him a moment to realize she must have left it in the box.

That was…strange.

Like something out of a spy film.

More curious than ever now, Vanko decided to stay where he was and let her drive away. He wanted to see for himself what was written in that note.

It was one of many mistakes he'd made in the last nine hours.

NINETEEN

THE OLD ABANDONED barn stood next to a little used road outside Slavne. The stone walls had been there for a hundred and fifty years. But though crumbling in spots, they still looked as if they had several more decades in them.

The roof was another matter. It had been made of wood, and had been missing since not long after the final shots of the Second World War.

The nearest other structures were those that made up Slavne Prison, a good four kilometers away. Because of this, the barn was the perfect place for Deuce and Cooper to use as headquarters.

With the exception of when they initially set up camp, they were never there at the same time. They traded duties at the prison lookout point in six-hour shifts.

The barn had the additional benefit of being within a ten-minute walk from the message drop that had been set up with Traz. The drop itself was an old metal box nailed to the trunk of a tree along the road. Messages weren't actually put inside the box, but in the crevasse between the box and the tree. It was the responsibility of the person at camp to check the drop every few hours in case something had arrived.

At 4:30 that morning, this duty fell to Deuce. When the alarm on his cell phone vibrated under his pillow, he was tempted to fling it at one of the stone walls. After relieving himself in the copse of trees outside the barn, he made a cup of barely passable coffee, then, mug in hand, headed out to the drop box.

The path to the box ran along the edge of the field, through some trees and into a shallow dale. As he headed down the slope, Deuce realized something wasn't right.

He paused.

For several moments, there was nothing, then he heard a muffled crunch—leaves under a foot.

He wasn't the only one out here.

Crouching, he peered through the bushes, but could see little in the darkness. Whoever had made the noise was somewhere ahead of him, by the road.

It could be anyone, really. A farmer getting an early start to his day. Someone out for a predawn stroll.

Zombies.

The thought gave him the creeps. He didn't actually believe in zombies, but, well, you never knew, right? And meeting one on a back road in the middle of nowhere in Ukraine seemed not entirely impossible.

Undead monster or not, he decided to move in for a closer look, and carefully picked his way through the undergrowth until we was about twenty yards from the drop box.

There was a woman standing there, wearing a white dress that screamed nurse. She looked to be in her late twenties, but the night could have been hiding a few years. Her head was cocked as if she was listening to something. Given the fact she was otherwise stone still, he was pretty sure she was doing exactly that.

Parked on the side of the road behind her was a dark sedan that could have been as old as the woman. She held her pose for half a minute, then took a couple deep breaths. With a quick look from side to side, she jammed a folded piece of paper under the metal box.

So apparently this was Traz.

The last thing Deuce wanted to do was scare the crap out of her, so he waited until she drove away, watching her taillights fade into the distance.

He was about to move when he heard the crunch again. Another footstep.

What the hell?

He froze in place, his legs bent.

Crunch. Crunch. Crunch.

A shadow detached itself from a group of bushes just down and across the road. A man. Not big, not small. But with a wiry, athletic frame that suggested he might be a threat.

As the man got closer to the metal box, Deuce saw he was wearing a uniform. A cop? No, Deuce realized, as the man neared. The uniform didn't look like the ones he'd seen worn by the police in this area. There was also no gun holster.

Military? Didn't seem right.

Private security?

Whoever he was, he was now interested in the box. He looked inside, and seemed surprised not to find anything. He checked again, and predictably came up empty once more. He started scanning the ground.

It was obvious that from where he'd been hiding, he had been unable to see where Traz had put the note. But, given his apparent keen interest, Deuce doubted it would be long before he found it.

And that would not be good.

Remaining crouched, Deuce thought for a moment. The mere fact that the guy was here right now meant he knew the nurse was up to something.

But did he know *what*?

Was he aware of her connection to Alex? And was he acting on his own, or working with someone else?

Deuce flexed his fingers, warming them up. Alex's safety was his number one job, and whoever this asshole was, he was a threat to that.

Staying low, Deuce made his way over to the edge of the road, where he could make faster time. He checked on the uniformed man again. The guy was still searching for the note, his back now to Deuce.

Four steps forward. Pause.

Four more. Pause.

The man had no idea Deuce was there.

As Deuce started moving again, the man finally checked

behind the box, and pulled the note out in triumph.

He suddenly cocked his head and listened, like Traz had earlier, but by that point, Deuce was already at his back.

"Turn around," Deuce said, not caring whether the guy understood English. "Slowly. And don't try anything stupid."

Turning quickly around, the man stuffed the note in his pocket, drew an arm back, and threw a punch.

Deuce leaned to one side before the blow could find his jaw, and countered by slamming his own fist into the guy's stomach.

The man groaned as he fought hard to keep from completely doubling over. Gritting his teeth, he made a grab for Deuce's head. He missed with one hand, but caught Deuce behind the ear with the other and shoved him to the side.

Deuce nearly tripped over a root growing out of the ground, but managed to keep his feet. When he turned around, the man was facing him.

In an unmistakably taunting tone, the guy shouted something in Ukrainian while waving at Deuce to come over. He then raised his fists like a boxer.

"You can't be serious," Deuce muttered, then in a louder voice, "I warned you. I did. Don't forget that."

He stepped toward the guy, feigned a punch, and pulled back, knowing he'd draw return fire. He was right. The guy came at him, both fists flying.

One blow glanced off Deuce's arm and the other missed completely, as he dodged to the side again.

Didn't this guy learn from his mistakes?

With a quick twist away from his opponent, Deuce kicked out with his left leg, his foot landing loud and solid against the side of the man's knee. The joint bent inward, knocking against the other leg, as most of its ligaments ripped apart.

Screaming in pain, the man fell to the asphalt. He clutched his knee and rolled back and forth.

"I told you, don't do anything stupid," Deuce said. "I swear to God I told you. This did *not* need to happen. Your fault, not mine. Right?"

He dropped down next to the man, and held him still long enough to take the note out of the guy's pocket. As he let go and took a few steps back, he pulled his phone out of his own pocket, and called Cooper.

While he waited for the line to connect, he read the note.

"What's up?" Cooper whispered.

"You should come back here. We have a bit of a situation."

"Did you hear from Alex?"

"Yeah, but…well, you'll see when you get here."

AS HE WAITED for Cooper, Deuce contemplated staying out on the road with his catch. Traffic was usually rare along the country lane, but rare didn't mean never, and there was always the chance of someone coming along before Cooper did.

That would turn an already complicated situation into a complete mess. So, without much effort, he located the injured man's car and used it to transfer them both back to the barn.

When Cooper walked in a few minutes later, his first words were, "Whose car is that?" Then he saw the man tied to the campstool next to the tent. "And who the hell is that?"

"You kind of answered your first question yourself," Deuce said. "Answer to the second's a bit tougher. I mean, unless you read Ukrainian." He tossed the guy's wallet to Cooper. "He's not talking."

"Okay, but what's he doing here?"

"Interesting story, that," Deuce said. He filled Cooper in on his trip to check the drop box. "He obviously knew about Traz. So there's a chance he knows Alex isn't who she says she is. No way I could let him go." Deuce waited, but when Cooper offered no response, he said, "Please tell me you agree with me."

"I suppose so."

"You *suppose so*?"

"No, I mean, I know," Cooper said. "It's just...Jesus. What a mess."

"It could have been a whole lot messier if I hadn't stopped him."

Cooper nodded absently. "Was he alone?"

With a disdainful snort, Deuce said, "Do you see two of them?"

"Maybe the other guy got away."

Deuce shook his head. "No, he was by himself. If there was someone else, they would have taken the car when my buddy here and I were having our little conversation."

"Let me see the note."

Deuce handed the piece of paper to him. There were only three words on it:

Message received. Complications.

Cooper frowned as he read it, then handed it back. "Wonderful."

"Did you really expect everything to go smoothly? You put her in a *prison*. In *Ukraine*."

Cooper looked back at their captive. "Is he the only one who knows about Traz, or is he working for someone?"

Deuce knew the question was rhetorical, but he answered anyway. "If you can get him to tell you, be my guest. But I don't think he speaks English."

"Then I guess we need a translator." Cooper pulled out his phone, dialed, and said, "Cooper for Olek Morrison." A long pause, then, "Hey, Olek, it's Coop. I need your expertise." Another pause. "Yeah, but FYI, he's injured and probably not exactly happy. I'm putting you on speaker." Cooper switched the device to speakerphone, and knelt down next to their visitor. "Olek, can you hear me?"

"Loud and clear," the voice on the phone said.

"Good. He's right here. Maybe we should go for a name first."

Olek's next words were incomprehensible to Deuce, but

the man on the ground didn't have any trouble understanding them. He looked surprised for a moment, then said, "Leonchuk. Vanko."

"First name, Vanko," Olek said. "Last name, Leonchuk."

"He's wearing some kind of uniform. Ask him what it's for."

Olek did, and Vanko responded.

"He works at a prison."

"Slavne Prison?"

The man perked up at the word "Slavne." Olek asked the question, and the man nodded, repeating several times a word that Deuce guessed meant yes.

"Ask him what he's doing out here."

After an exchange that lasted nearly half a minute, Olek said, "Well, that was fun. Let's see. He says he's going to call the police if you don't get him medical attention right away. He also says you're in big trouble. It was a little more colorful than that, but that's the gist."

"Tell him to answer the damn question."

Olek repeated the question, but before Vanko could plead his case again, Cooper tapped his damaged knee with the toe of his boot. The guard yelped in pain.

"Tell him if he doesn't want matching knees, he'll cooperate."

Olek told him. The response was nowhere near as long as Deuce thought it would be.

"He says he needs medical attention now," Olek explained. "He claims he'll tell you what you want to know, but you've got to get him to a doctor first."

"Oh, he's definitely gonna need a doctor. Surgery, too, is my guess. But they won't be able to do anything until the swelling goes down. A week or two at best. So I think we have a little bit of time."

The story, as Vanko finally told it, was an interesting one, involving Alex—whom he called "the prisoner Powell"—a prison doctor, and a nurse who was apparently the one Deuce had seen drop off the note. According to Vanko, the doctor and the nurse seemed to be working together. If true, that was news neither Cooper nor Deuce had known.

Vanko's reasons for following the nurse were a little sketchy, so he was either leaving something out or lying entirely.

When asked who else knew about his trip out here, Vanko hesitated before blurting out that his friend Danya knew all about it.

There was no either-or this time. It was clearly a lie.

When Cooper and Deuce had gotten all they could out of Vanko for the moment, they let Olek hang up, then moved to the other end of the barn to have a private conversation, just in case Vanko understood more English than he was letting on.

"What do you think?" Cooper said. "Is he working alone or not?"

Deuce glanced at their prisoner. "Alone would be my guess. Did you see the way he looked when he was telling us about the nurse and the doctor? I got the sense he had it out for them. But that's just a guess. I could be wrong. I could be *very* wrong."

Cooper frowned as he nodded. "That's the same sense I got, but there's one way to know for sure. If he's working with someone, sooner or later they'll come looking for him."

"Yeah, but before they do that, they might shut down Traz and go after Alex. Is there any way to get a warning to them?"

Cooper shook his head. "Only the dead drop."

"Right, but McElroy must have communicated with Traz somehow before this."

"Burner phone." Cooper pulled his cell back up and started going through the contacts list.

"You have the number?" Deuce asked.

"Yeah, but don't get too excited. They were instructed to only hold on to it until Alex arrived at the prison, in case something went wrong before then."

Cooper found what he was looking for and punched in

the number. But only a few seconds passed before he hung up. "Disconnected."

"So we're stuck with the dead drop."

"That's what it looks like."

Deuce sighed heavily and shook his head in disbelief. "I'm gonna say this again. Maybe it's time to call this thing off. I don't know about you, but I'm getting a real uneasy feeling, and the sooner we can get Alex out of there, the better."

Cooper was silent for several seconds. "McElroy won't approve it."

"Fuck McElroy. You're on-site mission chief, right? Don't you get final call?"

More silence. Then, after taking a deep breath, Cooper gave Deuce a nod. "I'll write the note."

TWENTY

WHEN ALEX WOKE the next morning, she could hardly believe that only two days had passed. She felt as if she'd been in this shithole of a prison for half her adult life.

Her ribs, shoulders, thighs, and calves were all screaming for more rest. The cut on her arm was worse. The medication Dr. Teterya gave her the night before had worn off, and the wound throbbed painfully with every beat of her heart.

It would have been great to just stay in bed, but besides the fact the guards would eventually rouse her, today was the big day. She would either make contact with El-Hashim, or lose that opportunity altogether. Sleep was not an option.

Down in the cafeteria, she found Frida eating breakfast by herself, so she sat with her. "Any more problems?"

Frida swallowed a spoonful of gruel. "I saw Kalyna last night right before dinner. She gave me...what do you call it? A dirty..."

"A dirty look?"

"A dirty look. Yes. But she leave me alone." She smiled now. "Thank you."

Alex retuned the smile, but didn't say anything. She knew Kalyna would be back at her old games before long, especially after Alex left.

Before they finished eating, Rachel joined them. Alex wasn't as surprised that the other two women had met, as she was by the fact Frida didn't seem to like Rachel. Frida greeted Rachel's questions with frowns and mumbled responses and seemed uncomfortable in her presence.

Rachel, however, didn't seem to notice, and Alex didn't

have time to question Frida privately about it. Once they all got out to the yard, she excused herself and left them to deal with their own problems. She had no interest in playing moderator.

Her first task involved a leisurely trip to the door in the back wall. The purpose of this was to see if she could hear anything coming from the other side. She knew that El-Hashim and her friends were over there somewhere, but the only noise she heard was that generated by the prisoners on her side of the wall.

Stepping forward, she gave the door a closer look. Made of metal, it was thick, heavy, and formidable. Meaning it would be impossible to get through without an explosive charge—unless you were authorized, which Alex most definitely was not.

Turning now, she started walking, heading directly for the administration building, counting the steps as she went. Give or take a few feet, it was just shy of a hundred and fifty yards. Adding that to the approximate distance on each end, she came up with an estimate of five hundred to five hundred twenty-five feet—a number she filed away for later use.

Scanning the back wall again, she focused on the guard towers. The observation areas were enclosed by clear glass or Plexi, and she could easily see there were two men in each. Three towers along the back, six men.

Although she couldn't see it from where she stood, she knew from the satellite photo that there was an additional outpost at the back of the isolation area. So potentially eight watchers could spot someone caught out in the open.

Another piece of info for her file.

She walked over to the exercise area, and pretended to watch a group of women kick a soccer ball as she mentally went over everything again.

And when the horn signaled the end of the outside hour, she was ready.

HER ASSIGNMENT THAT day was once again in the kitchen.

When lunch started, she quickly ate her food before getting back to work, washing the pots and pans that had been used to prepare the meal. She was in the middle of cleaning out a particularly grimy kettle when someone tapped her shoulder.

"You go." It was Oksana, the inmate who ran Building One's kitchen.

Behind her were two guards.

Finally.

While Oksana had a rudimentary knowledge of English, the guards apparently did not. They communicated with Alex using points and nods as they guided her back to the administration building and up to the infirmary.

The nurse who had been helping Dr. Teterya the night before glanced up from her computer, then stood and walked over. The doctor had called her Irina.

"We work together," the doctor had said the night before as they were finishing their discussion. "She starts her next shift tomorrow at noon. She'll send for you when she gets here to do a follow-up."

"That's not something that should take very long," Alex had said.

"Leave that to us."

Irina talked to the guards for a moment, then motioned for Alex to follow her. Unlike the guard from the night before, these two simply left, apparently having other, more pressing duties.

Irina took Alex to the examining table farthest from the lobby, and pulled the curtain around.

"My English not good," the nurse whispered. "Doctor come, look arm. Make like hurt, yes?"

"Sure," Alex said, though she wouldn't actually have to pretend.

It was several minutes before the older doctor—the one who had initially stitched Alex up—pulled back the curtain just wide enough to enter. Unlike the previous day, he looked pale and a little sweaty.

"Hello," he said, his tone brusque.

He pulled a stool over to the table. As he sat down, he shot out a hand, grabbing the edge of the bed to steady himself, then paused for a moment, panting.

"Are you all right?" Alex asked.

He frowned at her. "Arm."

She held it out.

As he examined the wound, she could hear low grunts and groans emanating from his throat, and knew that there was something definitely wrong with him. She winced as his fingers traced her stitches. When he got to the ones Dr. Teterya had redone, he paused, but went on without saying anything.

A moan this time, louder than the grunts that had preceded it.

"Wait," the doctor said, suddenly rising to his feet. With three quick steps, he was gone.

Alex sat silently. Five minutes passed, then ten. Finally Irina appeared with another nurse and said, "You must..." She struggled for a moment before continuing. "Not go. Doctor come...soon."

A smirk graced Alex's lips. "Like I have a choice."

DR. TETERYA HAD a hard time sleeping that morning, knowing that less than four hours after he laid his head down, he would need to be up again. Of course, the thing that was really keeping him awake was the prisoner Powell.

It had been less than a week ago when the doctor was approached outside his apartment building. The offer: money. *Lots* of money. Half upon agreement to help, and half upon completion. All he and Irina had to do was provide assistance to an inmate who hadn't even been arrested yet. This assistance, the man had told the doctor, would come in the form of information, communications relay, and most importantly, escape—but not just the new inmate.

There would likely be another.

Teterya and Irina had, of course, done this before. Once. It had been out of necessity. Irina's sister had been sick and quality medical assistance was far from cheap, so they'd helped a Hungarian woman escape, and made the needed cash.

As it turned out, the man making the new offer knew all about their previous assistance. And while he didn't say it directly, it was clear that if the offer was refused, the authorities would become aware of their earlier indiscretion.

Dr. Teterya was given two hours to think about it.

He went directly to Irina's home.

"How much?" Irina had asked.

He repeated the number to her, and knew exactly what she was thinking. The amount of money the man had offered was more than enough for them to quit their jobs at the prison and take the time they would need to find better employment in Sevastopol or even Kiev.

"The money is fantastic," Irina asked, "but how are we supposed to get them out? Anton can't fit two inside his truck. And more than one trip will be too much of a risk."

But the doctor had an answer for that. There was one other way. It was trickier than hiding in the compartment of a truck, but he had discovered it when he first started working at the hospital, and knew it would work.

He told Irina what he was thinking, then said, "In the end, it probably doesn't even matter. What are the chances that this woman will actually show up?"

Not much, they had agreed. Not much at all.

No one was that crazy.

It was a good thing neither Teterya nor Irina were gamblers.

When his alarm sounded at 11:30 a.m., Teterya was already staring at the ceiling, his stomach a bundle of nerves.

Sucking in a breath, he slapped the clock and silenced the buzzer.

As he crawled out from beneath the blankets, he realized his hands were shaking. Soon the spasms extended to his arms, then shoulders, and even his torso. He was shaking so hard it was as if he were freezing, yet his apartment was already warm with the growing day. He stumbled into the bathroom and managed to turn on the shower, and as soon as he was under the stream of water, his muscles began to relax.

By the time his phone rang at 12:20 p.m., he was sitting on his couch, dressed, his hands steady.

He answered the call. "Yes?"

"Dr. Teterya, it's Irina." They had managed to keep their relationship a secret from the prison staff, worried it might damage their careers if anyone found out. To that end, every conversation they had outside their private moments was cordial and professional.

"Hello, Irina. What can I do for you?"

"I'm sorry if I woke you, but Dr. Timko has taken ill and needs to go home. He would like you to fill in for him the rest of the day."

"Ill? What's wrong?"

"Stomach. Probably the flu."

"All right. I'll be there as soon as I can."

"Thank you, Doctor."

Teterya forced himself to wait five more minutes before heading out, then drove through town and out into the country. He was slowing to turn down the road to the prison when he remembered the message drop. It was his turn to check, and if he didn't do it now, Irina would be forced to handle it when she got off work.

He sped back up and continued down the highway. It would delay his arrival at the prison for another ten minutes, but that probably wasn't a bad thing.

To his surprise, there was a message behind the box. It was sealed in an envelope marked with the letter P. For Powell, he presumed. The sealed envelope also meant it was for the prisoner's eyes only—and that was fine by him. The less he and Irina knew at this point, the better.

He stuffed the envelope in his pocket and resumed his journey to the prison.

As was protocol, his first stop was the assistant administrator's office, where he would check in and learn of anything he might need to know.

He and the assistant administrator, Petro Doroshenko, had developed a friendly relationship that had on more than one occasion extended to drinks away from work.

"I heard Timko is sick," Petro said. "So you've got a long shift in front of you."

"Not the first time. Anything happen while I was gone?"

"All quiet."

"Good," Teterya said, "then I should probably get to the infirmary." He turned for the door, but then stopped as if he'd just remembered something. "Petro, yesterday evening I was informed that several prisoners had been taken to isolation, but no one told me why. Is there something I need to know? Any medical issues to be aware of?"

"No," Petro told him. "None that I know of." He hesitated as if there was something more, but he was unsure whether to say it.

"What?" Teterya asked.

A pause, then, "A rumor, really. I don't know anything for sure."

Teterya kept quiet, waiting for him to go on.

"There might be a threat on the life of one of the prisoners who was moved."

One of the doctor's eyebrows rose a millimeter. "What's so different about that? This is a prison. Inmates are threatened all the time."

"No, no. Apparently this news came from outside. Someone in the prison has been hired to kill her."

"An assassin?"

Petro kept his mouth shut, but the look on his face said *yes*.

"But why? Who is she?"

"A'isha Najem. At least that's the name she was brought here under. But…" He shrugged his shoulder.

"A false name? Is anyone checking to see who she really is?"

"The warden is handling the investigation personally."

The message was clear. Petro had been cut out of whatever was really going on. "Most of this is just rumor, of course. Best if you don't share them."

"Share what?" Teterya said, acting innocent, but feeling anything but as he turned for the door and left.

ALEX SAT QUIETLY for over forty minutes before she heard a new, male voice talking to one of the nurses. When the curtain surrounding her table moved to the side again, she was surprised to see Dr. Teterya.

"My apologies for wait," he said, his face tense. "The nurse call me because Dr. Timko not feel well, so has gone home." He sat on the stool Dr. Timko had been using. "You are here for check of arm, correct?"

"That's right."

"Please, may I see?"

Alex extended her arm.

Dr. Teterya made a show of giving it a thorough examination. When he was finished, he frowned and shook his head.

"This, I do not like," he said, pointing at a spot along the wound that looked no different than anywhere else. "Infection, I think. Very dangerous." He turned toward the closed curtain. "Irina!"

A few seconds later, the nurse was there. Teterya spoke rapidly to her in Ukrainian. She nodded and left quickly.

"You must stay here for watch," he told Alex. "Maybe go back to cell tonight, but give antibiotics first, see what happen. Okay?"

"Is it serious?" she said, acting worried.

"We treat now. Will be fine. Don't worry."

He stood up and disappeared for a moment. When he returned, he had a roll of gauze that he wrapped loosely around her arm, covering up her wound.

"Is painful, yes?" As he said this, he pantomimed cradling one arm in the other.

Alex got the message and mimicked him.

"It hurts like hell," she said. "What do you think?"

"Because infected. Please, stay here moment. Nurse Irina fix room where you can rest."

He left again.

So this was how they'd been planning to keep her here. She'd been wondering about that. She wondered also what they had given Dr. Timko to make him so sick. Whatever it was, she was pretty sure he wouldn't be enjoying life for a while.

Suddenly, the curtain was pulled all the way open.

"Come," Irina said.

She led Alex through a door at the back of the infirmary, into a large room with cluttered supply shelves along one wall, and three metal doors across the back. Each had a slot window in the upper half that could be closed off with a locking flap.

Irina took Alex to the open door on the left. The room inside was just large enough for a bed, a toilet, and the space needed to get from one to the other. A cell, in other words, for patients required to stay in the infirmary for treatment.

Dr. Teterya was waiting for her next to the bed. "Why you here?"

The sharpness of his tone took Alex by surprise.

"What do you mean?" Alex asked. "We talked about this last night. This is how you're going to—"

He moved around her so that he was between her and the door. "No. I mean Slavne Prison. Why?"

"To take the other prisoner out. You know that."

"I think you maybe come to kill her."

She stared at him for a moment. "What? Why would I kill her? I'm supposed to get her out."

"I just find out she and friends are in isolation because assassin come here to prison—come to kill her. Is you, isn't it?"

Alex closed her eyes. Now he made sense. It was only natural, she thought, that once he found out about the assassin he'd think it was her. She had kept the conversation she'd overheard between El-Hashim and the warden to herself.

When she opened her eyes again, she locked her gaze on his. In no uncertain terms, she said, "No. It is *not* me. The last thing I want is for that woman to be killed. She has information that's very important to me personally."

"So? You get information, then you kill."

"No," she told him, her voice rising. "My employers need to talk to her, too. None of us, *none of us*, wants her dead. Do you understand? If she dies, my time here has been wasted."

The doctor looked uncertain. Irina said something to him and he looked at her, then glanced back at Alex before walking out of the cell and shutting her alone inside.

Cursing under her breath, Alex moved over to the door and pressed her ear against it, hearing only muffled voices.

This lasted maybe two minutes before all went silent.

TWENTY ONE

"ARE YOU SURE Petro is right about this?" Irina asked.

"He told me it was a rumor," Teterya said. "But you know he's always aware of what's going on around here before the rest of us."

"Even if he is right, that doesn't mean this woman Powell is the killer."

"She came into this prison simply to get close to A'isha Najem. Isn't that proof enough?"

"But did you listen to her? Did you watch her? She wasn't lying. I'm sure of it."

"You can't know that."

Irina was silent for a moment. "You're right. I can't. But I *have* to believe it. And so do you."

"What are you talking about?"

"If we don't help her now, what do you think the people who sent her here are going to do?"

That stopped him. He knew very well what they would do. They would expose him and Irina, and the two of them would be arrested and undoubtedly given a severe sentence.

"So we go along with it?" he said. "What if she is the assassin?"

"If she kills Najem in the prison, the guards will get her, probably even kill her. You can say she coerced you, threatened your family. If she takes Najem out and kills her somewhere else, that's not our problem. Don't you see? We have no choice."

Teterya felt faint. "I…I need some water."

What he really needed was time to think, and since Irina knew him better than anyone, she didn't follow him when he left the room.

ALEX WAS ALL but certain Teterya and Irina were telling the guards right now that they had the assassin locked in an infirmary cell. When she heard someone grab the door handle on the other side, she stepped back, hoping to God that McElroy had some way of getting her out of this mess.

But instead of a squad of guards, it was just the doctor and the nurse. They stepped into the room, and Irina closed the door behind them as Teterya set a cloth bundle on the bed.

"Why is A'isha Najem important to you?" he asked.

Alex decided to be as forthcoming as possible. "That's not her real name. The name I know her by is El-Hashim. I'm not sure that's her real name, either. She launders money for terrorist organizations that then fund bombings and murders and God knows what else."

"Then you *do* want to kill her."

"No," Alex said quickly. "Killing her serves nothing. If she's alive, we can find out who she works with. She could be the key to unraveling a very large network. Who knows how many lives that could save?"

"Don't understand," Irina said.

The doctor translated for her, then said to Alex, "You said you have personal need to talk to her. Is same?"

Alex hesitated. "No."

"What is it?"

"Like I said, it's personal."

"Tell me."

"If you don't mind, I'd rather not."

Teterya considered her for several seconds. Then he pointed at the bundle on the bed. Clothes that looked very much like those being worn by Irina and the other nurse.

"Put them on," he said.

He turned to the wall to give Alex some privacy.

"The guard staff is told you stay here for observation," he continued. "Is standard. Happens many time. They never check."

Alex slipped out of the gray dress. "What about your other nurse?"

"She work here only short time. Irina in charge and you Irina's patient. Only Irina or me check you."

Alex would have to take their word for that. She pulled on the nurse's outfit.

"Okay," she said.

The doctor turned back around.

"What about this?" She raised her bandaged arm.

The doctor said something to Irina, who left the room for a few seconds and returned with a thin, cream-colored sweater. Alex donned it. It would make her a bit hotter than necessary, but hiding the wound was worth the price. Irina moved in behind her and started pulling at Alex's hair.

"Hey, what are you doing?" Alex asked.

"No move," Irina told her.

She attacked Alex's hair with a brush and comb and a few bobby pins, and in record time sculpted a whole new look. At least it *felt* different. When Irina was done, she took a step back and stared at Alex.

"So?" Alex asked.

"One moment."

She disappeared again. This time she returned with a pair of black, thick-framed glasses and a nurse's cap. She handed the glasses to Alex.

"Wear, please."

Alex put them on, relieved that the prescription wasn't too strong. There was only a minute distortion to her vision.

Irina fixed the cap to the top of Alex's head. This time, after she checked her handiwork, she pulled a small mirror from her pocket and held it up so Alex could see.

Alex had to admit that for a quick change, it wasn't a bad disguise. Still, she wasn't confident it would work, and said as much to the doctor.

"Will be fine," he told her. "We have many different staff come through infirmary. Some only work one time. Is too much for them." He handed her a laminated badge. "Is pass for temporary employee. Clip to dress."

She did so.

"Now take this." He handed her a file. "When walking, look at this as much as possible. You are ready?"

"Sure," Alex said. "Why not?"

TETERYA LED HER to the locked back exit of the infirmary.

"Take care," Irina told them.

Alex had the distinct impression the words were more for the doctor than for her.

They stepped through the doorway into a vacant hallway, moved quickly over to the central stairwell, and began their descent. They had nearly reached the first floor when the door below flew open and two guards walked in.

Alex immediately looked down at the file in her hands, pretending to study the sheet of paper attached to the cover. She felt acutely self-conscious, certain that her disguise would fool no one.

As the guards passed them heading up, one of them said something to Teterya. He responded with what sounded like a complaint, punctuated by an ironic laugh. The guards snickered as they continued their ascent without slowing.

Alex let out a breath.

When she and the doctor reached the first-floor landing, Teterya leaned in and whispered, "Stay close."

The corridor was bustling with activity. There were several guards present, a few escorting prisoners. There were also a couple of men in suits— administrators, Alex guessed—walking toward the far end on the right.

Following Teterya's instructions, she stayed directly behind him as he walked rapidly down the hallway toward another doorway she hadn't been through before. With every step, she was expecting someone to say something to her, shout at her to stop. At the very least, she was sure one of the prisoners they passed would recognize her.

But they didn't even look at her, and no one said a word.

There was a speaker box next to the door. The doctor

pressed the button at the bottom of the box, and a voice spoke. As the doctor replied, he tilted his head up to face a camera mounted above the door. When the voice spoke again, the doctor stepped to the side, giving the camera a view of Alex. Motioning with his eyes, he told her to look at the lens.

Steeling herself, she tore her gaze away from the file folder and looked up. Her heart was pounding.

The voice spoke again, and the doctor quickly responded.

A pause, then a buzz sounded as the door was unlocked.

The room on the other side turned out to be a stairwell that led to the basement, which was nothing more than a single long corridor that ended at a barred door. The walls were covered with green peeling paint, the floor made of bare concrete. Though otherwise clean, Alex was pretty sure it was a place that didn't see a lot of traffic.

There was another camera in the ceiling above the barred door. Just before they reached it, there was a loud *clank*, and the door swung open a few inches.

The doctor let Alex pass through first, then closed the door behind them. It clanked again as some unseen guard relocked it.

More concrete—walls, ceiling, and floor. Running along the center of the ceiling was an electrical line that was broken up at consistent intervals by glass-dome light fixtures, each with a single bulb inside. Cameras were mounted along the ceiling as well, about fifty feet apart.

The corridor curved to the right, and as they traveled through it, Alex realized that Teterya's attention was focused on the ceiling ahead. With a sudden stop, he looked back past her, then ahead again. One of the cameras was directly above them, but because of the curve of the passageway, the cameras behind and in front were well out of sight.

A blind spot.

Teterya quickly pulled an envelope from his pocket and handed it to her. "I forget before. This message come for you this morning."

"Have you read it?"

"No. Is sealed."

Alex started to open it.

"Read while walk," he said.

With a nod, she pulled the paper out, laid it against the file, and began following the doctor again.

The note was short and handwritten.

TOO DANGEROUS. RECOMMEND ABORT. PLS CONFIRM.

C

Now they think it's too dangerous?

It had been too dangerous since the day they'd laid out this plan. So had something happened? Had she been compromised? Should she get the hell out of here now?

"Hurry," Teterya whispered harshly.

She glanced up. The distance between them had increased to about twenty feet. She picked up her pace.

"A problem?" he whispered without moving his lips.

"No. No problem."

It didn't matter what the note said. She had to talk to El-Hashim. She had to find out what the woman knew about her father.

Soon the tunnel straightened, its pools of light fading off in the distance, giving the illusion the passageway went on forever. It wasn't long, however, before Alex could see another barred door. As they approached it, there was a familiar *clank*, but as they passed through the doorway, they weren't greeted by an empty corridor. Instead, two guards Alex had never seen before stood in the hallway, waiting.

Teterya shared a few words with them, then the guards led them to a staircase that took them back to ground level.

The building they found themselves in felt very much like the cellblock buildings in the main part of the prison—same gray walls, same oppressive feel. The difference came when they followed the guards onto the blocks. There were only six cells, three on each side, their open metal doors revealing they were only big enough for a single bed and a toilet.

They were also empty.

The same proved true of the cells in the second block. In block three, however, two of the doors were closed.

After block three, the guards led them through a double-gated security checkpoint that, given their escorts, went quickly and without incident. A couple of turns down a short hallway brought them to a wide corridor. One wall was lined with thick glass windows that looked out into the yard of the isolation area. Except for two more guards out for a smoke, the grounds were deserted. Alex noted that the three guard towers along the walls had clear views of every inch of the yard.

No-man's-land. All of it.

An elevator ride took their small group to the fourth floor. They went through another checkpoint, and two cellblocks identical to those below. The entryway to the third, however, was not open like all the others had been. In addition, a guard was sitting on a chair beside it.

As soon as he saw them, he jumped to his feet.

There was a quick conversation between the escort guards and the man at the door before it was opened. Teterya went through first, with Alex right behind him. When it appeared as if the escorts would join them, the doctor said something, and after a bit of back and forth, the guards stayed on the other side.

Another order from the doctor and the door was closed.

This new block was unlike any of the others. In fact, the only thing that gave it away as being part of a prison complex was the metal door they had just come through.

They were standing in a foyer that opened up into a large living room space, with a hallway on one side, and an open kitchen on the other. The décor was hotel chic—marble and silk and porcelain and bamboo—with beautiful paintings on the walls where windows would be, and a large-screen television sitting on a teak cabinet.

What the hell?

This was obviously the luxury suite for prisoners who could afford it, and Alex suddenly understood why the warden had been so accommodating. El-Hashim must have paid a fat wad of cash to be transferred here.

El-Hashim herself was standing in the living area. She and her three friends had all scrambled to their feet as Alex and Teterya entered, holding scarves up to hide their faces as they stared at their two new guests.

Alex kept a step behind the doctor, with her head tilted down in hopes she wouldn't be recognized right away.

"Good afternoon," Teterya said.

"What do you want with A'isha Najem?" one of the protectors barked. Alex guessed this must be the one called Marie.

The doctor moved out of the foyer and into the living room proper, Alex keeping pace.

"It is requirement," he said. "All prisoners in isolation have medical check every two days."

"Does it look like we are in isolation?"

"Does not matter. You are in isolation facility, you must have check."

El-Hashim and Marie huddled for a moment, then Marie said, "Okay, fine. Just make it quick."

Teterya bowed slightly. "I would like to use bedroom. Which one better for you?"

At the mention of bedroom, the women gave him a wary look, but the presence of a nurse seemed to stifle any objections they may have had. Alex half expected them to recognize her now, but they only seemed to see the uniform.

"That one," Marie said, pointing at a door on the left wall.

"Good," Teterya told her. "Who will be first?"

THERE WAS A small desk in the room. Alex opened the file

on it, then sat so that her back would be to the doctor and whomever Teterya was examining.

The order of the women was predictable: the two larger bodyguards first, followed by Marie, and finally El-Hashim.

During each check, the doctor would occasionally say something to Alex in Ukrainian. She would nod and pretend to write something in the file.

When El-Hashim came in, her hijab now wrapped around her head and covering her face, Marie didn't leave.

"You go now," Teterya told her.

"No," Marie said. "I stay. Where my friend goes, I go."

Alex was tempted to point out that her friend had been in the other room while *she* was in here, but held her tongue.

"Is not acceptable," Teterya said tersely.

"It is unacceptable for my friend to be alone with you."

"But we not be alone. Nurse is here."

Alex wished the good doctor hadn't pointed that out, but Marie simply said, "Same thing. I'm staying."

There was a pause, then Alex heard Teterya come up behind her. A moment later he was leaning over her shoulder as if to examine the file, his voice barely a whisper. "What you want to do?"

Alex had been expecting this. "It's okay," she said, matching his tone.

Teterya nodded as he continued to consult the file for another second or two before returning to his patient. "Very well," he told them. "If you'll both sit down, we can…" He coughed. Once, twice, and a third time. Then he said, "Excuse, please. I must get water."

He crossed to the en suite bathroom. As soon as Alex heard the door close behind him, she waited a beat, took a breath, removed her glasses, and turned around, finally facing the woman she had come here to see.

"El-Hashim," she said softly. "Excuse me for the intrusion. My name is Alexandra Poe, and I've come here to—"

"Assassin!" El-Hashim shouted, and lunged at her.

Alex dove sideways off her chair, not so much surprised by the reaction as by whom it had come from. She had expected any attacks to be launched by Marie, but the woman had stepped back against the wall.

El-Hashim rammed the chair and smashed it into the desk, barely missing Alex's hip. Spinning around, Alex grabbed her by the arm and tried to get behind to her to grab the other, but the woman was wiry and fast. She squirmed away and yanked her arm free. For a moment, they stood facing each other, El-Hashim's eyes narrow and wild.

"Listen to me," Alex said through clenched teeth. "I'm not trying to—"

The door to the room burst open, and the two bodyguards ran in. At the same moment, El-Hashim rushed at Alex, swiping a hand toward her face.

Alex jerked her head back, reflexively moving her elbow up to block the blow, and ended up with El-Hashim's nails ripping into the cut on her forearm. Alex cried out and tackled her to the floor, straddling her and pinning her arms down.

"Get off me!" El-Hashim screamed.

"I'm not trying to hurt you," Alex said.

One of the bodyguards grabbed Alex around the waist, as the other tried to pry her hands from El-Hashim's arms. But Alex couldn't be budged. "I just want to talk!"

"Liar!" El-Hashim cried.

"I'm *not* here to kill you, goddamn it. I'm here to get you out of this—"

Hot white pain shot through Alex's torso as a fist hit her kidneys. She immediately released El-Hashim and rolled onto her side, the pain so intense that she could barely breathe.

As El-Hashim got to her feet, Alex looked up, her words coming out in short desperate gasps. "I'm...here to...help you...escape."

The two bodyguards moved forward, but El-Hashim held up a hand and they stopped short. She crouched down next to Alex, her eyes full of curiosity. "What lie did you just tell me?"

Alex was finally getting her breath back. "It's not a lie. I'm here to help you escape."

"You expect me to believe this after you attack me?"

"*You* attacked me. All I did was defend myself."

El-Hashim studied her a moment, then shook her head. "Why should I trust you? I have no reason to."

Alex got up on her elbows, the move sending a jolt of pain through her. "I understand that," she said. "You're scared. You don't know me. But you do know my father."

"Your father? That's absurd." El-Hashim turned and looked back at Marie, who was still safely on the other side of the bed. "How would I know your father?"

"His name is Frank Poe. I'm his daughter, Alexandra."

El-Hashim scoffed and stood up. "I'm getting the prison guards."

She gestured for the bodyguards to grab Alex. They moved in quickly and roughly pulled Alex to her feet as El-Hashim headed for the door.

"Wait," Marie said. "Perhaps we should hear what she has to say."

El-Hashim stopped and studied her friend in confusion. "And why would we want to do that?"

Marie shrugged. "Curiosity?"

El-Hashim considered this a moment, then nodded. "I suppose the guards will still be there in a few minutes." She walked back to Alex, her eyes narrowing. "So who is this Frank Poe you think I should know?"

"I don't think," Alex said. She twisted around slightly, testing the grip of the bodyguards. They were strong, but not so well positioned. It wouldn't take much effort to free herself, but that could wait for the moment. "You met with him last week, along the waterfront in Yalta."

Marie took a step forward. "How do you know that?"

Alex shot her a glance. "Because I do."

"Who told you?"

Alex kept quiet.

"Your father?"

Alex glanced away. Lying without lying.

Marie, who seemed to have taken on the role of main inquisitor, said, "Even if this is true, why should we believe you're his daughter?"

"Look at me. I have his mouth and nose. My hair is darker, and my eyes, they're like my mother's. She was Persian—although I'm sure you already know that."

Marie seemed stunned. Her expression suddenly softened as she moved around the bed and walked over to El-Hashim. They huddled for several seconds, then El-Hashim said to the bodyguards, "Let her go and leave the room."

Alex could feel them hesitate, as if they were hoping they'd heard incorrectly.

"Go!" El-Hashim commanded.

As soon as their hands were off her, Alex rubbed her upper arms to get her circulation going again. There wasn't much she could do about her kidney, which was throbbing like a son of a bitch.

No one said a word until the bodyguards had left the room and shut the door.

Then El-Hashim looked at her. "You do have some of your father's features. I'll say that much. But tell us again. Why exactly are you here?"

"Because he sent me," Alex said. "To get you out."

TWENTY TWO

ALEX HAD ORIGINALLY intended to go with McElroy's plan of telling El-Hashim she was here because of her father's concern that the woman would not be able to easily extract herself from the Crimean judicial system. But considering what she now knew, she decided there was a better way to handle this.

"My dad discovered that there might be an attempt on your life," she said, and both women visibly tensed. "As a...business associate, he felt the need to do what he could to keep that from happening."

Alex hoped the label she'd used was accurate. Thankfully, it didn't seem to raise any suspicions.

"So he sends *you*?" El-Hashim said.

"He couldn't very well break in here himself—not without a round of reconstructive surgery."

"That's fairly audacious," Marie said. "Sending your daughter into a pit like this."

Excluding their present surroundings, of course.

"My father isn't a sentimental man, and he knows I can handle myself. I was the best person for the job, so here I am."

Marie grunted softly. "You sound like him, too."

The comment was unexpected, catching Alex off guard. She was lost in it for a moment, lost in the memory of her father—tough as iron when he needed to be, and sometimes when he didn't.

"Are you all right?" Marie asked.

"I'm fine."

El-Hashim studied her carefully, and Alex knew she

wasn't yet convinced. "If your father did send you, then he must have told you why we met last week."

There was only one way to deal with this question.

"He most certainly did not," Alex said, an edge to her voice. "Let's get something straight. I do not work for my father. I don't know what he does. I don't get involved. But when he asks for my help, which doesn't happen often, I'll do what he needs."

"An impressive speech," Marie said. "But if you don't work for your father, then what is it you do?"

Alex paused. This was something that was bound to come up. They had even discussed it at Stonewell, and decided it was best to stick as close as possible to the truth.

"I collect people who've skipped out on their bail," she said. "Car thieves, burglars, assault suspects. I work in and around Baltimore, Maryland. Real cream of the crop kind of people."

Marie frowned. "You're a...bounty hunter?"

Alex nodded. "And before that I was in the army for a couple of years. Didn't think to bring a resume. Sorry."

It was a make-or-break moment. The women could easily have walked out of the room right then and there—and that would've been the ballgame.

But they didn't walk out. Instead, Marie said, "How much do you and your father expect to be paid for this service?"

Hooked, Alex thought, and had to struggle to contain her relief. "Me, I want nothing. My father? That's between you and him."

El-Hashim sneered. "Of course."

Alex shrugged. "I'm sure you'll find a way to make it mutually beneficial. You're both resourceful people."

"This is an interesting proposal," Marie said. "But I think you'll understand that my friend here needs time to think it over."

"I do understand. But I'm afraid time is one thing we can't afford to waste. I'll need your answer before I leave."

The two women exchanged glances, then El-Hashim said, "Please give us a moment."

Alex nodded and watched them walk to the bedroom door, where they stopped and spoke together quietly.

As she waited, the door to the bathroom opened, and Teterya stuck his head out.

She'd been wondering how he was holding up in there.

When he saw Alex, he made a gesture indicating he was ready to come out, but Alex held out her hand, palm first, letting him know *not yet*. He nodded, retreated inside, and quietly closed the door.

Finally, the two women came back over and El-Hashim spoke first. "If we are to say yes, how would you get us out of here?"

Alex shook her head. "Not all of you. My instructions pertain to El-Hashim only."

"I'm not leaving here without Marie."

"You're not leaving at all," Alex said.

El-Hashim frowned. "I don't understand."

"The two of you have a nice little bait-and-switch thing going here, but I figured you out a while ago." She turned to Marie. "If I'm not mistaken, *you're* the real El-Hashim."

TWENTY THREE

THE WOMEN LOOKED at Alex, nonplussed, and the one who had been calling herself El-Hashim started to protest—

—but Marie waved her off. "Don't. It will only waste time. There's no point in denying it." She stared at Alex. "How did you know?"

"I suspected it when you let your friend here do your fighting for you. You confirmed it for me when you said I sound just like my father."

"This doesn't change anything," the fake El-Hashim said, stepping closer to Alex. "I won't let her go alone with you. It could be a trap. You could kill her the moment you are out of our sight."

"I could kill her now," Alex said, shifting her gaze to Marie, aka the real El-Hashim. "I could kill you both now. I could have killed you when your bodyguards were still here, and thrown them on the pile. But I didn't, did I?"

The friend, who may or may not have been named Marie—it was hard to tell around here—eyed her defiantly. "You boast, but can you deliver?"

"Try me."

The woman held her gaze for a moment, then finally looked away.

Alex dismissed her with a glance and returned her attention to El-Hashim. "You're in prison. Even without an assassin on your tail, there are thousands of ways you can die in here. I'm offering you a way out, sooner rather than later. Take it or leave it."

"There is still the question of how you propose to do this," El-Hashim said.

"You'll find out when the time comes, not before."

"Can you at least tell me when that time will be?"

A reasonable question, Alex thought. There were two factors involved in the timing. The first was that any escape would be best conducted at night. The second was that Cooper and Deuce would need to be in position on the outside.

This, of course, meant getting them a message and receiving their reply—a procedure that might take hours. There was no way it could be done in time to leave tonight.

"Well?" El-Hashim asked.

"Tomorrow night, or the night after that at the most," Alex told her.

El-Hashim considered this, then looked at her friend as if seeking advice. But Marie—or whoever she was—was already shaking her head. She leaned in toward El-Hashim and whispered something in French.

Alex could hear a few of the words—*not...crazy...now*—but most were said too quietly for her to pick up.

After several seconds, El-Hashim patted the air with her hand. *"Qui, je sais. Je sais."*

Yes, I know. I know.

She turned to Alex. "Ms. Poe, I understand your need for an answer. But you must understand that I cannot take this on your word alone. I need time to verify that you are who you say you are."

"I won't put this on hold. It's now or never."

"You say it will take at least a day before we can leave. I'd suggest you proceed as if I have said yes, and by this time tomorrow, I can give you a definitive answer."

Alex couldn't blame her for wanting to check her story. She would've done the very same thing. But while she hadn't lied about her background, what if El-Hashim tried to verify everything through her father?

How would he respond?

Would he sell out his own daughter?

Alex didn't think he was capable of that, but she had also never thought him capable of leaving her and Danny. And time and distance didn't always make the heart grow fonder.

A part of her wished she had just come in here and asked El-Hashim straight out about her father. Asked her where to find him. But she knew the woman would have told her nothing. The only way to get an answer was to gain her trust and get her away from this prison—alone. And when El-Hashim had no one else to rely on, that's when Alex could make the push.

She made a show of not being happy about the request, but finally nodded.

"I'll give you until noon tomorrow," she said. "No more. After that, you're on your own."

"That is most appreciated."

It had better be.

And this had damn well better be worth it.

"AGAIN?" DR. TETERYA said as they returned via the tunnel under the prison.

"Is that a problem?"

"I am not scheduled during day. Dr. Timko will be back."

Alex shrugged. "He seemed pretty sick today. Another day off shouldn't be surprising."

"Effects of drug will wear off by time he wakes up in morning."

"I'm sure you can arrange a prolonged illness. A home visit tonight, perhaps, to see how he's feeling."

She had no trouble sensing his reluctance. He was oozing it like sweat.

"Doctor, this is the job you are being paid well to perform. There's no backing out. You should know, if I'm pleased with how things go, I will recommend a bonus when I see my employer."

"Bonus?" The word bounced clumsily out of his mouth.

"More money," she explained. She wasn't lying. She

knew she was forcing the doctor to go miles beyond what he had expected to do, so recommending an additional payment wasn't unreasonable. She had no idea if McElroy would comply, but she'd do everything she could.

"I...I was supposed to work double shift," he said quietly, speaking more to himself than to Alex, as if he were trying to come up with a strategy. "Must get someone to cover tonight, so I come back tomorrow."

"See? No problem."

"Is no guarantee I find someone," he snapped.

"I'm sure you will."

He scowled at her and they walked the rest of the way in silence. When they finally returned to the infirmary, Irina took Alex into the back room and helped her change back into her gray dress.

"If we go out tomorrow night," Alex said once the doctor had rejoined them, "I'm going to need my team in place. I don't know where to tell them to go, though."

Teterya thought for a moment, then nodded. "Of course," he said. He gave her the location.

She asked for paper and a pen, and wrote Cooper and Deuce a note, sealing it inside the envelope Irina had brought her.

"Deliver this as soon as possible," she told them.

"I take," Irina said. "On way home."

"Thank you."

Irina called for the guards, and Alex was escorted back into the now full prison yard. The day was much warmer than the previous one, so any area in shade had, for the most part, already been claimed.

After walking around in the relentless sun for several minutes, Alex found a spot along the wall on the other side of the exercise area. If she pushed herself right up against the stone, she could at least partially avoid the direct sunlight.

She didn't last there for long, however. She was restless, all worked up. She wanted to act, get things rolling, do *anything*. The only way to keep from exploding was to start walking again.

What if El-Hashim said no?

It was a very real possibility. If that happened, Alex would have only two choices:

One, accept the decision and walk away.

Two, take El-Hashim by force.

The second option would entail neutralizing the other three women in El-Hashim's suite, and getting an uncooperative inmate past the regular prison guards.

Of course, with access to the infirmary, she could have the doctor bring some kind of drug that would knock El-Hashim out, making option two not quite as daunting.

Yeah. That might work.

It might be *preferable*.

They could pretend a fight had broken out while they were in the apartment, and that they needed to get an unconscious El-Hashim to the infirmary as soon as possible. Hell, they might even be able to get the guards to carry her.

But then what?

Whatever drug Teterya used would have to wear off quickly. Alex would need El-Hashim to be alert and able during the actual escape. But it would then again be a question of willingness to cooperate.

As Alex pondered this dilemma, she crossed into the middle of the yard and noticed Rachel heading quickly in her direction. The girl was half walking, half jogging as if she wanted to go faster but wasn't sure she should.

"Where have you been?" Rachel asked as soon as she was close.

"What do you mean?"

"I've been looking for you everywhere."

Alex, guard up, said, "I was in the infirmary. My arm."

"Oh," Rachel said as she glanced at the bandaged forearm, then just as quickly seemed to forget about it. "Come on."

She turned back toward the cellblocks.

"Where?"

"It's your friend, what's-her-name—Frida, right?"

"What about her?"

"She's hurt pretty bad."

TWENTY FOUR

ALEX FOLLOWED RACHEL into Building One, and to a cell on the first floor.

The only one inside was Frida, lying on a lower bunk.

Someone had beaten the hell out of her. Her face was bruised and bloody, her arms cut and scraped. Her dirty dress was ripped in several places, one across her belly exposing a welt at least two inches long.

Alex dropped to her knees next to the bed and said, "What the hell happened?"

Rachel, who stood in the doorway, held her hands up in surrender. "I wasn't here. I just found her lying right outside the cell."

"You didn't see anything?"

Rachel said, "It happened before I got here, okay?"

Frida's eyes were closed, her teeth clenched in pain.

Alex softened. "Frida? Frida, can you hear me?"

A low, almost imperceptible moan escaped the girl's lips.

"I couldn't get her to talk, either," Rachel said.

Alex looked back at her. "Why didn't you take her to the infirmary?"

"I thought moving her onto the bed was already taking a chance," Rachel said.

"You could have at least gotten a guard."

She started backing out of the cell. "Look, I didn't want to get involved, all right? I knew she was your friend, so I went looking for you."

"Well, get a guard now."

"I've already done my job. This is your deal, not mine."

With that, she left.

"God*dammit,*" Alex said under her breath.

Running her fingers lightly over Frida's skin, she summoned up her combat training and checked for obvious broken bones. Everything seemed to be in place, but who knew what kind of internal damage there was?

The sooner Frida received medical attention, the better.

"Frida, open your eyes."

The girl moaned again.

"Come on," Alex said. "Open your eyes."

A slit appeared across Frida's left eye as the lids parted. Her right, already swelling, wasn't going to open at all.

Alex touched the girl's forehead. "I'm gonna help you up, all right?"

Considering her own residual pain, she thought that might be easier said than done. But she had to try. Frida's face, however, became tinged with fear, and she moaned again.

"You need help," Alex insisted. "I've gotta get you to the doctor."

Gingerly, she slipped an arm under the girl's shoulder and another under her legs. Alex's forearm screamed in agony as she lifted Frida off the mattress, and hoisted her out of the bed. Grunting, Alex swiveled one of Frida's legs up so that her foot was flat on the ground, then did the same with the other.

A loud groan flew out of Frida's mouth as Alex stood all the way up.

"Hang in there. The hard part's done."

The size of the cell doorway forced Alex to shuffle sideways to pass through without banging Frida against the bars. Once she was in the common area, she moved as quickly as she could toward the exit.

There were dozens of prisoners right outside the entrance to Building One, milling around, bullshitting, and trying to stay out of the sun. When Alex made it outside with Frida, they all turned to look, their conversations dying mid-sentence.

One inmate moved in closer, trying to see who it was Alex was carrying.

"Out of the way!" Alex shouted as several more women moved into her path. "Move! Move!"

Most of them stepped to the side, largely because they had no choice the way Alex was moving, but the first inmate stood her ground.

"Who that?" she said, nodding at Frida.

"None of your goddamn business. Now get out of the way!"

Instead of moving, the woman scowled, narrowing her eyes.

Alex had no time to deal with this shit. She turned as if she was going to walk back the way she'd come, then suddenly kicked backward, ramming her right heel into the woman's stomach.

There was a sudden exhalation of breath and a thunderous groan. As Alex turned back around, the woman dropped to her knees, clutching her abdomen.

Alex moved around her without further incident and continued toward the administration building.

The guards finally showed up when she was about three quarters of the way across the yard. They shouted at her, probably to get her to stop, but she kept moving. It took two of them grabbing her by the shoulders to finally stop her.

The guard who had taken Alex to her cell when she'd first arrived pointed at Frida, and said, "You do?"

"Do you think I'd be trying to get her help if I did?"

It was clear she had far exceeded his ability to understand.

"Help," she said. "My friend needs help. Doctor!"

That seemed to do the trick. Two of the guards took Frida from Alex and hurried toward the entrance to the admin building. The two who had been holding Alex hadn't let go, however, and started shouting questions at her.

She rolled her eyes and looked up at the sky. "How many

213

goddamn times do I have to say this? *I don't understand you.*"

The employment exam for this shit box had to be a cinch.

After throwing a few more unintelligible phrases at her, they took her into the administration building and to a windowless room on the first floor. There were three chairs along the wall opposite the door, all bolted to the floor. A guard shoved her into one and they left her alone.

Twenty minutes passed before the door opened again. While it was no big shock that one of her new visitors was the warden, the presence of Dr. Teterya surprised her.

The warden spoke first, then Teterya said, "We would like to know what happened to girl."

"What does it look like? Someone beat her up."

Teterya looked uncomfortable as he translated this for the warden. Apparently the doctor was the best English speaker in the prison at the moment.

The warden asked another question.

"You did not do this to her?"

Alex shook her head in disbelief. "What is wrong with you people? Why would I be trying to get her help if I was the one who hurt her?"

The questions continued for several more minutes. Then Teterya said, "We would like to examine you to make sure what you say is true."

"Have at it," Alex told him.

The warden looked on as the doctor checked her face and hands. While she'd had more than her share of fights over the last couple days, none of her injuries equaled what had been done to Frida.

When Teterya got to her arms, the warden pointed at the gauze bandage that now had a bit of blood seeping through. He said something and the doctor replied, most likely explaining to the man that the injury was a day old and had nothing to do with Frida.

It took a while before the warden looked fully satisfied. Once that happened, he was quick to leave.

"I will send nurse to bandage arm again," Teterya said, keeping his voice formal even though they were alone.

"So you all believe me now?"

"You were being what they call Good Samaritan, yes?"

"That's right."

"Then okay. Is no problem."

He started to leave.

"The girl?" Alex asked. "Will she be all right?"

He stopped at the door. "She hurt very bad, but will be okay in few days." He hesitated before adding, "Night doctor watch her tonight, and I check her again when I come in tomorrow morning."

Message received. "Thank you."

"Tomorrow I send for you midday. Want to check your arm again."

Alex kept her face passive, but inside she cringed. The comment had been unnecessary, especially since it had come out more wooden than she would have liked. Hopefully, if anyone was listening in, their English wasn't good enough to pick it up.

"Whatever you say," she told him. "You're the doc."

As soon as her bandage had been changed—not by Irina, but another nurse—Alex was taken back outside, where the sun had begun to dip.

Unfortunately, the temperature hadn't. She was wiping sweat from her brow before she was even halfway back to the cellblocks.

As she walked, she couldn't help but notice that whenever she neared a group of other prisoners, several would glance at her as if they could see right through her false identity, and knew she was not who she claimed to be.

Way to keep your head down, Alex.

TWENTY FIVE

WHEN COOPER WENT to check the drop box, Deuce stayed inside the old barn. Their prisoner was out cold, the pain pills from the medical kit working exactly as advertised. The plan was to keep him under until they executed the abort mission later that evening. Then they'd drop him somewhere he could find help, and get the hell out of Dodge.

Deuce was a little surprised that Cooper hadn't simply put a bullet in the guy's brain. He figured Stonewell was a take-no-prisoners type of outfit, and Cooper was Stonewell through and through.

Or was he?

Maybe Deuce had been wrong about the guy. Maybe behind that cool, hard-ass exterior he was more of a human being than he liked to let on. Deuce had known a lot of former soldiers like him and had discovered that, unlike Deuce himself, they felt uncomfortable showing they had a heart, as if this somehow might compromise their manhood.

He also knew there had once been something between Cooper and Alex, something more than shared combat experiences. And he wasn't quite sure how he felt about that.

Had they been lovers?

Not that it was any of Deuce's business. But he cared about Alex, and didn't want this renewed contact to lead to anything that might hurt her.

If that happened, *he* would have to hurt Cooper.

He was in the process of heating up some canned stew when Cooper returned carrying an envelope, the top ripped open.

"What time do we pick her up?" Deuce asked.

Grimacing, Cooper handed him the note.

Deuce pulled out the sheet of paper and unfolded it, immediately recognizing Alex's handwriting:

NEGATIVE ON ABORT. CONTACTED AK THIS
AFTERNOON. EXTRACT TOMORROW APPROX.
9PM. RENDEZVOUS ABANDONED BUILDING,
WEST OF PRISON, OUTSIDE FENCE.

"Well, fuck me," he said quietly.

He handed the note and envelope back to Cooper, thinking that he and Alex would need to have a little talk when all of this was over.

A talk about unnecessary risks.

"Looks like we're still on," Cooper said.

"That it does," Deuce murmured. "That it does."

TWENTY SIX

THE GUARDS SHOWED up in Building One's kitchen right on schedule.

At a few minutes before noon the next morning, Alex washed her hands, removed her apron, and followed them to the infirmary.

"How's Frida?" she asked Teterya once they were safely inside one of the infirmary's secure cells.

"Frida?"

"The prisoner I helped yesterday."

"Ah," the doctor said. "Arcos. Come."

He took her to the cell two doors down. Frida was on the bed. While the blood had been cleaned from her face and arms, her bruises looked worse than ever. The good thing was that she was asleep.

"Ribs broken. Three," Teterya said. "Many, many, uh, brew?"

"Bruises."

"Yes, bruises. All over arms and body. But is lucky. No injuries inside." He paused. "You know who do this?"

Alex had a pretty good idea. It had to be that bitch Kalyna. But she shrugged and said, "Could've been anyone."

"Well, if happen again, think she not live. She very...delicate?"

Alex didn't want to think about it. She had enough issues to worry about without adding Frida's problems to the mix. But the girl had been kind to her from the beginning. It was hard to ignore what had happened to her, and what could very well happen again.

Back in her room, Alex changed into the nurse's outfit,

with Irina once more helping her with her hair. Once the hat and glasses were in place, she followed Dr. Teterya back down to the tunnel.

As expected, El-Hashim and her friends were sitting in the living area, waiting for them to arrive.

Alex said, "Shall we go to one of the bedrooms again?"

"Here is fine," El-Hashim told her, gesturing to a chair. "My friends are well aware of our discussions."

Teterya cleared his throat. "I need to use the toilet."

El-Hashim smirked. "Again, Doctor? You miss so much when you do."

He cleared his throat a second time, then headed for the bathroom.

Once the door closed behind him, Alex took the proffered seat. "What's it to be?"

El-Hashim smiled. "You are definitely your father's daughter. Always right to business."

"You believe me, then."

"I believed you yesterday, but, in my life, I have found it prudent to not always rely on instinct."

"Fair enough. So again, what's it to be?"

El-Hashim leaned back in her chair. "Do you know why I'm here?"

"You were arrested."

"But do you know why?"

"No," Alex said.

"Your father didn't mention it?"

"Not a word. We don't...talk much."

"Interesting." She smiled. "He was there, you know."

Alex froze, all other thoughts forgotten. "What?"

"Yes. He was arrested, too."

It took a second for the words to sink in. Dear God, was her dad also sitting in a Crimean prison at that very moment?

Alex tried to gather herself. "Funny. He didn't mention it."

"Oh? How do you communicate with him?"

"Online. Dummy accounts. E-mails. The occasional

text."

"No phone calls?"

Alex shook her head. "Like I said, we don't talk much. What happened?"

El-Hashim studied her face, then smiled again. "Your father and I were meeting in Yalta. The nature of what we had to discuss involved getting together several times over a two-day period. Our last meeting was to take place at a café a few blocks from the sea. He was there first. Upon seeing me when I entered, he stood to greet me. As we were saying our hellos, the police moved in. Not only did they take your father and me but also my friends who were stationed along the street." She gestured toward her three companions. "We were all processed at the police station, then my friends and I were sent here."

"And my father?"

"He really didn't tell you any of this?"

"I told you before, we lead separate lives. I'm not involved in his business unless he really needs me. I usually don't *want* to know what's going on."

"But now you're curious."

"I am this time, because I'm an active participant. It's not so much that I want to know, but that I *need* to know, in case it has a bearing on how we proceed."

A perceptive grin. "And because, deep down, you really do want to know."

Alex kept quiet.

After a moment, El-Hashim said, "Your father was supposed to be taken to a prison in the middle of the peninsula. But one thing Frank Poe has at his disposal is a very capable network. The car transporting him turned up full of bullet holes at the bottom of a hill about forty miles away. The driver was still strapped behind the wheel and your father was gone."

Alex hadn't realized she was leaning so far forward. She sat back, trying to act as if the news wasn't all that surprising.

But she was hurting inside.

Her father escaping at the cost of a policeman's life? That wasn't the man she knew. That wasn't the dad who taught her how to swim or change a tire or swing dance. It especially wasn't the dad who'd taught her how to know the difference between right and wrong.

"Too bad you don't have as capable of a network," she said.

"Our areas of specialty are...different," El-Hashim said. "My job is more subtle, behind the scenes. We rely more on our clients' help when necessary."

An opening. "And hence the reason I'm here," Alex said.

"So it would seem."

"I need your answer. Are you coming with me, or are you going to stay and take your chances?"

"It would be very difficult to leave my friends behind."

"The only reason the Ukrainian government hasn't been bragging about your capture is because they haven't yet figured out who you are. My guess is that it was my father they were really after and you just got caught up in it. But now that he's gone, their attention's going to turn to you sooner than you want, and when they *do* realize who you are, that egg on their faces for losing my father will be a distant memory. You'll suddenly become a very big fish to a government that has little reason to boast." She smiled. "Then again, if you *also* disappear, how much will they be able to pin on your friends? Another month, maybe two, and they'll all be released."

"There is no way we can know that for sure," El-Hashim said.

"You're right. Life is full of uncertainty. It's up to you."

Silence descended, then Marie leaned in and whispered something in El-Hashim's ear.

"My friends are concerned about my safety," El-Hashim said.

"As they should be."

"They want you to know if anything happens to me, it is you who will pay."

"I'm afraid I can't guarantee anything, and I don't respond well to threats." Alex stood up, not in a huff, but in a manner that indicated business was business. "We won't simply be walking out of here. This is dangerous, and if you get hurt, you get hurt. But it won't be because of something I've done." She took a breath. "Consider this a missed opportunity."

As she stepped away from the chair, El-Hashim said, "I did not tell you no."

"You haven't really told me *anything*. I've laid out the ground rules, so you either live with them or you don't."

El-Hashim stood up. "If something happens to me, it happens. Does that work for you?"

Alex purposely hesitated, then nodded. "So that's a yes?"

"Correct."

Alex studied her a moment, and sat back down. "Then this is what I need you to do."

TWENTY SEVEN

TETERYA SUGGESTED THAT Alex stay in the infirmary for the duration. If she were to leave, he would have to summon her again, and that might raise unnecessary attention.

He had a point, but Alex shook her head. "I need to do something first. Send for me right after dinner. I'll be ready then."

Before she left, she requested two items to take with her.

"Why?" the doctor asked, surprised.

"Better if you don't know."

He looked nervous. "I cannot have this as problem for me later."

"It won't be."

She could see that he wasn't sure if he could believe her, but he collected the things she wanted and gave them to her.

Back in with the general population, she moved in and out of the crowds until she found who she was looking for. Instead of approaching her, however, Alex held back and watched.

When dinner came, she fell in line three people behind the woman. Dinner was a variation of the slop from the night before. It might well have been the very same batch, doctored up to look new. Who could tell? Alex took her share, grabbed a stale roll, and loitered beyond the end of the serving area until the woman had taken a seat.

Approaching casually so as not to draw any attention, Alex surreptitiously slipped a note next to the woman's plate. She then took a seat three tables back where she could watch.

For several minutes she wondered if the woman would even notice the piece of paper, but finally the side of the inmate's palm brushed against it. She picked it up, opened it, and read the two numbers inside. One was the number of her own cell. The other was a time: twelve minutes from now.

The woman crumbled the note in her fist, and glanced side to side. Alex ducked down, but it wasn't necessary. The woman never looked behind her.

Quickly, Alex rose and left the room, then hurried up to the fourth floor, stepping into the cellblock directly adjacent to the one in which the woman's cell was located. Leaning against the wall by the door, she pulled her arm into her dress and reached into the waistband of her panties.

Removing the two items Dr. Teterya gave her, she brought her arm back out, uncapped the needle at the end of the syringe, stuck it into the bottle, and drew the liquid into the cylinder.

Now she just had to wait.

Right on schedule, she heard the woman clomping across the concrete at the far end of the fourth floor. When the steps neared the neighboring cellblock, they slowed for a moment then picked up again, heading for the row of cells on the left side.

The steps grew muffled and stopped. The woman was in her cell, exactly where Alex wanted her.

Pushing away from the wall, Alex quietly entered the block and approached the woman's cell from the side so as not to be seen. She stopped at the edge of the bars, set the syringe on the floor next to the wall, and stepped out.

"You came," she said.

Kalyna was standing only a few feet in. The moment she realized it was Alex who'd passed her the note, her eyes shrank to slits. She spat out a word.

Alex felt safe to assume that if it was a greeting, it wasn't a friendly one.

"Nice to see you, too."

"What you want?" Kalyna said. "Same your friend? Is why you here?"

"I *am* here about my friend, but—"

"Good."

Kalyna rushed toward the doorway of the cell, her arms outstretched so she could grab Alex. Alex took a half step back, and ducked down right before Kalyna could reach her.

Using her whole body, Alex thrust her palm up into Kalyna's chin and smashed the woman's teeth together, the loud clack echoing through the block.

Kalyna staggered backward into the cell, stunned.

Not waiting for her to regain her senses, Alex punched Kalyna in the gut, just below the rib cage.

Doubling over, Kalyna fell against the end of the bunk bed.

Alex hit her again and again, punching her like one of the bags back at Ackerman's Gym.

Stomach.

Arms.

Ribs.

A cartilage-cracking blow to the nose.

Kalyna tried feebly to block the first few hits, but was soon using whatever strength she had left to stay on her feet.

"When you have someone on the ropes, you can never let up," Emerick had preached over and over.

He would have been proud of Alex at that moment. She didn't let up until Kalyna started to slide to the floor.

"No, you don't," she said, grabbing the woman under the shoulders.

She forced Kalyna to walk around the end of the beds.

"Which one's yours?" she asked.

Kalyna, her head hanging low, said nothing.

Alex slapped her across the face. "Which bed's yours?"

With effort, Kalyna looked up and glanced at the lower bed of the rear set of bunks. Alex walked her over there, then pushed her onto the mattress. Kalyna fell onto her ass, and leaned back against the wall with a moan.

Alex retrieved the syringe and moved back into the cell.

"You're not a very nice person," Alex said, crouching down to Kalyna's eye level. "I don't like people who aren't nice."

Kalyna eyed her through half-open lids. There was fear now in her gaze, not likely an emotion she experienced often. But there was also still a bit of defiance.

"I know what you're thinking. I know you're telling yourself that tomorrow, or the next day, you're going to find me and return the favor. But sorry, that's not gonna happen. What's gonna happen is that your habit of beating on others is gonna stop. Maybe you don't believe me, but here's the thing. People already know I beat you once. They're gonna see you now, see your broken nose there, and know I did it again. They'll know you aren't as tough as you pretend to be. And they'll stand up to you. And they'll come at you. And there will be *nothing you can do about it*." She paused. "Nod if you understand me."

Kalyna stared at her, unmoving, for several seconds, breathing raggedly through her open mouth. Finally she nodded.

"Good," Alex said. "I have one more surprise for you." She lifted her hand and wiggled the syringe in the air.

Kalyna's eyelids opened wider. She pressed herself against the wall, as if hoping she could push through it.

"Don't worry," Alex said. "This is gonna help you sleep, for a nice long time. Hell, it might even be lunch tomorrow before you wake up. It'll give your pain some time to dull." She smiled. "Consider this a favor. You're welcome."

Alex made like she was about to lean in and stab the needle into the woman's arm. The moment Kalyna tried to twist away from her, Alex changed directions and drove the tip into the woman's thigh.

Kalyna cried out and tried to snatch the syringe, but Alex shoved her in the chest, knocking her against the wall. As soon as all of the drug was administered, she pulled out the needle.

"You might want to lie down," she said.

Kalyna, drawing on whatever energy she had left, lunged forward. Alex stepped to the side, easily avoiding her.

With an angry growl, Kalyna staggered off the bed and onto her feet. The moment she was standing, she began to sway, and only kept from falling by grabbing the top bunk.

As Kalyna took an unsteady step toward Alex, the woman began to blink slowly. She thrust her other hand out, placing it against the wall. She blinked again, her eyes remaining closed for nearly a second this time. When she opened them, she looked back at her bunk, took a half turn toward it and promptly fell on the floor.

"Dammit," Alex said under her breath.

The last thing she needed was for someone to find Kalyna passed out in the middle of her cell. It would most likely mean a trip to the infirmary for the night, and drug or no drug, Alex didn't like the idea of the woman being anywhere near that place on this particular evening.

"I *told* you to lie down," she said as she manhandled Kalyna back onto her mattress.

Rolling the woman toward the wall, Alex pulled the blanket over her, then stood back and surveyed her work.

Other than Kalyna seeming to have fallen asleep so early, nothing looked out of the ordinary. It would undoubtedly be a bit of a problem come cell-check time, but at most, Dr. Teterya or Irina would be called out to check on the unresponsive inmate, and could massage the story appropriately.

With a satisfied nod, Alex left the cell and turned for the exit. But the second she stepped out, she saw she was not the only one on the cellblock. Rachel was there, standing just inside the cellblock door.

"That's not your cell," Rachel said.

As Alex slipped the hand holding the syringe and bottle behind her back, she wondered how long Rachel had been there. Had she heard any of the fight?

"Just helping a friend," Alex said, keeping her expression neutral, and continuing toward the door. "She wasn't feeling well."

"Who?"

"Just a friend. I doubt you know her."

As Alex passed, Rachel followed. "I might."

Alex paused in the doorway. "Elena. From Bulgaria. Know her?"

A frown and a shake of the head. "No. I don't."

Alex shrugged. "It's a big place." She then asked the question that was uppermost in her mind. "So what exactly are *you* doing in here? Your cell's not up here."

Rachel looked embarrassed. "I saw you come into the building and got curious. I've been looking for you."

"Why?" Alex asked calmly, but inside she was far from relaxed.

"I felt...bad about earlier," Rachel said. "You know, with Frida. I wanted to apologize, and, well, ask if you knew how she's doing."

Alex shook her head. "They were still examining her when they sent me back out. And as far as feeling bad, don't worry about it. It's fine."

Rachel looked relieved. "Thanks. This place just gets to me sometimes."

"It gets to all of us."

Rachel nodded and walked over. "Don't take this wrong, but I'm glad you're here. It's good to have a friend like you."

"Thanks, I think," Alex said, then stepped through the door.

Rachel followed her, all interest in Kalyna's cell apparently gone, which was certainly a relief. "You wanna play some cards before they lock us in?"

"Thanks, but not tonight. I'm not feeling too good myself. Think I'll just head back to my bunk and lie down."

"Jesus," Rachel said, "is something going around?"

"Could be."

As they approached the door to the fourth-floor toilets, Alex said, "I need to make a pit stop."

"Okay, I'll wait here for you."

"You don't have to do that."

"No problem," Rachel said.

Alex flashed her a smile, and stepped inside the restroom. Moving to the toilet farthest from the door, she flushed the syringe and bottle, then waited a few extra minutes for authenticity's sake before heading back out.

Alex parted with Rachel at the third-floor landing. Rachel continued down the stairs while Alex went to her cell, breathing the sigh of relief she'd been holding in for the last several minutes.

Twenty minutes later, the guards arrived with orders from Dr. Teterya to take her to the infirmary.

TWENTY EIGHT

"WE'RE CLEARING OUT now to the observation point," Cooper said into the phone. "Will move in for extract at the appointed time."

"Let me know the second you have El-Hashim," McElroy told him.

"Will do."

"Don't fuck this up."

"Thanks for the vote of confidence."

Cooper clicked off before McElroy could reply.

Asshole.

Their camp had already been struck and packed into the back of the car. The only thing left in the roofless barn was the unconscious guard they'd taken prisoner.

"I was thinking maybe we should leave him tied up," Deuce said. "That way it gives us a little extra time if he wakes early."

Cooper doubted that would happen, but Deuce's concern was sound. Still, they couldn't leave the guy behind with no way to get loose. Out here, he might starve to death before anyone found him. They had no idea how much of a threat the guard really was, but killing an enemy with a gun in your face was one thing. Leaving a man to potentially die simply because he'd made a few bad choices was something else altogether.

Removing the hunting knife from his belt, Cooper drove it into the barn's hard earth floor a good thirty feet from where the guard was tied up. The guy wouldn't see it when he first came to, but he'd eventually find it.

Cooper thought it was the best they could do.

As he stood back up, Deuce gave him a nod of approval.

"All right," Cooper said. "Let's get out of here."

They drove out to the main highway, and continued exactly half a mile past the prison turnoff before veering onto a dirt access road between two fields.

The copse of trees they had been using for cover was another two hundred yards in. They parked the car out of sight behind it, and hiked to the top of the hill that overlooked the prison.

When they reached the summit, they stretched out on their stomachs, and Cooper gave Deuce one of the two sets of binoculars in his pack. The other he used for himself, training it on the facility below.

All looked as it should.

He swung the glasses to the right, following a gently sloping field to where it suddenly dropped off into a shallow ravine in the west. Butted up to the side was a stone building that bore a passing resemblance to the barn they'd been camping in—old and roofless. From their current position, they could see almost the entire structure, but from most everywhere else, the ravine would hide all but the very tops of the walls.

Cooper switched his binoculars to night vision, and saw exactly what he expected.

No one.

That would soon change.

Hopefully.

TWENTY NINE

DR. TETERYA'S FEET tapped rhythmically as he paced the infirmary's tiled floor.

He had never in his life felt so tense. For the millionth time that day, he wished he had said no to the man who had approached him about assisting in the escape. He was sure now that something would go wrong, and instead of being a doctor at a prison, he'd be a doctor *in* one.

And then there was Irina. Bringing her into this made it even worse. If they were caught, it was likely she'd be incarcerated in this very facility.

Teterya had tried to think of a way they could back out, but Irina had been right. Their only choice was to move forward and do their part, praying it would come off without a hitch.

Behind him, the door to the back room opened. He turned as Irina stepped out.

"Is everything okay?" he asked, keeping his voice low.

Other than the two women in the isolation cells, he and Irina were the only people in the infirmary, but the nature of this night called for caution.

"She's changed and ready," Irina said.

"And Arcos?"

"Still asleep."

He nodded, and began pacing again.

The waiting was killing him. The phone call he was expecting hadn't yet come.

Why, he didn't know.

Had something gone wrong? Were guards on their way at this very moment to arrest them?

Teterya involuntarily flicked his gaze toward the infirmary's main door. Through the window beside it, he saw that the hallway was empty.

But how long would it stay that way?

How long before—

Stop, he told himself. He halted in the middle of the room and closed his eyes, taking several deep, calming breaths.

Relax. Everything will be fine. Everything will—

The phone rang.

He exchanged a startled look with Irina, and nodded. The phone on the wall was closest to her, so she went over and answered it.

"Infirmary," she said, and listened. "One moment."

She held out the receiver to him.

Teterya took one more breath, accepted the phone, and put it to his ear. "This is Dr. Teterya."

"Doctor, this is Captain Balanchuk, Isolation."

Teterya swallowed. "Yes, Captain?"

"We have an inmate in need of medical attention."

The doctor tried to calm himself. "Her name?"

The guard gave him the name the prison had for El-Hashim.

Teterya waited several seconds to give the impression he was consulting the prisoner log. "Oh, yes," he said. "What's the complaint?"

"It seems to be stomach related. She appears to be in a lot of pain."

Teterya did his best to feign annoyance. "Appears? Or *is?*"

He didn't want it to look too easy. This wouldn't be the first time an inmate had pretended to be sick in hopes of getting special treatment, and Teterya's skepticism would further sell their ruse.

"That's why I'm calling," Balanchuk said. "I thought you might be able to advise me before we take this any further."

Teterya had to play this very carefully.

"I can't diagnose a patient over the phone, Captain, but if she has an upset stomach, you have medicine for that. Give her a dose and send her back to her cell."

"It isn't nausea," Balanchuk said. "She's claiming outright pain, a severe tenderness in the abdomen."

"Oh? And where is it located?"

"On the right."

Teterya paused, mentally counting to three. "I see," he said, now feigning a touch of concern. "If this is legitimate, it could be serious. Perhaps I should come take a look."

He waited, half expecting Balanchuk to dismiss the idea, but Balanchuk said, "Very good, Doctor. Please make it a priority."

"I'm on my way."

Teterya moved to the wall, hung up, and turned to Irina. Now that the game was on, he felt focused and alert, no longer distracted by his fears.

"You'd better get Powell," he said. "And make doubly sure she looks the part."

Irina nodded, walked over, and hurriedly kissed him. "Be careful."

ALEX FOLLOWED TETERYA down the stairs to the first floor, but instead of using the underground passage to the isolation unit, the doctor moved toward the exit that led to the yard.

"Where are you going?" she whispered. "What about the tunnel?"

"Look strange, we try take now. We use when prisoners in yard only."

She put a hand on his arm, stopping him. "But won't the guards at the security check be the same ones who were there when I was brought in tonight?"

"Yes."

"*Hello?*" she said, pointing at her face. "This isn't a mask."

She had her file folder and was wearing the glasses

again, with the hat topping Irina's expertly rendered hairstyle. But she felt far from confident that it was enough to fool someone who had seen her only an hour earlier.

"They not expect prisoner to be dressed like nurse," Teterya told her. "Last thing on mind. I go first, keep attention on me. You come through quickly, keep eyes on file, not them."

In other words, the same drill as before, but a lot riskier this time. "And if they look at me?"

"They bored and lazy men. They see glasses, not face."

Teterya couldn't guarantee this, of course, but what choice did Alex have?

She nodded and felt a knot taking shape in her intestines as they started walking again.

When they neared the security gate, she fell a few steps behind Teterya and opened the file folder, keeping her head down as she flipped through the pages. The doctor said something to the two guards manning the station, then laughed. They chuckled in return. A reply by one of them was followed by loud laughter from all three, and somewhere in the middle of it all, a buzzer sounded and the gate swung open.

The doctor kept talking, turning to face the guards as Alex slipped past behind him and went through the gate, not stopping until she was several feet beyond.

There were a few more laughs, then the doctor stepped through and joined her on the other side. He touched her arm, and they continued to the exit.

They had nearly reached it when one of the guards called out to them—sharp and abrupt.

Alex froze, but Teterya squeezed her arm and turned. He and the guard had a quick exchange, then he turned back to Alex, looking relieved.

"What did he want?" she asked quietly.

"He ask me play cards tonight." Teterya paused with a slight grimace on his face. "He tell me bring pretty nurse, too."

As the knot in Alex's stomach hardened, the exit door buzzed open without incident, and they stepped into the yard.

Floodlights lit the grounds, leaving no corner of darkness, and making it impossible for anyone to cross without being seen from one of the towers.

Dirt crunched under their feet as they walked around the east side of Building Three, toward the door in the back wall that led to the isolation section.

Alex couldn't see any of the guards in the towers, but felt their gazes on her. If any of them was using a scope or binoculars, she could only hope he was concentrating on her body and not her face.

Just before she and Teterya reached the door, it swung open, revealing three guards waiting inside. Teterya shared a few quick words with them before they walked as a group into the isolation building.

When they stepped into El-Hashim's suite, her two bodyguards were in the living area.

"Where is the sick prisoner?" Teterya asked them.

One of the women pointed toward a bedroom door.

The doctor spoke quietly to the three prison guards, and they stayed back as he and Alex went inside.

El-Hashim, still clad in her hijab, was lying in bed, Marie sitting in a chair beside her. As soon as Alex closed the door, El-Hashim threw her blanket off and stood up.

"You're late," Teterya told her.

El-Hashim and Marie shared a look. "Marie is coming with me."

"That's not the plan," Alex said.

El-Hashim held up a hand. "To the infirmary. If everything is as you have said, she'll stay there. This is not a negotiable point."

"We have very limited room," Teterya said.

"Nonnegotiable."

"Fine," Alex told her.

She didn't like it at all, but they didn't have time to argue. And if Marie was only going as far as the infirmary, then that shouldn't be a problem.

They gave it a few more minutes before El-Hashim lay back down and started groaning softly as the doctor called in one of the guards. They had a quick conference and the guard made a call on his radio. The back and forth lasted only seconds, then the guard nodded to Teterya.

Looking over at the three women, Teterya said in English, "We go now." He pointed at Marie. "You will help."

"Of course," she said, bowing her head.

Once El-Hashim was propped between Marie and Alex, they headed out. As much as they all wanted the trip to go as quickly as possible, they had to keep up the appearance that El-Hashim was ill, which necessitated a much slower pace.

With known prisoners now in their party, two of the guards stayed with the group as they reentered the general population section and slow-walked their way to the administration building.

Passing through the checkpoint was much easier this time, the attention of the gatekeepers directed at Marie and a groaning El-Hashim.

Rather than take the stairs, the group squeezed into a small, rarely used elevator, and took it up one floor to the infirmary level. As they were exiting the car, the infirmary door opened down the hall, and Irina stepped into the corridor, looking nervous.

Something was wrong.

While Alex, El-Hashim, and Marie maintained their slow pace, Teterya rushed ahead. Irina started speaking to him before he reached her. Teterya looked past her into the infirmary, and glanced back at Alex and the others.

There was concern in his eyes, but he was trying to hide it.

Alex hoped the guards didn't notice.

Addressing El-Hashim, he cleared his throat and said, "Another inmate is sick and come here while we getting you. Is okay. Not problem. We still have room for you."

Alex glanced at El-Hashim and Marie, and saw the

questioning looks on their faces. She smiled, trying to put them at ease.

As they entered the infirmary, Alex saw that a curtain had been drawn around one of the examination stations, and sitting on a chair in front of it was another guard, reading a newspaper.

But it wasn't just any guard.

It was the one with the birthmark. Who knew her by name.

Wonderful.

Teterya spoke to her in Ukrainian and gestured. Alex nodded, and she and Marie guided El-Hashim toward the back room.

The problem was, they couldn't get there without passing the guard. And the way they were positioned—with El-Hashim between them—Alex was on the guard's side of the aisle. There was no way she could switch sides without calling attention to herself.

The knot in her stomach returned.

As they neared the guard, Alex moved half a step in front of the others and twisted her body slightly, so that her back was partially toward him. They were only a few feet away when the guard peeked over his paper, then jumped to his feet to give them room as he said something to Alex, sounding annoyed.

Keeping her back to him as much as possible, she made a grunting sound that she hoped would convey her thanks, but he repeated himself as if expecting an answer.

Fuck.

Alex had no earthly idea how to reply to him. But before she could grunt again, she heard Teterya call out and the guard suddenly turned away from her, his footsteps clacking on the tile.

Relieved but still tense, Alex picked up her pace, forcing the other two to also speed up. The moment they stepped into the back room, she swung the door shut.

"Off to the side," she whispered, motioning them away

from the door's window.

Once out of the line of sight, El-Hashim scowled at Alex. "What is going on? Who is this other pri—"

"Shh," Alex said, raising a finger to her lips.

Without explaining, she tiptoed over to the room Frida was in and peeked inside. The girl was still asleep. Alex shut the door and turned back to the others.

"Another one?" El-Hashim said incredulously. "Who is in that room?"

Alex held up a hand. "Relax, it's just a patient. No one who will be a problem."

El-Hashim didn't look reassured.

"And the one behind the curtain?" Marie said. "Who is she?"

"I don't know," Alex whispered. "But again, not an issue. The doctor will take care of her, send her back to her cell, and then we'll be out of here."

She moved over to the main door and peeked through the window. While the guard with the newspaper had returned to his chair, the ones who had been part of their group seemed to have left.

She wanted to go out there and find out what was going on, but she knew the minute she stepped through the doorway, the guard would recognize her for sure. So she was stuck in here until he left.

Glancing around, her gaze landed on the two small stacks of clothes on a shelf just outside the isolation room she'd been using earlier.

No sense in wasting time.

She grabbed the clothes and gave one set to El-Hashim. "Put these on."

"Why?"

"That gray dress marks you," Alex said. "When we get out, that's the last thing you want to be wearing." She gestured toward the empty isolation cell at the far end. "You can change in there."

With a brief hesitation, El-Hashim carried the clothes

into the cell. Alex went into her temporary cell, shucked her nurse's garb, and changed into the pair of dark pants and black, long-sleeve T-shirt that Irina had provided. When she stepped out again, El-Hashim was waiting for her, dressed in a similar outfit.

There was one problem, however.

"You're gonna have to lose the scarf," Alex said.

Involuntarily, El-Hashim put a hand to her cheek. "No. Impossible."

"Do you want this to work or not?" Alex said. "You wear that thing, you'll be a neon target. You'll be spotted and taken back in before you even get a chance to breathe free air. Besides, I'm told the route we're taking gets pretty tight. I can't have you choking to death if that thing gets hung up on something."

"It stays on," El-Hashim told her.

They locked gazes. "It comes off, or you're not going."

El-Hashim was the first to blink. "A compromise. It stays on until it needs to come off."

"It needs to come off now."

"No, it doesn't. You know that."

Alex pressed her lips tightly together, then said, "Fine. But when I say it's time, it's time."

"Very well."

Alex was about to check the window again, when she heard footsteps heading their way. "Get in the cell," she said. "Both of you."

The two women moved hurriedly into the isolation cell that El-Hashim had used to change clothes, Alex right behind them. Making sure the door's observation window was open, Alex pulled the door shut behind her, stopping short of engaging the latch.

She looked through the narrow window. Across the room, Teterya entered and looked around, confused. "Powell?"

"Wait here," Alex told El-Hashim and Marie.

She exited the cell, and met Teterya near the center of

the room.

"We have problem," he said.

"What now?"

He tilted his head in the direction of the examination area. "Prisoner having pain in head and chest."

"Well, give her something for it and send her back to her cell."

"She complain very strong, you know? It not look good I send her back. Guard will think something wrong. Better she stay here."

Alex thought for a moment. This was more a nuisance than anything else.

"Okay, okay," she said. "Put her in the room I was using. I'll stay with the others."

He looked relieved.

As he turned away, Alex said, "And make it fast. I don't want us to be here any longer than we have to be."

"Not worry," he said. "I feel same."

THIRTY

TETERYA PULLED THE curtain back and smiled.

"You stay tonight so can keep check on you," he said, and handed her two pills. "For sleep, will make less your pain, too." He gestured. "Water and glass on table beside you. One moment, take you to room, okay?"

The prisoner nodded, her voice strained. "Thank you, Doctor."

He closed the curtain again as he left. To the guard he said, "The prisoner will be staying here. Please put it in the log to have someone check with us in the morning. She should be fine by then."

The guard stood up. "Yes, sir. I will. Would you like me to wait until she's in one of your cells?"

"Does she have any history of violence?"

"None that I'm aware of."

"In that case, I think we'll be fine. You can go."

The guard left, and for a second, Teterya let his shoulders sag, belying the confident front he'd been projecting. The game may have been on, but it wasn't going as smoothly as it should be, and his focus was wavering.

Irina approached and touched his arm. Keeping her voice low so that the prisoner wouldn't overhear, she said, "Are you okay?"

"I'll just be glad when this is over."

"Me, too."

He took a deep breath, knowing he was only wasting time. "You'd better check to see that the others are out of sight. I want to move our new patient into an isolation cell."

With a squeeze of his arm, she nodded, and left.

The doctor grabbed the curtain and pulled it all the way open. The prisoner was sitting up now, a half-empty glass of water in her hand.

"How is head?" he asked.

"Still hurts."

"Pills work soon. Do not worry."

He heard the door to the back room open. Looking over his shoulder, he saw Irina stick her head out. He raised an eyebrow and she nodded.

"Everything is ready," he said to the prisoner. "You need help?"

She rose unsteadily to her feet. "I'm okay, I think."

"This way, then." He motioned toward Irina waiting at the door, then trailed behind as the prisoner walked gingerly across the floor and into the back room.

"Door in the back corner," he said, indicating the isolation cell Powell had vacated, where Irina was now waiting.

The prisoner looked around. "Popular place, huh?"

"I do not understand," Teterya said.

"The other two rooms are closed. They must be occupied, right?"

"Ah. Well, yes, we almost always have someone here."

She paused and closed her eyes, letting what appeared to be a wave of pain pass over her.

"You are all right?"

"Sorry. That one was bad." She started walking again.

Once they were in the cell, Irina explained that the button on the wall near the bed would summon her, should the prisoner need assistance.

"Medicine help you sleep through night," Teterya said. Once Irina had helped the woman into bed, he added, "But we check you every hour. So no worry."

"Thanks," the woman whispered, sounding quite sleepy.

"I'm sure you be fine by morning, Miss Norman."

"Call me...Rachel."

"Goodnight, Rachel."

Teterya and Irina left the room. Once the door was closed, he raised the window flap and looked through the slit.

Yes, the pills had worked. The woman was already asleep.

After replacing the flap, he moved quickly down to the cell at the far end and opened the door.

"ALL RIGHT," TETERYA said, sticking his head into their cell. "It is time."

Alex exited first, but when the others started to follow, she blocked Marie's passage. "This is the point where you stay behind."

Marie looked at El-Hashim, speaking in French. "I need to stay with you. We don't know if it's safe yet."

"Of course it's not safe," El-Hashim said. "It won't be safe until I'm away from here."

"That's not what I meant."

"I know what you meant." She gestured for her friend to step back. "Stay, Marie. I will be fine. Frank Poe's daughter would not hurt me."

The nod was reluctant, as was the step backward, Marie eyeing El-Hashim with what looked like genuine concern.

Standing in the doorway, Alex said, also in French, "She's right. The last thing I want is to hurt her."

Which was only partly true. She didn't hold any soft spots for a woman who aided terrorists, and she wouldn't hesitate to hurt El-Hashim if it came down to it. But not before she found out everything she could about her father.

Looking not even remotely reassured by Alex's words, Marie just glared at her as Alex closed the door.

"Please. Over here," the doctor said after the door was shut.

He stood at a metal table along the front wall. There was a stack of files and loose papers to one side, along with a few magazines. He picked one up, flipped to the back, and removed two sheets of paper that were definitely not part of the publication. He set them side by side on the table.

It was a map, hand drawn and crude.

"Prison is old," he said. "Stalin make before war. Simple place, yes?"

Both Alex and El-Hashim agreed that it was.

"But sometime prisoner for...political reason, more problem alive. Sometime many prisoner. Understand?"

"They needed to disappear," Alex said.

"Yes. But if kill here in prison, make other inmate angry and..." He paused, holding his fists up in the air and shaking them.

"Rise up? Fight?"

"Yes. These things. So make building half kilometer away. Big wall, you know? Keep sound inside. When want to take someone there, tell everyone prisoner be transferred. But not transferred. Take them here." He pointed at a line on the map that led from inside the prison walls to a square representing the aforementioned building.

"A tunnel," Alex said, realizing it couldn't be anything else. Teterya had already hinted that their escape would involve a secret exit. "Like the one we took to isolation."

"Yes," he said. "Tunnel. Built same time as one you and me take, but is different. Much deeper." He raised his left hand and held it out flat at eye level. "Isolation tunnel here." Then he raised his right hand, holding it flat several inches below the left. "Kill tunnel here. Understand?"

Alex and El-Hashim nodded.

Teterya pointed to the crude drawing, running his finger along a line that marked the tunnel. "Is not used for many year. At far end, is some mud and...and...garbage. Collect from storm in winter."

"But we can still get through it?" Alex asked.

"I think so, yes."

This wasn't a definitive answer. "How many times have you been down there?"

He hesitated. "Two."

Two? "When was the last time?"

"I go from other end five days ago to make map."

"You didn't have any problems?"

He shook his head. "No."

"All right," she said. "Sounds easy enough."

"Not easy," he said quickly. He pointed to several more lines that branched off from the main one. "These tunnels, like here, here, and here, they built to trick prisoner if try to run. Lead to...dead stop."

"Dead end."

"Yes, dead end. Also they look like main tunnel, easy to confuse. Understand?"

"I got it," Alex said. "If we stick to the map, we'll be good."

"Yes."

"Okay. So that's getting *through* the tunnel. How do we get *to* it? We can't go through any checkpoints dressed like this."

"There is way," Teterya said. "But must be very careful. I take you."

A buzzer sounded—short, then long. Alex tensed, her gaze shooting to the door into the examination area. Teterya, on the other hand, was looking toward the back of the room.

Alex twisted around, following his line of sight. There was a small yellow lightbulb blinking above the center cell door.

Frida's cell.

"Your friend wake up," the doctor said.

El-Hashim looked at Alex. "What friend?"

"An inmate. She got beat up earlier, is all."

El-Hashim's eyes narrowed. "What is this, some sort of ambush? You've got Marie locked up and—"

"Do we really need to go through this again?" Alex said. "If I wanted you dead, you'd be dead."

"I knew I shouldn't have trusted you."

"Calm down, all right? Even if she wanted to, Frida couldn't hurt anyone right now. If you don't believe me, look for yourself."

Alex headed for Frida's cell. The doctor, already a few

steps in front of her, was reaching for the handle.

"Hold it," Alex told him.

He paused.

Alex looked at El-Hashim, who had followed cautiously. "Let her look inside, first."

"Is that really necessary?" the doctor asked.

"Just let her look in."

Obviously irritated, Teterya lifted the flap covering the window. Alex stepped out of the way so El-Hashim could move in for a look.

El-Hashim hesitated, then stepped forward and peeked inside. After several seconds, she stepped back again and said, "What happened to her?"

"There was another prisoner who liked to use her as a punching bag."

"Liked?"

"The problem's been remedied."

Teterya gestured, not hiding his annoyance. "May I check patient now?"

Both Alex and El-Hashim moved to the side so Frida wouldn't see them as the doctor opened the door and went in.

They heard Frida say, "Can I...get some water?"

Her words punctuated by pain.

"Yes," Teterya said. He called out in Ukrainian.

Irina, who was waiting nearby, rushed over to the sink and started filling a pitcher.

"I thought...I heard my...friend's voice," Frida said.

"Friend?"

"Maureen. She's another prisoner. Is she here?"

"No. Am sorry. Probably only medicine. Will sometimes make head think things."

"Are you sure?"

"Yes," Teterya said.

Irina entered the cell with the pitcher and a glass.

"Here you are," the doctor said. "And please to take this. Will help you back to sleep."

For several seconds, Alex heard only subtle sounds of

movement.

Then Teterya said, "Okay. Just rest. Tomorrow you sore but feel little better. Am sure."

The doctor and nurse exited and shut the door.

"We need to get out of here, now," Alex whispered.

Teterya nodded. "Yes. Now would be good." He said something to Irina, then looked back at Alex and El-Hashim. "Follow me."

"Wait a second," Alex said. She gestured to El-Hashim's scarf. "Time to take it off."

"Now? But—"

"No excuses this time."

After a brief hesitation, El-Hashim reached up and removed the hijab from her head, revealing for the first time more than just her eyes.

If there was an ounce of Middle Eastern blood in the woman, that's all it was. An ounce. The gray-streaked blonde hair and pale skin both belied those brown eyes. Contacts, undoubtedly. Her eyes were more likely blue or even gray. If Alex had to guess, she'd say the woman was northern European or Scandinavian.

She eyed Alex defiantly. "Happy now?"

"Surprised," Alex said. "I guess you're lucky the Crimean authorities are very tolerant when it comes to religious garb."

"The Crimean authorities are pigs," El-Hashim—or *whoever* she was—said. She rolled the hijab into a ball and tossed it into a nearby corner. "Can we go now?"

The doctor stared at El-Hashim in surprise.

"Doctor?" Alex said.

"Sorry," he said, blinking. He grabbed two flashlights off the counter. He gave the miniature one to Alex, retained the larger one for himself, and led the two women out the back door of the infirmary. Instead of heading left toward the stairwell, though, he went right. There were only a few more rooms in this direction. The one he took them into turned out to be a storage room stuffed full of shelves and boxes.

"Is this way," he said, weaving a path through the mess.

When he finally stopped, he stood in front of a set of double doors to what looked like a cabinet built directly into the wall, about three feet above the floor. He opened the doors and revealed what amounted to a large, empty, wooden box.

"Is for moving…items, you know? Up and down."

"Supply elevator?" Alex suggested.

He nodded. "But only work if person here and person downstairs. See button?" He pointed at a red button mounted beside the jamb just inside the door. "I go down and push. When you see button light up, you push, too, and everything work."

"Okay," Alex said. "I got it." She looked at the box dubiously. "Is this strong enough to hold both of us?"

"I think no problem."

"You *think*?"

He shrugged, and made his way out of the room.

Alex was pressing a hand against the box, checking how sturdy it was, when El-Hashim said, "What happens once we're on the outside? Will your father meet us?"

"No. A couple friends of mine are waiting to help us."

"So where *is* your father?"

Alex couldn't help but laugh at the irony. "Not a clue. He's not that great at keeping me informed." Satisfied that the box was strong enough, she looked at El-Hashim. "Maybe *you* can tell *me*."

"Why would I know?"

"You've talked to him more recently than I have."

"But he sent you here."

"Text messages and e-mails, remember?"

El-Hashim shook her head. "Your father is…unusual."

"You think?"

"I was actually surprised he sent you here to help me."

"Why's that?"

"The deal we were working on, I'm fairly sure he was not as interested in it as he was pretending to be."

Alex shrugged. "Not my area." She wanted to bring the

249

conversation back to her father's potential whereabouts, but didn't know how to do that without making El-Hashim suspicious. She changed the subject. "I'm sorry we couldn't bring your friend along."

"She'll be out soon enough. She knows that I'll make sure of it."

Then she's about to be very disappointed, Alex thought.

The red button suddenly glowed and Alex waved at El-Hashim. "Get in."

El-Hashim climbed into the box, and pressed against the back wall so Alex could squeeze in next to her. Once Alex was sure she was all the way inside, she reached out, pushed the button, and snapped her hand back in.

The doors closed automatically and the box began a slow, steady descent, plunging them into darkness. It was several seconds before a set of closed doors appeared, light seeping in around the edges.

This would be the first floor. They continued their descent and soon everything was dark again. When they reached the next floor down, the elevator jerked to a stop, and the doors opened, revealing the waiting doctor in a dimly lit room. As the women climbed out, he put a finger to his lips, telling them to be quiet.

The room was about half the size of the storage space upstairs. It smelled of musk and dirt, and was packed with decaying cardboard boxes. Cobwebs clung to the corners and draped over the cardboard. The room looked as if it hadn't been disturbed in several decades.

The doctor leaned in close and whispered, "We need go two doors. Must be *very* quiet. Three doors down is main part of basement."

As soon as Alex and El-Hashim nodded, he went over to the door and opened it.

The hallway was low and narrow. Like the tunnel to the isolation area, single lightbulbs hung from the ceiling at consistent intervals, creating pools of light surrounded by areas of shadow. About thirty feet down the hall, more light spilled out from a window mounted in a closed door. Alex assumed this was the main basement entrance the doctor had mentioned.

Teterya stepped into the hallway first and headed in that direction. Alex motioned for El-Hashim to go next, then brought up the rear. They'd gone only a few feet when they passed a darkened doorway.

That would be door number one.

Alex hoped number two would come as quickly, putting them as far from that lit doorway as possible, but her wish was not to be. The second door was only a handful of steps from the third.

It also had the added bonus of being closed.

The doctor approached it quietly, then turned the handle and pushed. The squeak that followed was brief, but to Alex it sounded like an explosion that reverberated down the hallway. Her gaze shot over to the lit window, expecting to see the shadow of a guard at any moment. But the light remained undisturbed.

A tap on her shoulder snapped her attention back. El-Hashim gave her a wave, then turned and walked through the now open doorway. Once Alex was inside, Teterya shut the door behind them, the creak once more setting Alex's nerves on edge.

With a click, the doctor's flashlight came to life, its beam cutting through the darkened space, revealing that they weren't in a room, but another corridor.

"This way," he whispered.

Alex turned her light on, and panned it through the corridor as she followed the others. The hallway looked even less used than the nearly abandoned one they'd just been in. What Alex could see of the floor was covered with dust. There were cobwebs along the ceiling, and what paint hadn't already fallen off the walls was slowly peeling away. There were boxes and discarded furniture and twisted pieces of shelves strewn about, turning their route into an obstacle course primed to twist an ankle at the first misstep.

They came to an archway on the left. The doctor turned, stepped through it, and immediately backed out.

"Sorry," he said. "Not right way. Next one."

He found the archway he was looking for another twenty feet in. On the other side was a stone-walled room, with a ceiling so low that Alex found herself ducking despite the fact she had about a half foot of clearance.

The doctor swung the beam through the space, stopping on the back corner, where the stones were built into a six-inch-high, four-foot-square pedestal.

As they drew near, Alex saw a metal grate centered in the top. She shined her light through the slits, but could see nothing. She could, however, hear the trickle of water.

"The tunnel?"

"Yes," Teterya said. "Down and go left."

Alex listened to the water again. While it sounded as if it was coming straight up from below, it also sounded as if...

"How far down?" she asked.

"Six meter. Maybe little more."

Almost twenty feet.

"Is there a ladder?"

Teterya shook his head. "Cable on other side. Metal, yes? Go down maybe three and half meter. Climb down, drop."

The drop would still be close to eight feet onto who knew what. But if they were getting out, this was the way they were going. And Alex was sure as hell getting out.

After turning off her light, and stuffing it in her pocket, she reached for the grate. "Does this come off?"

Teterya nodded.

Alex gripped two of the thick slats, bent her knees, and pulled upward. The metal groaned loudly as it fought to remain where it was. The doctor gave the flashlight to El-Hashim and bent down to help Alex.

They raised it about half an inch before the doctor lost his hold, and Alex was forced to set it back down.

Resting her hands on her thighs, she took several rapid,

deep breaths. "When was the last time...someone...pulled it out of there?"

"I open first time here," the doctor said. "Two year ago. Think no one open since."

Two years?

She shot El-Hashim a sideways glance. "You don't have to just stand there looking pretty, you know. If you give us a hand, we should be able to do it."

El-Hashim looked surprised at the suggestion.

"I'm not asking you to do it alone," Alex said. "A little help is all. Or would you rather we just go back and turn ourselves in?"

El-Hashim frowned. "I didn't say I wouldn't do it."

"Good," Alex told her. She took a long, deliberate breath and straightened up. "Shall we try again?"

THIRTY ONE

KEEPING BUSY HADN'T distracted Irina as much as she had hoped it would.

While Symon was risking his life for two people they barely knew, she had gone out to the reception desk and tried to work through the ever-present stack of files. Within moments, however, her nerves got the best of her. She stared blankly at the wall, as her mind counted the many ways this could all go wrong, and land her and Symon in very serious trouble.

When the buzzer went off, she jumped in surprise, knocking her knees against the bottom of her desk. She looked toward the door, then the window, then down at her desk before she finally realized the buzzer had come from one of the isolation cells.

She rubbed her knees, calmed herself, and stood up. Before she could take a step, though, the buzzer sounded again.

"Yes, yes," she murmured. "I'm coming."

Walking into the back room, she saw the yellow light glowing above one of the cells. As she crossed to the door, the buzzer sounded again.

"I'm *coming*," she repeated, this time raising her voice, not caring if the patient understood her or not.

She made a stop at the medicine locker to get a pain pill, filled up a glass of water, and opened the cell door.

"Good evening," the prisoner said.

Irina jerked back in surprise, some of the water splashing out of the cup and onto the floor. The prisoner was standing right on the other side of the door, an odd smile on her face.

She glanced at the pill and cup in Irina's hand and said, "I won't be needing those."

It suddenly occurred to Irina that the woman was speaking Ukrainian. Quite capably, in fact. Flustered, Irina said, "You should lie down. You'll feel better."

"Oh, I feel fine," the prisoner told her. "Excellent, even. How about you?"

She stepped out of the cell, forcing Irina to take a step backward.

"You—you can't come out here," Irina cried. "You need to go back inside and lie down. When the doctor returns, I'll have him check in on you."

"That won't be necessary," the woman said. She smiled again. "Your name's Irina, right?"

Irina's eyes widened in shock. "How do you know that?"

"I wouldn't be any good at my job if I didn't." The prisoner continued moving forward, forcing Irina to back further away. "I need you to pay attention, Irina. First you're going to put that cup down before you spill any more water, then—"

Irina didn't wait to hear what "then" might be. She tossed the cup at the woman's face and ran for the alarm next to the door. As she was reaching for it, a hand clawed at her shoulder and yanked her back.

"Let go of me!" Irina cried.

The prisoner spun her around and slapped her squarely across the face.

"Let's not do that again, shall we?" the woman said, her calm, almost unconcerned manner only frightening Irina all the more.

Suddenly someone started pounding on one of the other cell doors, the inmate inside demanding to be let out, to know what was going on. It was the friend of the woman who had gone with Symon and Powell.

The prisoner holding Irina's arm ignored the shouts. "I need you to listen very carefully to me, Irina. Are you listening?

She was too frightened to respond.

"I asked if you're listening."

Irina didn't trust her own voice, so she nodded.

"Good. Now, here's what I want you to do. I know your friends are headed for a tunnel. I want you to show me how to get there. Right now. And you won't be making any wrong turns that might lead to some of your friends working in the building." She smiled again. "Are we clear?"

This time, Irina managed to eek out a yes.

"Excellent," the woman said. She nodded toward the door. "After you."

IT WAS AT moments like these that the assassin loved her work. The assigned killing itself was often routine, but it was what led up to it—a series of moves and counter moves that forced her to use her wits and often improvise—that she relished.

Her instincts about Powell had proven to be correct. And her decision to keep close tabs on the woman had led her to the exact place she needed to be, at the exact moment she needed to be there.

She had assumed there was some sort of escape plan in the works, and listening at her cell door as the doctor and Powell spoke had confirmed this.

The assassin had waited until she was sure everyone was gone, then had pushed the button to call for help. And while she often got a kick out of scaring the crap out of people, sometimes even hurting them—slowly—in the process, she knew tonight was not the night to indulge her baser desires. Prolonging the nurse's terror would only keep the assassin from the task at hand.

And time was of the essence.

After telling the nurse to find a flashlight, she followed her down a hallway into the storage room, and immediately became suspicious. "*This* is the way?"

"The tunnel starts in one of the basements."

"So why are we in here?"

The nurse gestured to a set of double doors at the rear of the room. "Elevator for supplies," she said, looking even more frightened than before. "It will take you to the proper basement. But…but it can only be operated if there is a person at each end."

The assassin nodded, then went to the doors and tried them.

Locked.

"Why won't they open?"

"The elevator car must not be here," the nurse said. "They remain locked if it's on another floor. For safety."

The assassin examined the doors for several seconds before turning again to the nurse. "And once you get to the bottom, where is the tunnel entrance?"

"I'm not sure. I've never been down there. Symon…Dr. Teterya said it's in one of the rooms close by. That's all I know."

"You've never seen it?"

"No."

Disappointing, the assassin thought, but not the end of the world.

Smiling again, she thanked the nurse, and for a moment the poor girl looked relieved. The assassin let her hold on to that feeling for a few seconds, then reached out and snapped her neck.

Never one to disrespect the dead, she gently laid the nurse on the floor, out of the way.

Then she returned her attention to the elevator doors.

THIRTY TWO

IT TOOK THEM a couple minutes—and more than a few grunts and groans—to finally pull the grated cover free and drop it to the stone floor.

Alex retrieved her flashlight, flicked it on, and shone it through the hole they'd just uncovered.

The opening was a cement cylinder about three feet long, stopping where the roof of the tunnel began. As she'd been warned, it was a leg-breaking drop down to a damp floor. The tunnel walls seemed to be oozing water. The passageway was so old and decrepit it was leaking groundwater.

Badly.

There was no missing the smell, either—dank and tinged with rot.

The cable the doctor had mentioned was embedded in the cylinder about half a foot up from the bottom. What it had been used for, there was no telling, but Alex did notice three other evenly spaced points around the tube where other cables had most likely been anchored.

She pulled herself back up, and stuffed the flashlight into her pocket. "I'll go first," she said, looking at El-Hashim. "Wait until I'm down, then you start. The trickiest part will be shimmying down the tube. Take it as slow as you need to, and make sure you have a good grip on the cable before you commit yourself. When you reach the end, I'll be there to help you."

El-Hashim peered into the hole. She looked as if she were unsure she could actually do this, but she said nothing.

Alex turned to Teterya. "Thank you, Doctor. After you help her into the hole, your job is done."

She held out her hand for him to shake. He hesitated, then took it.

"You are welcome. Please not to come back."

Alex grinned. "I promise."

Alex swung her legs into the opening and moved down, bracing herself against the cement. Reaching the cable, she grabbed on, then carefully relaxed the tension that was holding her body in the tube. As her legs dropped down she swung a bit from side to side, so she hooked a foot around the end of the cable to arrest the movement.

Hand over hand she lowered herself until she was just a few feet from the end of the line. She peeked down to get a glimpse of the tunnel floor, but without the use of the flashlight, all she saw was black. Hoping there was no stone beneath her that might trip her up, she bent her knees in anticipation of absorbing the shock, and let go.

Barely a second passed before her feet touched the ground. She started to fall to the side, but a quick hand to the stone floor helped her maintain her balance.

She pulled out her flashlight, turned it on, and looked up at the hole in the ceiling. "All right. Come on down."

She could see only shadowy movement as El-Hashim entered the tube, but could clearly hear the woman's nervous breathing. At one point, a short cry of surprise echoed through the chamber, and Alex was sure El-Hashim would come crashing down on her. But whatever had prompted the noise, El-Hashim seemed to have gotten things under control, and was soon lowering herself down the cable.

"Just a bit more," Alex said, "and I can grab your feet."

"There's not much cable left."

"It's okay. You can go all the way to the end of it if you need to."

"I'm not sure. I don't want to—"

"Don't worry. Just a few more inches."

The surprised cry again, this time lasting as long as it took for El-Hashim to fall through the air and land in Alex's not quite ready arms.

Alex staggered back a step, before slipping on the wet stone and falling to the ground. The flashlight skittered away, its beam spinning around a few times then settling on an unhelpful view down the tunnel.

"Are you okay?" Alex asked.

El-Hashim's hips lay across Alex's stomach, while her shoulders and head were tipped back against the floor of the tunnel. She groaned, then twisted as she tried to push herself up. "I think so."

Alex scooted out from under her and climbed to her feet. She could feel the aches from the spots that she was sure would bruise later, but the pain in her shoulder, which had taken the brunt of El-Hashim's fall, was the worst. She moved it around, trying to stretch it out, and hoped that nothing was torn inside.

When this job was over, she was going to need a month's stay in the VA hospital to recover.

She reclaimed the flashlight, and turned back to El-Hashim, pleased to see the woman had risen to her feet again.

"Ready?" Alex asked.

"Yes. Please, let's go."

Alex consulted the hand-drawn map again, and started down the tunnel.

WHEN DOCTOR TETERYA heard the crash, he looked down the hole, but could only see the beam of the woman's flashlight along an empty patch of the tunnel floor. He was about to call out to them when he heard them speak.

They were all right. Of course, if they weren't, what would he have done? He certainly wouldn't have crawled down the cable. There would have been no way for him to get back.

No, the moment they descended into the tunnel, they were out of his hands.

Thank. God.

Never again would he agree to something like this.

He stood up. There was still much to do. The infirmary

needed to look like a violent escape had occurred, then he and Irina would take sedatives so they could later be found unconscious. A bruise or two wouldn't hurt, either, though he wasn't looking forward to that part.

But first he had to get the damn cover back over the hole.

He positioned himself so that he could pull it into place without lifting it, grabbed the edge, and started to give it a yank.

THERE WAS NO trapdoor in the top of the elevator car.

Getting to it had not been a problem. The doors above were old and had been easy enough to pry open. A pair of rags the assassin had found, and tied around her hands, had allowed her to grab hold of the cable and slide down to the top of the car with little risk of injury.

The assassin had then crouched down, put her ear to the wood, and listened.

Silence.

Which was a good thing. It meant the car itself and the room beyond it was empty.

Unfortunately, the absence of a trapdoor made getting *into* that room a bit complicated.

Not that she minded. This was all part of the hunt. The part she so loved.

It took her less than thirty seconds to find a way in.

There was, she noticed, a gap on either side of the elevator car that would allow her to access the braking tracks. Untying the rags from her hands, she was able to use them to hook the elevator stops and pull the release.

As she had hoped, there was enough play in the cable that the car dropped half an inch. This was just enough to expose the top of the basement opening, the gap the perfect size for her to slip her fingertips through. Setting her feet firmly against the top of the car, she grabbed the lip of the opening and pulled upward, putting all of her strength into it.

The ancient cable groaned as it stuttered a few more inches down. She kept this up until she heard the next set of stop latches engage.

Using the same technique as before, she released them, then started pulling again. It didn't take her long before the gap was wide enough for her to slip through.

The assassin smiled, feeling quite proud of herself. She took a quick look around, and spotted the tracks on the dusty floor, leading to the doorway. She was happy to see they continued into the hallway beyond, too.

Though there were several doorways along the corridor, light was only spilling out of one. The footsteps, however, didn't go all the way to the light, instead stopping a doorway short.

The assassin listened at the closed door. More silence. As she was about to open it, she heard a noise from the next room down, the lit one.

She contemplated what to do for a moment, but knew she needed to make sure she left no potential problems behind her. So she abruptly changed course and continued down the hallway.

The light was actually coming through a window in the door. On the other side was a hallway with several more doors along it—a hallway that looked as if it saw far more traffic than the one she was in.

The source of the noise, she discovered, was a guard walking away from her down the hall.

The assassin gently took hold of the handle and tried to turn it. Locked. Just as she suspected. The part of the basement she was currently in was likely little used and mostly forgotten.

Good, then. Nothing to worry about.

She returned to the other door, and turned the knob. Within the first few inches of movement, it squeaked. She paused, listening again, but there was no noise indicating that someone had heard her on the other side. She continued pushing the door open, glad that the squeak didn't return, and found herself in a dark corridor, save for some light spilling out of a doorway further back.

Choosing each step with care, the assassin moved quietly down the corridor. It turned out the light wasn't coming out of a doorway so much as an arched opening in the wall that led into a wide room.

At the far end, on his hands and knees, looking at the floor, was the doctor.

No. Not looking *at* the floor.

Looking *through* it.

The tunnel entrance, she guessed. That would explain the absence of Powell and El-Hashim.

The doctor suddenly leaned further down, as if straining to see something. After several moments, he put a hand to his mouth. The assassin thought he was going to say something, but he sat back, his hand falling away.

Then she heard a voice. Faint, coming from…below the man.

Definitely the tunnel.

Dr. Teterya repositioned himself, and grabbed on to a grated metal plate sitting nearby. There was no question what he was about to do.

Before he could proceed, however, the assassin stepped into the room and said, "That actually won't be necessary."

One of the doctor's hands slipped from the cover as he twisted around in surprise, throwing him off balance. He fell backward, and managed to miss tumbling through the hole only by inches.

The assassin was on him before he had the chance to get back on his feet.

"What…what are you doing down here?" he asked.

She smiled. "What does it look like I'm doing? I'm following you."

His confusion lasted several more seconds, then his eyes widened in understanding. "It's you, isn't it?"

"Me, what?"

"You. You're the one…you're the one who—"

To answer his question, the assassin reached forward and dispatched him with the quick, deadly efficiency that had made her reputation.

After appropriating his flashlight, she took a look into the hole.

It was quiet down there, no sense of movement. She shone the light and moved it around. She could see that an area on the wet ground directly below had been disturbed very recently, the slowly advancing water already starting to reclaim it.

Someone had fallen, she thought.

Good. Maybe that'll slow their progress.

The assassin climbed into the hole and used the cable to descend into the tunnel. Once her feet were firmly on the stone floor, she masked most of the light with her hand, paused, and listened.

Footsteps. Echoing back.

Coming from…

…the left.

THIRTY THREE

"BUILDING THREE SECURE," Danya said into his radio.

There was a hiss of static, then Plachkov, manning the desk at the prison control center, repeated in a bored monotone, "Building Three secure."

"Moving to Building Two," Danya said.

"Moving to Building Two."

Danya Sosna had long ago stopped rolling his eyes when his messages were repeated back to him, and hardly even noticed it anymore. It was, after all, procedure. But tonight the practice grated on his nerves, like almost everything else.

Because tonight he wasn't supposed to be here.

This was Danya's night off. The one night every week he could spend in his beloved Ivanna's bed and eat her wonderful dinners, two finely tuned skills that had always kept him coming back for more.

But instead of lying in Ivanna's arms with a belly full of expertly prepared *chee-börek*, Danya was stuck here in this prison, forced to work another man's shift.

This was all Vanko's fault. Vanko, who, at the best of times, was a terrible card player and lovestruck fool. Vanko, who, for reasons unknown to anyone here, had decided not to report for duty tonight, and could not be found in his sleeping quarters.

Danya himself had tried calling the man, but the stupid fool hadn't answered.

Where had he gotten to?

Danya could only guess. Saw him drunk and sprawled out on a mattress with some local whore, undoubtedly imagining that she was the object of his obsession, the lovely nurse Irina.

Danya hoped he was enjoying himself, because the money he had used to hire such companionship would soon be very hard to come by.

It wasn't likely that Vanko would have a job after this.

Cursing the man's name as he checked Building Two, Danya called it in, did the same for Building One, then made his way to Administration. He briefly chatted with the guards at the security point, airing his complaints about Vanko, before heading inside to check and double-check the doors and windows, as he had so many times before.

He was on the second floor when he noticed something wrong. The door to the infirmary was unlocked and no one was manning the reception area.

The empty desk by itself wasn't unusual.

The night shift would typically consist of only two people—Vanko's crush, Irina, and one doctor. But when Irina left the desk, she always closed and locked the door.

Had she forgotten this time?

If so, it wasn't like her. Not only was she an attractive woman—although nowhere near Ivanna's part of the stratosphere—she was also quite professional and extremely efficient. And, in Danya's experience, she was not one to forget things. Especially when it came to safety.

Danya waited for a moment, checking his watch, wondering if she would return. He listened, hoping he might be able to hear her moving around back there, but it all was quiet. *Too* quiet. And as the seconds ticked by, he began to feel more and more uneasy.

Something wasn't right.

Stepping past the reception desk, Danya went inside and found that the main examination area was still and lifeless, all of the curtains pulled back to reveal nothing but empty beds.

When he reached the door to the back room, he peered through the window. He didn't see Irina inside—or the doctor, for that matter—but then he couldn't see the whole room from here.

Putting a smile on his face, he tapped the glass.

No one answered.

Even if Irina had gone to the cafeteria, the doctor would have remained on duty. The guidelines were very clear on that. Someone on staff had to be present in the infirmary at all times.

Danya opened the door a crack. "Irina? Doctor?"

He wasn't sure which doctor was on duty. Probably Teterya, a cold man who, according to Vanko, was his biggest rival for Irina.

When no one answered, Danya stepped inside, but a quick look around revealed he wasn't alone.

"Irina?"

Worse yet, the door to one of the isolation cells was open, and there seemed to be some water on the floor in front of it.

As he walked over, he noticed a plastic cup lying to the side. There had obviously been a spill here, but why hadn't anyone cleaned it up?

"Irina?" he called out, louder now.

At the sound of his voice, someone pounded against one of the other cell doors and called out in English, "Hello? Hello? Who's there?"

It was coming from the cell at the opposite end.

Danya walked quickly over and moved up to the door. Raising the window slat, he looked in and saw a prisoner staring back at him.

Summoning up his best English, he said, "Is nurse...with...you?"

It was unlikely, but he supposed it was possible that Irina had somehow managed to lock herself inside.

"Only me," the prisoner told him. "The nurse is gone."

He processed her words. "Gone? Where gone?"

"I don't know. It sounded like a fight. What happened, it wasn't good."

The word that stuck out to him was "fight." Had Irina and the doctor had words? Or was it something much worse than that?

"Where go?" he said. "Where go?"

The prisoner shook her head. "I...I don't know."

Danya looked around, hoping to find some clue to where Irina or the doctor was, but saw nothing. He ran back into the examination area, and was starting to do the same there, when he caught sight of something he hadn't noticed the first time.

The rear exit was ajar.

Danya had never seen it left open before, and was sure there was something in the guidelines about that as well.

He pushed through to the corridor, found it empty.

Which way did they go?

Right led to the stairs, the elevator, and the main part of the prison—all just as easily reachable through the main infirmary door. To the left was a handful of storerooms and a few unused offices, none of which held any medical equipment or supplies.

Why would either of them go there?

For a moment, Danya considered phoning for help, but what if the explanation for their absence was something as simple as a medical emergency, or just a bathroom break?

That would *not* score him any points with his boss.

Danya took a breath. If they went to the right, then everything was fine and they'd show up soon. So, Danya went left, opening each door he passed and checking inside.

He immediately knew there was something different about the storage room when he opened its door.

It was the only room with a light on.

"Irina? Doctor?"

He stepped inside. Though the room was stuffed with boxes and discarded pieces of what appeared to be telecommunications equipment, none of it looked as if it had been disturbed in a very long time.

"Irina?" he said again as he moved around the end of a storage rack.

Though she would have surely answered if she were here, he kept going, drawn forward by a sense that something was wrong.

The first thing he saw when he passed the last shelving unit was the rectangular hole in the wall. There was a partially open door covering half of it, but the other door had been pried away and lay against the wall, hanging by a single hinge.

The second thing he saw was the foot.

A woman's foot.

For a full two seconds, he didn't move, unable to fully grasp what he was seeing. Then he rushed forward, nearly tripping over himself. He gasped.

Irina! Oh, God!

He dropped to his knees beside her. "Irina! Irina!"

Her head was tilted to the side, her eyes closed.

"Irina!" This time, shaking her shoulder.

He checked her pulse, but could feel nothing. He looked at her chest to see if she was breathing, but of course she wasn't.

She had no pulse; how could she be breathing?

All guards had rudimentary first-aid training, and Danya knew he needed to get her heart going and air into her lungs. He reached over to turn her head so it faced upward, giving him better access to her mouth. But he realized with horror that no matter what he did, he would never be able to bring her back.

Her head flopped in his hands, her neck clearly broken.

Which meant this was no accident. She hadn't simply fallen.

Someone had done this to her.

Someone had *killed* Irina.

THIRTY FOUR

"**WHERE THE HELL** are they?" Deuce said.

It wasn't the first time he had said it, or even the third, so Cooper didn't bother to reply.

From their vantage point on the hill, Cooper watched the prison, while Deuce kept an eye on the abandoned building in the ravine. The moment Alex and El-Hashim appeared, the two men would head for the rendezvous point.

So far, there had been no movement at all in the ravine.

"I don't like this," Deuce said. "Maybe we should go see if we can—"

"Just relax," Cooper told him. "We're still well within the scheduled time frame."

Deuce grunted his dissatisfaction, but said nothing more.

Cooper slowly scanned the complex again. It looked exactly as it had when they arrived. Quiet. Tucked in for the night.

He lowered the glasses and was reaching for one of the energy bars in his pocket when a sudden siren pierced the stillness.

There was no question where it was coming from.

The prison.

As Cooper snapped up his binoculars, spotlights came alive in the guard towers, some sweeping their beams through the prison yard, others lighting up the landscape outside the facility walls.

"I *told* you I didn't like this," Deuce said.

Cooper ignored him, his attention caught by movement in the parking area in front of the prison. Several people were running toward the facility's entrance. From the angle of their approach, he figured they were coming from one of the outbuildings. The barracks, no doubt, guards who'd already been awake rushing to help. Others would soon follow.

"This is not good," Deuce said. "We need to go get Alex."

Cooper kept his eyes on the prison.

"Cooper! Hey, are you listening to me? We need to go get Alex!"

"Do you see her yet? We can't risk getting any closer until she shows."

"But if we wait, we'll waste time we probably don't have anymore. We need to be down there when she shows up." When Cooper didn't say anything right away, Deuce added, "The purpose of us being here was to keep an eye on the prison in case anything happened. Well, something has! We don't need to stay here any longer."

Cooper pulled away from the binoculars and looked at Deuce. "We *do* need to know if anyone is heading in our direction, and this is the best place for that." He paused, knowing there was also merit to Deuce's argument. "Stay here. I'll go see if she's getting close."

"No way. *I* go. She's *my* partner!"

Cooper could sympathize, but he was the running the show. "No, you stay. Is your radio on?"

"Yeah," Deuce grumbled.

"Good. Let me know if anything more changes."

THIRTY FIVE

TWICE DURING THEIR trek, Alex and El-Hashim had come upon ramps that lowered the level of the tunnel before flattening out again. When they reached the bottom of the second ramp, they found the ground covered in three inches of water.

"Not so fast," El-Hashim said. "Please."

Alex glanced back. The woman was a good dozen feet behind her.

The water alone made it difficult to walk, but that's not where the problem ended. The stone floor was also slick with algae or some kind of vegetation, so to keep their legs from flying out from under them, they had to take each step with care. Alex had been able to maintain a decent pace, but her companion was apparently not as sure-footed.

She sloshed back to El-Hashim.

"Here," she said. "Hold my arm."

El-Hashim grabbed on, sighing in relief. "Thank you."

Their new pace was not as fast as Alex would have liked, but it was better than what El-Hashim had been doing on her own.

"How much farther?" the woman asked.

"I'm not sure."

Dr. Teterya's map wasn't exactly drawn to scale, but so far it had helped them avoid one of the false branch tunnels.

There was something Alex was sure of, however. Once they reached the end, her chance to learn what El-Hashim knew about her father would be over.

"Whoa," El-Hashim said as she slipped, her free arm flying into the air to steady herself.

Alex paused for a moment, allowing the woman to regain her balance.

"You're doing great," Alex said. "Ready?"

El-Hashim nodded and they started walking again.

As they skirted a piece of floating debris, Alex said, "Can I ask you a question?"

"What?"

"How long have you worked with my father?"

A sideways glance. "This is something you should ask of him, not me."

"It's not a subject we usually discuss."

"Business is business. If he wants you to know, he'll tell you."

Alex had expected this answer, and knew she wouldn't get much further with a lie. It was time to finally be honest.

"Actually, the truth is," she said, "my father and I don't discuss anything at all."

"Yes, texting and emails. You told me that."

"That wasn't entirely accurate. The last time I had any communication with my dad was a decade ago, before he fell off the map."

El-Hashim's face screwed up in confusion. "I don't understand. You haven't heard from him? But you said…"

"That he sent me to get you?"

"Yes."

"That was a bit of a lie," Alex told her. "Actually not even a bit. I made it all up."

El-Hashim released Alex's arm and took a step back. She started to lose balance again and Alex grabbed her, gripping her bicep. "Careful. You don't want to break anything down here."

El-Hashim tried to pull away, but Alex wouldn't let go.

"Who *are* you?" she demanded.

"You know who I am. You checked me out yourself. I didn't lie about that."

El-Hashim continued to struggle. "Then what do you want from me?" Her eyes opened wide in realization. "You *are* here to kill me, aren't you?"

Alex held her steady and swung the flashlight beam, taking in all of the tunnel. "Do you seriously think I'd go to all the trouble of getting you down here just to kill you? I could have done it in about two seconds flat back at the prison."

"So then why are we here? Why are you helping me escape?"

"The answer to that is very simple. You were with my father just a handful of days ago, and I want to find him. I want to talk to him. I haven't seen him in over a decade, and you're the only one I know who has."

"And how do you know this? Who told you about us?"

Time to start lying again. "I have a lot of friends. They know I've been looking for him."

"You're friends with the Crimean police?"

"No," Alex assured her. "My father is a wanted man, and I have no interest in associating with the people who are out to get him. But I do have friends who have connections to the police, both in and outside the law." She paused. "I know this is a lot to process right now, and I know you have no real reason to trust me, but I need your help, El-Hashim. I need to know about my father."

El-Hashim stared at Alex, clearly not quite buying it.

"These friends," she said. "There's much more to them than you're letting on. You couldn't have done all of this alone. Someone's waiting outside, aren't they?"

Alex said nothing. She didn't have to.

"Who are you working for?"

"That's not important."

"It is to me."

Alex hesitated. "I only took this job because of your contact with my father."

"And yet, even if I tell you what I know, you'll turn me over to your colleagues."

Again Alex was silent. But at least El-Hashim had stopped struggling, probably because she knew there was no point to it. She was physically outmatched and had no chance of getting away.

The corner of the woman's mouth turned up. "What if we were to make a deal?" she said. "One that's mutually beneficial?"

"Can you help me find my father or not?

"I honestly have no idea where he is," she said. "But I do know how to contact him, and I would be willing to give you that information."

"In exchange for what?"

"For letting me free as soon as we're out of here. For not turning me over to your employers."

"Come on," Alex said, and dug her fingers deeper into the woman's arm, pulling her forward.

"What? You're not even going to consider it?"

"I don't need to consider it," Alex said. "Before we're out of this, you're gonna tell me."

"Oh, I highly doubt that."

Alex gave her a jerk. "I don't."

THE ASSASSIN STOPPED at the top of the second downward ramp. She had heard the two women's voices on and off for several minutes, but had been too far away to understand what they were saying.

Now, the words were clear, if a bit distant. And the fact that they weren't fading out told her that Powell and El-Hashim must have come to a stop. Perhaps if she were to go to the bottom of the ramp, she'd be able to see them.

Of course, they might see her as well, and she wasn't yet ready for that.

She listened to their conversation and was surprised to find out Powell had tricked El-Hashim. While on one level this admission amused the assassin—even impressed her—she knew it was also a problem. Though Powell had not actually confirmed that anyone was waiting at the end of the tunnel, her non-denial was proof enough. The assassin would have no choice but to take care of the two women before they reached Powell's friends.

And then there was the whole father thing that Powell had been whining about. What a sentimental fool. Obviously, she was one who allowed her emotions to dictate her actions. That wasn't much of a surprise, considering the way she had conducted herself in the prison.

But who her father was, and, for that matter, who *Powell* actually was, made no real difference to the assassin. The only thing important about the revelation was that it appeared the women's reluctant partnership was quickly deteriorating.

The assassin waited until their voices grew distant, indicating they were walking again, before she made her way down the ramp.

The water that covered the floor was cool, but not uncomfortable, and walking silently through it was not a problem. She had been trained to function in a multitude of environmental situations, and before long, she closed the distance between them, until she could see their silhouettes backlit by Powell's flashlight.

After a few minutes, the two women stopped again, and in the beam of their flashlight, the assassin saw the beginnings of what looked like an intersecting tunnel. Powell looked down at something in her hand, then pointed to the left and headed that way, pulling El-Hashim along with her.

The moment they were out of sight, the assassin increased her speed. When the tunnel straightened out again, she was only twenty feet behind them.

She felt a sudden rush, wanting very much to savor the moment. But she knew that all good things must come to an end.

It was time.

THIRTY SIX

COOPER WAS ALMOST to the abandoned building when his earpiece came alive with Deuce's hushed voice.

"You there yet?"

"Just about," Cooper said. "Anything new?"

"Two jeep patrols have started circling the perimeter."

UAZs, Cooper knew—the Russian equivalent of the Jeep. "Terrific. Inside or outside the fence?"

"Inside."

That was good. The rendezvous building was right outside the prison's double fence, so unless the patrols actually headed out the gate, they weren't an immediate threat.

"Let me know if that changes," he said.

There was silence for a moment, then, "You see any sign of Alex?"

"Not yet."

When he reached the building, Cooper looked around, trying to figure out exactly where Alex would be coming from. There was no obvious route to the outside that wouldn't require them to run over hundreds of yards of open space before they reached the ravine.

Not exactly a stealthy way to escape.

And then, of course, there were the two fences. How would they get over those?

Again wishing that Alex had given them more details, Cooper studied his surroundings, and it suddenly struck him that maybe there was no need to get over the fences.

Why not go *under* them?

That had to be it, right? A tunnel. Maybe one that led

directly from the prison to the building?

All other possibilities would come with an almost zero chance of working.

So if there was a tunnel, where would it come out?

Inside the building?

Wishing he could block out the sound of the siren, Cooper removed a flashlight from the bag on his back, then found an opening in the side of the building that had once had a door, and made his way inside. He spent the next several minutes exploring, and discovered that the interior of the building was little more than a collection of crumbling walls.

He moved room to room, finding nothing here that would support his theory. Until, that was, he stumbled across an enclosed space no bigger than a supply closet, its badly dilapidated door barely clinging to its hinges.

Unless he was wrong, most supply closets didn't have a manhole in the center.

So was this it? Given the complete lack of other candidates, it seemed a pretty good fit.

Cooper stood there, studying the manhole. If he was right about this, it might be wise to get the cover off so that Alex and El-Hashim could crawl out quickly and save precious time. But the task would take more than a simple grab and pull. He needed something to assist him, a crowbar or a piece of pipe that he could stick into one of the holes atop the cover and pry it off.

There was nothing in the immediate area, but two rooms over he found a three-foot section of rusted rebar lying atop a pile of rubble. It wasn't quite as long as he would have liked, but he thought it might work.

He returned to the room, and slotted the tip through one of the holes. As he pushed on the rod, he was afraid it was going to bend before the lid canted up. It did, but only a small amount, and he was able to lift the edge of the cover just high enough to twist it so that it was sitting partially out of the hole. A couple of intense shoves later, the opening was cleared.

Cooper shone his flashlight into the hole. On the left was a wall with a built-in ladder of metal hoops leading up to the opening. To the right was a tunnel, its floor about ten feet below.

Cooper leaned through the opening and cupped his free hand at the side of his mouth. "Alex? Are you there? It's Cooper."

Nothing.

"Alex?"

Still dead quiet.

He pulled back up and thought for a moment, then swung his legs around, and lowered himself down the ladder.

THIRTY SEVEN

IN THE CHAOS surrounding the discovery of not only a dead nurse, but three missing inmates and a doctor, it took an extra seven minutes before someone had the wherewithal to send a guard to check the floors that the supply elevator serviced.

The guard's initial stop was naturally the first floor, where he wasted an additional four minutes determining there was no sign of anyone recently exiting the cramped elevator there. He lost even more time in the basement, where the elevator was housed in a rarely used section of the building that he had no idea how to get into. A full six minutes passed before he located someone with the correct key and unlocked the right door.

The guard navigated a dusty corridor, stepped through an open doorway, and saw that the elevator car was indeed there, but the room itself was empty.

He radioed the information in, and was told to report back to the main floor where a room-by-room search was underway. He was so focused on joining the search upstairs as he headed back the way he came, he didn't notice the dark door to his left that was slightly ajar.

A door that, when opened, was prone to an initial, loud squeak.

THIRTY EIGHT

AS THEY CONTINUED down the tunnel, Alex tried to figure out how to get El-Hashim to talk, short of beating the crap out of her. As much as she would have liked to give in to her more primal nature, Alex knew El-Hashim was having a hard enough time navigating the tunnels without the complication of black eyes and a broken rib or two. Besides, she wasn't keen on beating up the defenseless, no matter how repugnant they were.

She needed an alternate strategy. Something along the lines of...

...fear.

Ahead, another fork in the tunnel appeared. She studied the map for a moment, and pointed toward the left passageway, which, according to Teterya's map, was a false tunnel.

"This way," she said.

The plan she'd thought up was simple. When they reached the dead end, Alex would leave El-Hashim there with a quick word and the sound of retreating footsteps. Left alone with no map, no light, and the potential of being lost in the labyrinth for God knew how long, the poor woman would realize the advantages of cooperation.

Would it be enough to get her to open up?

It was worth a try.

There was a sharp bend to the tunnel for the first several yards, before it eased into a relatively straighter path. Alex thought she could just make out the dead end at the far reach of her flashlight beam.

Just a little closer now.

She was going over what she'd say, trying to get the words exactly right, when she heard a low noise behind her and started to turn. Her head had only moved a couple inches when something smacked into the side of her skull.

At first there was no pain, only confusion, as she staggered to the left, the flashlight slipping from her hand. Then the whole side of her head began to scream.

She put a hand over the spot and felt something sticky and wet. Blood, she realized. How...?

Something grabbed her shoulder and twisted her around. She could see the outline of a person only a couple feet away, but whether it was the darkness or blurred vision, she couldn't make out any details.

She could, however, see a hand flashing toward her face. She ducked, not in time to completely clear the blow, but enough that it glanced off the top of her skull.

Without missing a beat, she swung out with her left as her training with Emerick kicked in, and followed with an upper cut from her blood-covered right.

Both blows found their targets.

There was a yell, loud and angry—definitely not El-Hashim.

Alex stepped backward, knowing her attacker was about to make another assault. The move would have been a good one if not for the slippery stone that her foot first found, then quickly lost.

Alex twisted sideways as she tried to keep her balance, but there was no way to avoid the fall. She hit the wet ground with an *oomph*, but before she could even move, a foot connected with her gut. A second later she heard splashes of someone running away.

Alex fought through the pain and pushed herself to her feet. She looked around for the light of her flashlight, but all she could see was dark.

Had the water shorted it?

"El-Hashim," she said. "Where are you?"

No response. The only thing she could hear now was her

own breathing. She was completely alone without a light.

The steps had gone...that way.

Her head throbbing, she turned to her right. She could still hear the steps faintly in the distance. She moved within arm's length of the wall so she could touch it with her fingertips, and began to run.

THE ASSASSIN KNEW her target wouldn't get far.

It wasn't a complete surprise to her when El-Hashim snatched up Powell's flashlight and made a run for it. The woman was no idiot, and saving her own skin would be the only thing that mattered to her.

But running wouldn't do her much good. Hers was a world of clandestine meetings and backroom deals, not fleeing for her life from someone whose sole purpose—for the moment, at least—was to take it.

Unfortunately, the assassin hadn't had time to completely finish off Powell before El-Hashim took off. After choosing to neutralize whom she considered the more dangerous of the two, she was now paying the price by having to abandon the job halfway through.

A gun would have been nice, but, sadly, prisoners don't get to have firearms.

She'd been right about Powell. The woman definitely had had some training. The sting along the assassin's rib cage was proof enough of that. She couldn't remember the last time anyone had been able to lay a hand on her.

As she ran through the tunnel, she didn't bother masking the beam from her own flashlight. El-Hashim already knew she was coming.

She could hear the woman ahead of her, both the splashes of her feet and the desperation of her breath.

A few seconds later, there was a gasp, then the rate of the splashes increased, and she knew that El-Hashim must have looked back and seen the light reflecting off the curved tunnel walls.

The assassin had a brief moment of surprise when the

tunnel straightened again. She had expected to see El-Hashim's light, but the passageway ahead was completely dark.

She could still hear the footsteps, however, and the breathing—off to her left.

A dozen feet farther on, she figured out what had happened. El-Hashim had reached the fork in the tunnels and had taken the correct one this time.

Sure enough, when the assassin took the turn, the other light came into view less than fifteen yards ahead.

The assassin picked up her speed.

Time to finish this.

ALEX SAW A brief flash of light reflecting off the tunnel wall, then it was gone.

As she ran, she tried to figure out who her attacker had been.

If it had been a guard, the person would have been armed, and a quick gunshot would have taken care of things. But there had been none. The attacker was a woman, she knew that much. The yell had confirmed that. But the brutality of the attack suggested it wasn't just any woman.

The assassin. It had to be.

Her head pounding mercilessly, Alex reached out and again felt the wall with her fingers, tracing the curve until it came to a stop, indicating she was approaching the fork again. Since there were no lights in front of her, she figured they must have gone down the other tunnel, in the direction of the exit.

Switching to the opposite wall, she slowed her pace until she reached the corner, and carefully made her way around it.

Sure enough, up ahead were two lights. The closest, about fifty feet away, would belong to the attacker. The other, not more than thirty or forty farther on, would be El-Hashim.

Alex took another step, and nearly stumbled when her foot landed on a loose rock. Recovering, she started to step over it, but stopped, leaned down, and picked it up. It was heavy and solid and a little larger than palm size—but manageable. Probably around the same size as the stone the assassin had used on *her*.

Well. Two can play at that game.

THIRTY NINE

COOPER TOLD HIMSELF he would only go fifty feet down the tunnel, but when he reached that point, he heard splashes in the distance. The kind of splashes someone would make slogging across water-covered stone.

Another fifty, he decided.

This time when he reached his goal, he stopped and cupped a hand to his ear.

Footsteps. No doubt about it. They were regular for several beats, then they would slow or speed up randomly.

He was just about to call out Alex's name, when he heard a faint voice shout, "Come on!"

That was enough to get him to yank the Beretta 9mm from the backpack and get moving again.

THE ASSASSIN SMILED when El-Hashim turned back to look at her.

It had to be a frightening sight—a killer, only ten feet away and closing fast.

Heart-attack stuff.

Hopefully, El-Hashim's heart was sturdier than that. This hunt wouldn't have a satisfying conclusion if the woman just dropped dead.

El-Hashim screamed and tried to run faster. She gained herself an extra half-second of freedom, but that was about it. The assassin lunged, clamped down on the woman's shoulder, and jerked her backward, off her feet.

The flashlight flew straight up into the air. On its way down, the assassin snatched it—just because she could.

Damn, she felt invincible right now.

She pointed both beams at El-Hashim, lying now in the water, her body trembling.

"I bring a message from your employer," the assassin said. "Your services are no longer needed."

The fear suddenly turned to shock. "The committee sent you?"

"Life's a bitch, ain't it?"

The assassin reached down and put a hand on each side of El-Hashim's head. The woman grabbed at them, trying to pull them off, while rolling side to side.

The assassin dropped her knee onto the woman's chest, pinning her down. "Just relax," she said. "This will be nice and easy."

"No! No! Let go of me!"

AS SHE RAN, Alex discovered that the edges of the floor curved up into the wall. If she traveled along them, she could minimize the amount of water she stepped in. This helped her increase her speed while making little noise. Her new pace wasn't fast enough, however, to keep the attacker from reaching El-Hashim.

Alex saw El-Hashim go down and the woman jump on her, grabbing for El-Hashim's head.

There were some words, but Alex didn't try to listen.

She raced forward, the rock gripped tightly in her hand. As she angled herself to circle around them, she pulled her arm back and swung it forward, flinging the rock into the attacker's forehead.

Right before the stone connected, she registered the woman's battered face.

Frida.

Alex had no time to consider what this might mean as Frida flew backward with a watery thud against the stone floor.

Grabbing the flashlights, Alex pulled El-Hashim to her feet.

"Come on!"

FRIDA REMEMBERED THE feel of the woman's head in her hands. But what she *didn't* remember was how she had ended up on her back, with El-Hashim gone.

Pushing herself up on her elbows, a wave of dizziness swept over her, nearly sending her back down. She gritted her teeth through it, then stood up.

Pain radiated through her forehead, and there was water trickling down her face. She reached up to wipe it off, winced, and jerked her hand away, looking at her fingers.

Though it was too dark to see them, she knew they were covered in blood.

How long had she been out?

Minutes? Hours?

Listening carefully, she heard rapid footsteps moving away. Two sets.

Powell, goddammit. Frida knew not finishing her off before would be a problem.

At least they hadn't gone far, so that meant she must have been out for only a few seconds.

She didn't care that she didn't have a flashlight.

She could operate in the dark.

She had *always* operated in the dark.

"HURRY," ALEX URGED.

El-Hashim had been limping since they left Frida behind, but that wasn't what was slowing her down. She seemed distracted, even stunned.

"What did she say to you?" Alex asked, still hardly believing that Frida was the assassin.

El-Hashim didn't respond, lost in her own thoughts.

"What did Frida say to you?"

El-Hashim came around now. "Frida?"

"The woman who was sitting on your chest. Frida was the name she used in the prison."

"She's...the one they sent to kill me."

"*Who* sent to kill you?"

288

It was obvious El-Hashim had descended into thought again, so Alex decided to drop it for now.

The map was soaking wet as she pulled it from her pocket, but at least the lines were still visible. According to Teterya's directions, there was one more false tunnel, then a straight shot to the end of a passageway that would lead to the rendezvous point, where hopefully Deuce and Cooper would be waiting.

Before they reached that point, though, she still had to get them through this godforsaken tunnel, *and* get El-Hashim to tell her how to contact her father.

She pointed the light ahead, and spotted the split with the last tunnel.

"Come on," she said, giving El-Hashim a tug. "We're getting close."

WITH EVERY STEP, Frida's mind cleared a little more.

She knew Powell and El-Hashim had to be getting near the end of the tunnel. She also knew if they were able to reach it, her job would become exponentially much more difficult.

So she was surprised when she saw the beam of the flashlight less than a minute later. El-Hashim and Powell were walking not nearly as rapidly as Frida had expected. As the gap between her and her target narrowed, she thought she could hear Powell urging El-Hashim on.

And a moment later she saw why.

El-Hashim was limping.

Hurt when I took her down. Good.

Frida was only twenty feet away from them when her toe caught on a hole where a stone should have been. She grabbed at the wall, searching for a handhold, but her momentum was already carrying her toward the center of the tunnel.

With a loud splash, she stepped into the water, and started to fall to the ground. She jammed a hand down onto the stone floor, catching herself at the last second.

As she shoved herself back up, the beam of light caught her in the face.

"Go!" Powell yelled. "Run!"

ALEX WOULD HAVE liked to take the final false tunnel and execute the plan she was going to do before, but with Frida somewhere behind them, that wasn't an option. As they passed the junction, she noticed that El-Hashim's limp seemed more prominent than before.

"Is it your knee?" she asked.

"Yes," El-Hashim said, pain lacing her voice. "It's hard to bend it now. I think maybe it is swollen."

"We'll take a look at it when we get out. And the faster you go, the sooner that'll happen. Lean more on me." Alex slipped her arm around El-Hashim's back. "There. That help?"

"Yes."

"Let's see if we can pick up the pace."

They had taken no more than three steps when Alex heard a splash in the tunnel behind them.

She let go of El-Hashim and twisted around, bringing the flashlight with her.

Frida.

There was blood on the assassin's forehead where the rock had smashed into her, but it didn't seem to be fazing her.

"Go!" Alex said to El-Hashim. "Run!"

El-Hashim got the message. Though she didn't exactly run, she took off at a faster speed.

Frida charged. By the angle she took, it looked as though she intended to run right past Alex and go after El-Hashim.

But Alex wasn't about to let that happen.

She waited until Frida was five feet away, then launched herself, knocking into the other woman's shoulder, and slamming the crown of her head against Frida's jaw. In a tangle, they crashed against the wall, the flashlight falling to the floor, its beam now pointing across the width of the tunnel.

Frida tried to pull herself free, but Alex kept her arms wrapped around her as she turned her back toward the center of the tunnel, and hooked her foot behind the killer's. Down they went, Alex on top, water soaking both of them.

Frida screamed in rage. She jerked side to side, trying to get her arms free, then jammed her knee up into Alex's thigh. The sudden pain was enough to momentarily loosen Alex's hold.

Frida ripped her arm from Alex's grasp, and shoved her hand into Alex's face, pushing her back. With her other fist, she repeatedly jabbed Alex in the ribs.

Alex could feel her hold on the woman slipping away. Frida must have sensed it, too. With a final, extra hard push, she sent Alex tumbling to the side.

Alex rolled with it, popping onto her hands and knees, then rapidly to her feet. Frida was already up, looking like she was about to run. Fortunately, Alex had ended up between her and El-Hashim.

"So you were faking it all the time, huh?" Alex said.

Frida snickered. "And you weren't?"

"The fights? The injuries?"

"It's not hard to get into a fight in a prison. Of course, I couldn't always rely on others. Sometimes I had to inflict a little of my own pain."

Through the indirect light of the flashlight beam, Alex could see Frida smile. The woman's gaze flicked down the tunnel in the direction El-Hashim had gone, then back at her.

"That's right," Alex said. "You're not getting to her unless you get through me."

"Good," Frida told her. "I wouldn't want it any other way."

She charged again. No yell this time, no scream.

Only focused anger in her eyes.

COOPER RAN AS fast as he could through the wet tunnel. He could hear splashes ahead, and what sounded like shouts and grunts. It all added up to one thing in his mind—a fight.

It was only a few more seconds before he realized there was something odd about the sounds. The big splashes and fighting noises seemed to be originating from a fixed point, but there were other splashes, rhythmic—*splash-splash, splash-splash*—coming closer and closer.

Someone was headed his way. If the tunnel didn't have a slight bend, he was sure he would have seen them by now.

He stopped and raised his gun, filling the tunnel ahead with the beam of his light.

There were no breaks in the pace of the splashes, and now that they were right around the corner, he could hear heavy breathing, too.

Instead of continuing, however, the splashes came to an abrupt stop, just out of sight.

"Who's there?" Cooper called out.

When no one responded, he took a few steps forward, his gun ready.

"I said, who's there?"

Still nothing.

Instead of walking forward this time, he ran, hoping to surprise whoever it was. As soon as his flashlight beam fell on the woman around the curve, she turned and started to go the other way.

"Stop!" he ordered. "I'm armed."

For half a second, he thought maybe she didn't speak English, but then she halted. He approached her, stopping just outside of arm's reach.

"Turn around."

Slowly, she did as asked.

She was blonde, wearing a black shirt and pants. Maybe not quite middle-aged, but working on it.

"Who are you?" he asked.

She hesitated, then said in a heavy French accent, "Marie."

"What are you doing here?"

"That is not business of you."

Though he knew he'd never met her before, there was something familiar about her.

"Did you come with Alex?"

"Alex?"

Her answer was a tad too quick for his liking. There was also something in her eyes, a forced innocence.

Her eyes.

They were brown, which didn't exactly go with her hair—assuming her hair was naturally blonde.

Still, it *was* her eyes that were familiar. Why?

Another shout from down the tunnel broke into his thoughts.

Alex. She had to be involved with whatever was going on down there.

He grabbed the woman's arm.

"What are you doing?" she asked.

"You're coming with me."

Whoever she was, he wasn't about to let her get past him until he found out. But Alex came first.

Pulling her after him, he headed toward the fight.

"Please," she said. "My leg. I cannot go so fast."

"You were doing all right a minute ago. Pick it up."

There was a small S curve in the tunnel. When they came out of it, there was a light about sixty feet away, low and focused on the wall. He could still hear the fight, but couldn't see anyone.

Then suddenly two shadows danced into the beam. They struggled with each other, twisting and turning, pulling and punching.

"Alex!" he called out.

The fighters, both women, paused and looked toward him.

"Cooper?"

Alex's voice. But he wasn't sure which one it had come from, their silhouettes far from distinct.

Before he could answer her, the fight resumed.

He let go of the blonde woman. "Don't move," he told her, and raised his gun.

Because he couldn't tell who was who, there was no way he could shoot Alex's opponent, but he might be able to stop them for longer than a second.

Aiming the barrel in the direction he'd just come, he pulled the trigger.

The boom was deafening in the confines of the tunnel.

As he'd hoped, the fight ceased again, the women pulling apart.

He aimed the gun back toward them, making sure it could be seen in his flashlight beam.

"You don't want to make me do that again," he shouted. "Alex, over here."

"Two seconds," she said.

A fist suddenly flew out from the woman on the left. The sound of flesh smacking flesh was loud even at this distance, as the punch connected with the other woman's cheek. The woman on the right fell against the wall.

"Okay, I'm done," Alex said, and began walking toward Cooper and the blonde. She was about halfway to them when Cooper was able to make out the features of Alex's face.

"Looks like prison treated you well," he said.

"Regular holiday," she told him. "I see you found my friend."

"So she *was* with you. El-Hashim?"

"One and the same."

He hadn't figured the terrorist money launderer for a blonde, but it looked like he—and a lot of other people—had been wrong.

"She told me her name was Marie."

Alex stopped a few feet away, and gave Cooper a relieved smiled. "She woo you with French?"

"French accent, anyway."

"She doesn't have a French accent."

"Figures." He jutted his chin down the tunnel past Alex. "What about that one?"

"She doesn't have a French accent, either."

"That's not what I meant."

Alex glanced over her shoulder. "She was sent in to eliminate your arm candy there."

In the distance, the woman Alex had punched began rising back to her feet.

"Give me," Alex said, gesturing to Cooper's pistol.

"I'm not sure that's such a—"

He could have put up a fight, but when she grabbed the gun, he let her take it.

As she swung around and pointed the Beretta down the tunnel, the other woman pushed off the wall and ran in the opposite direction, into the darkness.

Swearing under her breath, Alex fired a shot down the tunnel as she started running after her.

"Alex, stop!" Cooper yelled. "Let her go. There's no time."

It was as if she hadn't even heard him.

"The alarm went off at the prison," Cooper went on. "We have to get out of here now!"

Holding on to El-Hashim, he turned and headed toward the exit of the tunnel. A few seconds later he heard Alex run up alongside him.

"The alarms?" she said. "When did they start?"

"Five, ten minutes ago."

She glanced back in the direction the other woman had disappeared. "Dammit." She turned back and moved around to the other side of El-Hashim. "It'll be faster if we carry her."

Without another word, they lifted El-Hashim into the air, and ran.

FORTY

INSTEAD OF JOINING the others on the search of the administration building, the young guard was ordered to show his supervisor the basement room where he'd found the elevator.

He, of course, thought this was a waste of time. If the missing prisoners had gone there, they would have had to come through the main part of the basement, and someone would have seen them.

But as he escorted his boss along the badly lit, little-used corridor, he noticed two other doors that he had missed in his haste the first time around.

Could the prisoners have gone through one of *them*?

Temporarily dismissing the thought, he showed his supervisor the dingy room where the elevator car was waiting.

The older guard pointed at the floor. "Did you make all this?"

The younger man looked down but didn't understand what he meant. "Make what, sir?"

"Look. There's a lot of dirt on the floor. Someone has moved it around. If it was you, you must have been dancing." The last words came out harsh and accusatory. "Were you dancing?"

Dancing? the young guard thought. What kind of foolish idea was that?

"Of course not."

"So someone was here."

"Well, perhaps there was—"

The sound was low and distant.

"Was that a gunshot?" his supervisor asked.

That was exactly what it had sounded like to the younger guard, but to be safe, he said, "I'm not sure."

They paused where they were for several seconds, waiting for a reoccurrence of the sound. When none came, they went back into the hallway and listened there. Still quiet.

"Someone else must have heard the noise," his supervisor said.

He and the young guard headed over to the door leading into the main basement area. Just as the supervisor was reaching for the handle, there was a second, distant bang.

It had come from behind them and was slightly louder than the previous one. The young guard moved quickly back the way they'd come, trying to follow the echo.

It seemed to be coming from beyond the nearest door they'd bypassed on their way to the elevator room. It was already open a couple centimeters, so the guard pushed it the rest of the way. On the other side was a dark corridor.

"Is this where it came from?" his supervisor asked as he joined the guard.

"Yes. I think so."

The supervisor retrieved his flashlight, and drew his pistol out of his belt holster. While the guard wished he could do the same, he was not armed. That, however, didn't prevent his boss from indicating with a nod that he should go first.

Every nerve of the younger man's body was on edge as he crept down the silent corridor. They came to an archway and carefully peeked around it. The large space beyond was empty.

They did the same at the next archway—

—only what they found this time was not an empty room.

There was a man, slumped on the floor.

The guard shone his light in the guy's face.

"Dr. Teterya," he whispered, feeling for a pulse and getting none.

"What is that?"

The young guard looked around and saw his supervisor

pointing his flashlight at something across the room.

A hole in the floor.

DEUCE WATCHED ONE of the prison jeeps come around the far side of the facility and reenter the parking area. Its companion jeep was already there, waiting. There was a quick conference between the two crews, then a man from each vehicle headed into the building.

He keyed the mic on his radio. "Cooper, any sign of Alex yet?"

He waited, but there was no response.

"Cooper? You read me?"

Nothing.

"Cooper?"

When there was still no answer, he trained his binoculars on the abandoned building where Cooper had gone. There was no movement anywhere. Cooper must be inside. Perhaps there was something in the walls interfering with the radio signal. Not likely, but possible.

Dammit, he thought. He should probably go check.

He swung the binoculars back to the prison for a final quick look, then froze.

One of the jeeps was racing for the prison gate. He watched as it passed outside the fence, then turned off-road, heading for the building in the ravine. Back at the main building, the second jeep started heading in the same direction.

Son of a bitch.

COOPER WENT UP the ladder first, then El-Hashim, and finally Alex.

As she poked her head out of the hole, she saw Cooper off to the side, head bent, hand to his ear.

"What?" Cooper said. "When?…How much time do we have?…Okay, okay. We'll see you there." He looked over at Alex. "We've got to move. Now!"

Alex scrambled the rest of the way out of the hole.

"How's the leg?" she asked El-Hashim.

"Not great," the woman replied.

"No choice, then. Sorry in advance."

"What?" El-Hashim said, confused.

Instead of answering, Alex bent forward, put her shoulder into the woman's waist, and lifted El-Hashim in a fireman's hold.

"What are you doing?" the woman cried.

Since the answer was obvious, Alex shot Cooper a look and nodded.

As he led them through the building, he said, "Deuce says there's a couple vehicles heading our direction right now."

How the hell do they know we came this way? Alex wondered. She was sure Teterya and Irina wouldn't have talked. Not unless they'd screwed up and been caught—

Wait.

Oh, God. Frida.

The only way she could have found the tunnel as quickly as she had was if she'd gotten Irina or Teterya to show her.

Perhaps the doctor was caught afterward, but there was a second, more likely possibility. Once Frida knew which way Alex and El-Hashim had gone, she'd have no use for the doctor anymore.

She was, after all, a trained killer.

Alex hoped she was wrong, but a part of her knew she wasn't, and it made her sick to her stomach that she may have played a part in the doctor's or Irina's death.

Outside, they saw the jeeps coming their way. They ran down the ravine in the opposite direction, toward a large copse of trees that spread up the bank opposite the prison. They reached the protection of the woods just seconds before they heard the first of the vehicles pull to a stop in front of the building.

"You want me to take her, or are you okay?" Cooper asked.

"I'm fine," Alex said. "Keep moving."

The slope of the ravine was steep but not impassible. Once they reached the top, the trees thinned a bit. If they'd been doing this during the day, they'd have been spotted for sure, but the darkness helped conceal their presence.

A gunshot back at the house stopped them in their tracks. There was a pause, then a second shot, and a third, and a fourth, before silence returned.

Frida, Alex thought. She must have tried to make a run for it.

"Come on," Cooper said.

They moved through the trees until they came to a one-lane dirt road. Instead of going down it, they crossed over into the field on the other side. They were in the open now, but out of direct line of sight of both the prison and the search party at the abandoned building.

As they circled around the backside of a small hill, Alex heard the distinct sound of an idling car engine. Though its lights were off, the shape of the sedan soon revealed itself in the darkness.

They were still a dozen yards away when the trunk suddenly popped open, its interior light coming on, and revealing Deuce standing beside the vehicle.

"Finally," he said with a grin as he jogged out to meet them.

"Good to see you, too," Alex said.

"Let me help you."

Together they carried El-Hashim over to the trunk. The woman's eyes went wide as they set her inside.

"Hey! What are you doing?" she said.

Cooper answered by leaning in and cuffing her wrists and ankles with plastic ties.

"You can't leave me in here! What do you think—"

Before she could protest further, Deuce slapped a piece of duct tape over her mouth. She tried to scream but it only came out muffled and incomprehensible.

"Scoot over," Cooper told her.

Her brow furrowed.

"Scoot. Over." He reached in and pushed her to the back of the trunk. He looked at Alex and motioned to the open space that had been created. "All yours."

"Can't wait," Alex said.

As soon as she was in the trunk next to El-Hashim, the lid closed. She listened as Deuce and Cooper climbed into the car. With a quick rev of the engine, they were underway.

Alex knew this was the last time she and El-Hashim would be alone together, so her last opportunity to learn what the woman knew about her father.

She shifted onto her side. Not able to see El-Hashim in the near total darkness, she felt for the woman's face and pulled the duct tape from her mouth.

"My father," she said. "How do I reach him?"

El-Hashim spit, drops of her saliva splattering Alex's neck and shirt.

Alex resisted the urge to jam the heel of her hand into the woman's nose. "Just tell me. He's my *father.*"

"I don't care who he is to you."

"You owe me."

"What?" She let out a quick, surprised laugh. "*Owe* you? Thank you very much for taking me from one prison to another."

"I saved your *life.* If I hadn't gotten you out, Frida would have killed you. You know that. I know that. How do I get ahold of my *father?*"

The car began to slow, forcing Alex to reapply the duct tape, just in case El-Hashim tried to call out in hopes of getting someone's attention.

The stop was brief, a traffic sign of some sort, most likely. Once they were moving again, Alex pulled the tape free.

"Please," she said. "I just want to talk to him."

"Why?"

Why?

What kind of question was that?

"I need to know why he left," Alex said.

"I should think that's obvious. He didn't want to spend the rest of his life in prison."

That was an easy answer, one that Alex had dismissed so many years ago it made her angry to hear El-Hashim say it now. It didn't apply to the man who had raised her.

Nor would it ever.

She counted to ten and got her feelings back in check before she spoke again.

"You said you have a way of contacting him. It's all I ask. There's a very good chance he won't respond to me, but I need to try. I *have* to try. This will mean nothing to you one way or the other."

A beat. Then El-Hashim said, "You're right. It will mean nothing to me one way *or* the other."

FORTY ONE

FRIDA FOLLOWED POWELL, El-Hashim, and their new boyfriend all the way to the end of the tunnel, staying just far enough back to not be noticed.

She knew taking El-Hashim's life in the tunnel was no longer an option, but she had never aborted a job before, and wasn't about to now.

Once they had all exited out of the hole in the roof of the tunnel, she stood below it and listened to their conversation. When the man expressed the need to get out of there as soon as possible, Frida knew it could only mean that guards had begun searching for the missing prisoners. They had probably discovered the body of the nurse. Not really unexpected.

She waited until she was sure they gone before climbing up. She found herself in a small room in what turned out to be a stone-sided building. She hadn't made it very far from the room when she heard the motor. To get a better view, she headed up to the rickety second floor, and moved over to one of the holes where a window had once been. Staying out of view, she peered outside. There were two vehicles, heading toward the building she was in. The first was about two minutes ahead of the other.

More than enough time, she thought.

She was in position well before the first vehicle arrived. As she had guessed, the four guards who had been inside split up so they could cover more ground. She targeted one at random, and moved in behind him.

It was so simple, it made her brain hurt from inactivity. She came at him from behind, and swung to the side, grabbing his gun hand and pointing the barrel of the weapon at his chest before he even knew what had happened.

"Bye-bye," she whispered as she forced her finger over his and pressed the trigger.

As he fell to the ground, she ripped the gun from his hand, and moved around the corner of the building.

His buddies came quickly, first one, then the other two.

Bam. Bam-bam.

It wasn't even a fight.

She took off in their vehicle a full minute before the second group of guards arrived.

NO MATTER HOW Alex asked the question, El-Hashim kept her mouth shut.

There had always been the possibility that this mission would end without Alex learning any more about her dad, but she never truly thought that would happen. This was why she had come here. This was why she had said yes.

But short of jamming a gun down El-Hashim's throat—a tactic that probably wouldn't work, either—Alex now knew she would come up empty. She should have followed Deuce's advice and stayed home, taken Danny to the ballgame, and not had her hopes raised.

Knowing she'd receive the same nonresponse again, she decided to ask one more time, for her brother's sake.

No, for her own, too.

"My father left us when we were teenagers. My mother was already dead. He's the only parent we have. I'm not asking because—"

She heard the revving of a motor. A second later, the car leaped forward with a loud crunch as something smashed into the back of their sedan. Alex flew into El-Hashim, her knees slamming against the bottom of the trunk.

Before they had a chance to recover, there was another crash.

Wind suddenly whistled through the trunk as the lid buckled upward an inch on both sides. Alex could hear Cooper and Deuce shouting in the front of the car, but there was too much other noise to understand them.

Without warning, their sedan swerved to the side, as if dodging an obstacle in the road. At the same time, Alex heard the sound of the second motor again, racing back toward them, but instead of once more smashing into their rear end, it passed alongside them.

Metal crunched again as the other car swerved sideways into the sedan's back panel. Alex could feel Cooper fighting for control of the vehicle, the tires skidding sideways before finally biting the road again.

Another side slam, but while the car didn't fishtail as much this time, the trunk popped open. Alex grabbed the lid to keep it from flying all the way up. As she did, the vehicle that had been ramming them swung back and behind again.

It was one of the prison jeeps. The sedan's taillights illuminated enough that Alex could see it wasn't a guard behind the wheel, but Frida.

The jeep came forward again. Alex tried to hook the trunk lid down, but the latch was bent and wouldn't catch. Something pierced the lid only a foot away from her, punching a hole in the metal.

"Are you kidding me?" Alex said under her breath.

Frida was armed.

The jeep started rushing forward again.

"Hold on!" Alex yelled as she let go of the lid and ducked down.

Frida smacked into their rear bumper again, sending the lid of the trunk flying all the way up.

As the jeep fell back a few feet, Frida stuck a gun out her window and let off another shot. This one went into the trunk itself, puncturing the floor right where Alex had been lying moments before.

As soon as Alex saw Frida pull the gun out of sight, she hopped up on her knees and reached for the lid to pull it back down.

The jeep sped forward again.

Realizing there was no way she'd get hold of the lid in

time, Alex did the only thing she could. She crouched, her feet poised and ready. Right before Frida's vehicle hit them again, she jumped.

She almost blew it. Her jump had been too good, sending her all the way over the jeep's hood into its windshield, nearly bouncing her off the vehicle altogether. The only thing that saved her was throwing her arm around the top of the windshield at the last second and hanging on.

"If only I had a camera," Frida shouted. "YouTube gold!"

She pointed the gun directly through the glass at Alex, but instead of pulling the trigger, she jerked the steering wheel first one way, then the other.

Alex's feet swung out over the edge of the car, then slammed back into the front fender, but she didn't let go.

Frida smiled. "Oh, you're good. How about we go again?"

When Frida jerked the wheel again, Alex was ready. Using the swerving vehicle's momentum, she swung around the windshield and dropped into the front passenger seat. Caught off guard, the grin on Frida's face disappeared as she whipped the gun toward Alex. Alex shot her hand out, grabbing the woman's wrist, and pushing it into the dash. The gun went off, the bullet slicing its way through the passenger door and into the night.

"Stop the car!" Alex yelled.

Frida laughed. "Does that really work? Do people listen to you when you say stupid things like that?"

Alex slammed Frida's wrist against the dash again, trying to dislodge the weapon, but the assassin held on tight. Realizing she needed a different strategy, Alex swung her left leg into the driver's side footwell and shoved it toward the brake.

Frida blocked it with her own foot, kicking it to the side. That was fine by Alex. She hadn't thought it would work, but she knew it would provide the distraction she needed to grab the emergency brake handle.

She yanked it up.

The tires screamed and the smell of rubber filled the air. Frida let up on the gas as she tightened her one-handed grip on the steering wheel and fought for control. Alex moved her foot over to the regular brake and slammed it home.

The car came to a screeching halt in the middle of the road, the vehicle spinning sideways until it was almost perpendicular to the lanes.

Frida let go of the steering wheel and twisted to the side, pulling with all her strength to free the hand holding the gun. When she was finally able to yank it away, the momentum brought her arm upward, pointing the gun at the sky.

Alex thrust forward and reached for it. She wasn't able to get hold of the weapon, but she *was* able to knock it out of Frida's hand, sending it tumbling onto the jeep's floor.

Both women scrambled for it. Alex got there first, but Frida's hand was right on top of hers. The gun rocked back and forth on the floor of the vehicle, its barrel pointing skyward again. Alex felt Frida's finger slip over the trigger, so she shoved at the weapon just as it went off.

The bullet passed through the front lip of the driver's seat before cutting a hole through Frida's thigh. The second shot entered Frida's body, just below her rib cage, traveling through a lung, nicking her heart, and finally coming to rest against the C4 vertebra of her spine.

She didn't die right away, but it was only a matter of seconds.

FORTY TWO

FOR THE REST of the ride, Alex used a rope to hold the trunk lid closed from inside. Eighty-five minutes later, they reached the secluded bay southwest of Slavne with no further incident.

The arranged fishing vessel was waiting for them.

By the time the sun came up, they were twenty-five miles off the coast, where they met up with the *Nanu*, a Belgium-registered, oceanic science vessel. The *Nanu* was owned by the Teetaert Institute, a research firm that was itself owned—after a few additional corporate layers—by Stonewell International.

The scientists aboard the *Nanu* were a bit miffed that their research trip to the Black Sea had to be put on hold for several days, while the ship made its way back through the Bosphorus and then to a Greek island in the Mediterranean Sea. The purpose of the side trip was to ferry a group referred to as VIPs who had suddenly shown up on the ship one day. But a promise of adding the missing time to the end of the voyage seemed to mollify most of the researchers.

Alex never got the name of the island where they were dropped off. They were met at the pier by a blue sedan with black-tinted windows, and whisked away to a private airfield where a Stonewell jet was waiting.

El-Hashim was assigned to the back row of the plane, where she sat with the two Stonewell security officers who had been waiting for them at the airfield.

Alex took a seat in a row by herself near the front of the jet. She tilted her chair back the moment she was able and fell fast asleep.

"Miss Poe?"

Someone touched her.

"Miss Poe?"

She opened her eyes. It was one of the security men, his hand on her shoulder. She thought at first she had slept right through the landing, but no, she could hear the engines still droning.

"Yes?" she said as she tried to blink the sleep from her eyes.

"The prisoner has asked if she can speak with you."

"Uh, sure. Okay."

She followed him to the back. As she passed through the cabin, she could see Deuce passed out a couple rows behind where she had been. Cooper was on the other side of the plane, reading a book.

El-Hashim sat in the middle of the back row, holding a cup of water. When she saw Alex, she nodded a greeting and gestured to the seat beside her.

She then looked at the guard who'd brought Alex back. "May we have a bit of privacy?"

The man didn't move for a moment, but finally said, "Five minutes. That's all."

"It's more than enough."

The security man nodded to his partner, and they both moved a few rows up.

"What do you want?" Alex said.

"You asked me a question."

"One you didn't feel the need to answer, if I remember correctly."

El-Hashim tilted her head, conceding the point. "I've had time to think."

"And?"

"I will tell," she said, glancing at the two security men. "*If* you will do me a favor."

"I don't do favors for terrorists."

"I'm not a terrorist."

Alex shrugged. "Semantics."

"I simply want you to deliver a message."

"That doesn't do much to change my mind."

"Maybe this will. The person I want you to deliver the message to is your father."

Alex narrowed her eyes, but said nothing.

"All you need to say is, the committee should know that El-Hashim never forgets."

"And what's that code for?"

"I assure you, there's nothing coded in that message at all."

"You will, of course, forgive the fact that I have a hard time trusting what you say."

"So, will you do this for me?"

Alex looked away, shaking her head to herself.

"You realize," El-Hashim said. "All you need to do is say yes. I won't actually know for some time if you delivered the message."

"And maybe the contact information you give me won't even be for my father. Maybe it's a way of sending a message to someone in your network."

"You asked me for the information. And now I am offering it to you."

Alex was surprised by her own hesitation. Now that she was potentially this close to contacting her dad, was she actually scared?

"All right," Alex said. "I'll do it. *If* I decide to use your information."

"That doesn't concern me. It would be very difficult to never try and reach him, I think."

Alex didn't respond.

"How's your memory?" El-Hashim asked.

"Excellent."

"Like your father's, then."

Again, there didn't seem to be the need for a reply.

El-Hashim leaned over and whispered an e-mail address—a seemingly random mix of letters and numbers—in Alex's ear.

"Would you like to repeat that back to me?"

Alex shook her head. "I've got it. Is that all?"

"You want more?"

"Do you have more?"

"Unfortunately, no," El-Hashim said.

Alex stood up.

"You'll remember the message, yes?"

"I'll remember," Alex told her, then headed back to her seat.

MCELROY WAS WAITING for them at the airport when they landed. With him was a squad of black-suited men who screamed government agency. Which one, Alex wasn't sure.

He smiled and shook each of their hands as they exited the aircraft.

"Excellent work," he told Alex. "Well done."

She said thanks, then stood to the side as El-Hashim was escorted off the plane.

"It's certainly a pleasure to meet *you*," McElroy said.

El-Hashim frowned. "Am I supposed to know who you are?"

"I'm the one who sent the team to pick you up. But that's not important. We won't be spending any time together, so no need to become buddy-buddy. These men, however..." He gestured to the group of suits. "I have a feeling you'll be getting to know them quite well." He turned to the oldest-looking one in the group. "I remand El-Hashim to your custody."

"Transfer accepted," the man said. "Ms. El-Hashim, you will come with us."

As the woman was led away, Cooper walked over to Alex. "Nice working with you again. It's...been too long."

She gave him a quick smile. The truth was, being around him again had been better than she expected. Nice, even. The residual anger she'd felt over the last several years had receded. Maybe disappeared completely.

"It has," she said. "Thanks. You know, for saving my life and all."

"If you'd died back there, I'd be buried in paperwork. Nothing I hate more than that. I should be thanking you for staying alive."

"Glad I could keep the writer's cramp away."

"Hey," Deuce said, walking up and dangling Alex's car keys in the air. "They moved your car here, so we can go. I mean, you know—*now*?"

"Good working with you, too, Deuce," Cooper said, holding out his hand. "I'd trust you to have my back anytime."

Deuce looked surprised by the compliment. He shook Cooper's hand. "Thanks, man. You take it easy, huh?"

"You, too."

Cooper turned to Alex. She thought he was about to hug her, but after an awkward moment, he held out his hand again.

"Keep in touch, Alex. I mean it."

"I will," she said.

Deuce took hold of her arm. "Come on, already. I want to get home."

As they walked toward the parking lot, they heard footsteps running up behind them. Alex looked back to find McElroy heading their way.

"Hold on," he said.

"Do we have to?" Deuce whispered.

"Do you want to get paid?" Alex whispered back.

"Fine."

They stopped and turned to wait.

When McElroy reached them, he was slightly out of breath. "I meant what I told you when I first saw you back there. Great job. I know it wasn't easy."

"It's what you paid us to do," Deuce said. "Speaking of which, when can we expect the check?"

McElroy cocked his head. "The money is already transferred to each of your accounts."

"Crap," Deuce said under his breath. "You mean we didn't have to stop?"

Alex felt the urge to elbow him in the side, but refrained

and said to McElroy, "You're welcome. Now, if you don't mind, we're pretty tired, so we're—"

"Can I ask you something?" McElroy said.

"What?"

"Were you able to find out anything about your father?"

Alex frowned and shrugged. "No. She didn't have anything beyond what you already told me." Her father was personal business.

"I'm sorry to hear that."

"I took a chance. It didn't pay off. But we got her for you. So..." Another shrug.

"Listen. About that. I might have some other projects coming up that you might be great for. Can I call you?"

"Sure. You can always call."

"But what? That doesn't mean you'll answer?"

The corner of her mouth tilted up. "Hey, Deuce, didn't you say something about going home?"

"Once or twice."

"Mr. McElroy," Alex said. "Thank you for the opportunity. We'll show ourselves out."

EPILOGUE

London, England
Two weeks later

"ZETA FIVE, CLEAR."

"Zeta Six, clear."

After the last watcher reported in, the surveillance van fell silent.

"I don't think he's coming," Duncan said.

McElroy stared at the main monitor. "He's close."

"If you say so, sir."

McElroy looked over at Duncan, his eyes narrowing. "I *know* he is. He's gotta be. This is too tempting for him."

He looked back at the monitor.

Alexandra Poe was center screen, still sitting at the table outside the Weary Horseman Pub in west London, as she had been for nearly two hours.

Once McElroy had listened to the taped conversation Poe had had with El-Hashim on the plane, he knew this chance would come. It would have been nice if the mic had picked up whatever El-Hashim had whispered in Alex's ear, but it wasn't the end of the world. At some point, Alex would use the information to contact Raven, so all McElroy had to do was keep an eye on her, and monitor her electronic communications.

The last part was actually easier than the first. Stonewell's connection with the government gave McElroy access to eavesdropping methods ninety-nine percent of the population didn't even know about. Following her every day was a bit more difficult. More than once she had lost her tail for hours on end.

Cooper would have been the best person for the job, but McElroy was worried about Cooper's personal history with Alex, and thought it best not to test the man's allegiances at this point. He had told him nothing about the hunt for Raven.

It was the electronic surveillance that finally paid off when, the day before, Alex suddenly booked a round-trip flight to the UK, leaving at midnight that night and returning the next afternoon. They already knew she had yet to take on another job, so the trip couldn't have been tied to work. Which, in McElroy's mind, meant she was making the journey for one reason only.

This was what McElroy had been waiting for, and he was more than ready. He and his team were in the air a full two hours before Alex even stepped into Baltimore/Washington International Airport.

While in flight, his techs back in the States pored through the data on Alex's phone. Though they could find nothing pointing to a time and place for a meeting, they did uncover a Google Map search for the Weary Horseman. It wasn't a guarantee of where the meeting would occur, but McElroy was confident enough to send most of his team to the pub to set up while tasking two of his men to follow Alex when she arrived in London.

And now, here they were—Alex, McElroy, his team.

All except Raven.

Where the hell was Frank Poe?

ALEX CHECKED HER watch again.

If she didn't leave soon, she would miss her return flight.

Her father was already over an hour late.

She wondered, not for the first time, if maybe it hadn't even been her father who replied to her e-mail. There was no way to know if El-Hashim had been telling her the truth. That's why it had taken close to two weeks before she finally gave in.

Knowing she couldn't actually e-mail him from her own account, she had driven around the city until she spotted an internet café, and used one of their terminals to create a dummy account to send the message.

She actually stopped and started over a dozen times before just writing:

Dad,

It's Alex. Are you there?

As much as she wanted to check every ten minutes after that for a reply, she knew she shouldn't use any of her own devices, so she limited herself to finding other random computer locations every four or five hours.

It was almost a full day before she received a reply. She was surprised when she saw it in her inbox, and stared at it for what seemed like an eternity before finally clicking it open.

Weary Horseman Pub. London.
4 p.m. tomorrow.

While there was no greeting or signature, there was also no question whether she would go.

But now it appeared she'd come all this way for nothing.

The waiter approached her table. "Another pint, miss?"

"No," Alex said. "No, I think just the check."

She paid with cash she'd exchanged at the airport, then stood up, took a quick look around, and pulled on her jacket.

As she dropped her arms to her side, her wrist brushed against something sticking out of one of the pockets.

She looked down, confused, and saw it was a white envelope. She started to pull it out, but stopped when she spotted her name on the outside, written in a handwriting she could never forget.

She scanned the other patrons sitting on the patio. Had one of them delivered it? No one was paying her any attention. Then again, she had been here for a while, so it could have been any of two or three dozen people who had slipped it into her pocket.

Feeling suddenly exposed, she went inside the pub and walked back to the WC. She entered one of the stalls and closed the door. Alone now, she removed the envelope and tore the top open.

There were three items inside: a piece of paper, and two field-box tickets for the Baltimore Orioles game the next day.

She unfolded the piece of paper. The handwriting was the same as that on the envelope.

One for you, and one for the little lieutenant.
Wish I could go with you. Enjoy the game.

The little lieutenant. The nickname her dad had given Danny.

RAVEN WATCHED FROM the backseat of his hired car as his daughter left the pub and flagged down a taxi.

She looked good. So grown-up.

And so very much like her mother.

A cab pulled to the curb, and like that she was gone.

He had hoped he would have actually been able to met with her, to tell her in person how sorry he was that he had left. But, as he'd feared, she'd been followed, and sitting down at the table with her was out of the question.

Raven looked down at his hand. In it was the third ticket to the ballgame.

He wouldn't go, of course. It would have to be enough for now to know that he could.

One day, he thought. *One day*.

He leaned toward his driver and said, "Victoria Station."

Alexandra Poe will return

LB	9/13

CPSIA information can be obtained at www.ICGtesting.com
Printed in the USA
LVOW08s1452150813

348090LV00002B/138/P

9 781483 986838